Uncharted

T&L Pampeyan

UNCHARTED

This is a work of fiction. Names, characters, places and incidents herein are the product of the authors' imagination or are used fictionally. Actual historical persons, businesses or agencies are named only in ancillary reference. Any other resemblance to real persons living or dead, events, business establishments or locales is entirely coincidental.

Cover and authors' photos: PinkNosePix
Cover art and design: Blac Spacader

ISBN: 9781731090041

Printed in the United States of America

What they said…

Ted and Linda Pampeyan have experienced and observed much about life's raw reversals and the mysteries and angst of man-woman relationships. They grasp the eternal verities their characters long to discover.
Harold Myra, Author & Publisher

A uniquely written marriage story. But not just a story. *Uncharted* clearly communicates the value others can have in our marriage journeys when we allow committed, authentic and intentional people to influence us. This is a wonderful read. Had a hard time putting it down!
Monique Woodward, Marriage Mosaic

Uncharted is a story about love gained, love lost, love redeemed. In a world of throw-away relationships, *Uncharted* reveals characters that are flawed, intensely human and struggling with the countless changes of marital relationships. However, they take a turn into the light of hope, not to return to the past glory days of their marriage, but to a better more enduring future.
Miley Rose, Teacher

In *Uncharted*, the authors tell the compelling story of compassion and love for others. This is the story of a couple befriending another couple and building a trusting relationship, through patience and persistence, where God and his grace can heal, restore and bring hope to a broken marriage. From our experience in 15 years of marriage ministry, this is the most effective way to help marriages thrive.
Vic Woodward, Marriage Mosaic

To Caroline, Grace, Halle, Elijah

Uncharted

Prologue

1864

SOUTHERN GOLD.

Hopeless resolution to the War of the Rebellion a near certainty, Southern politicians and landholders foresaw deteriorating interests. In their fervor to withhold Confederacy wealth from the victorious Northern aggressor, those more alert secreted bullion and bills for safekeeping until a convenient future for a proper uprising against Lincoln's toadies. Avarice being what it is, just as much gold and currency found its way into private reserves, first come first seize. The paper was soon reduced to the value of kindling, but the gold appreciated, justifying the lust of those in its grip.

Dozens of Southern novice depositors commended their newfound acquisitions to one Roy Davis Phillips, stately in demeanor and therefore trusted. He would become the forebear of a patriarchal line of overseers of others' wealth.

With secrets of gains held in confidence, Roy Davis quietly moved about from state to state, slipping under countless fences, his investors losing track of his meanderings and their contraband savings. With uncontested millions, he settled himself in a Northern locale maintaining sympathy to Southern viewpoints, and came to be regarded as the town's new banker and eligible bachelor. His carriage of dignity accompanied by indicators of wealth granted him sufficient license to court the sought-after village princess. A subsequent family man, he eventually owned the right front pew of the Redeemer Methodist Church after humbly funding much of the building's post-war reconstruction. Roy Davis was one whom people naturally wanted to believe in. For his custodial management of others savings, he discreetly repositioned substantial percentages under his own table from new and always trusting investors. He believed God helped him because he certainly helped himself.

Civil War Phillips sired a son, G Fletcher, who relocated the cache to new concealment, recording in unreserved prose its exact location for his single offspring. The Phillips plunder passed through four generations of bankers in the family tree, each augmenting more than extracting occasional shares to boost his personal comfort in the community.

Eighty years after Roy Davis began his entrepreneurial exploits, fourth-in-line Banker Phillips—as he preferred to be addressed—formed a plan for the grand employment of his inherited treasury brought about by devious procedure. Converting all but a baker's dozen of small gold bars into spendable currency under the guise of virtuous citizenship and scrupulous banking, he amassed—an inadequate word—substance more than enough to purchase an island paradise of his dreams.

One early misty morning, Banker Phillips with ambitious visions, took his first steps toward a final visit to his ancestors' fortune. Fantasies of relocating it, and himself, filled his head:

away from detection, his boring little town, and his devoted but dull little wife.

His vision of flight to freedom and tropical seclusion was stopped short just outside his bank's backdoor.

NINETEEN FORTY-NINE.

World war was long over, done with.

Everyone remembered the sailor kissing the nurse in Times Square and all was declared good again. The nation, her people and economy relaxed, hopeful.

But Shaw's Bow, Kentucky, a musket's reach from the Tennessee border, languished. Quietly, solemnly, unnoticed people foraged for basics because they simply ran out. Animals called by name from the backdoor disappeared and a family ate for three days. Those who escaped the torture of living by dying before their time were buried in rags to provide for a relative needing a Sunday best.

JT Shiller, unremarkable in the small community but appreciated by friends for his fair dealings, dreamed of a return to stability. He felt a responsibility for his town, for his friends. Clean-living people, mostly. Even better, he was sure of it, if they could stand tall with decent jobs and cash in their pockets.

A real savings account. Now wouldn't that be a wonder? About the only one in Shaw's Bow with money was Banker Phillips himself. He seemed to have an endless supply of greenbacks, a fresh boutonniere in the lapel of his tailored suits, all the lights burning in his mansion on the hill. The rest of the town struggled below to save a little tallow to make candles. But the people had heart, often pooling their depleted resources to help avert a good neighbor's foreclosure. That was the nature of the folks JT Shiller called friends.

JT's younger brother, Edwin, achieved a personal low that winter of '49. Gainful employment only a mist, Edwin's trade was reduced to drifting the alleys. Layered and safety-pinned as best he could against the cold, he stepped out of his two-room shack in search of anything not bolted down. He might receive a handout from a kind soul who couldn't afford to spare, but he expected no new finds.

His luck took a turn when he happened to pass under a back window of the Shaw's Bow National Bank, opened unseasonably wide for a winter's day. He overheard a short hushed conversation between the esteemed president, Banker Phillips, and his guard, Jimmyboy Wheeler.

The strongbox would be carted under a canvas wrap tomorrow morning, out at six. Heavier this time, ingots no paper.

That was enough for Edwin. The next day before dawn, sleepy but anticipatory of new gain, he waited behind the bank admiring Mr Phillips' new pickup. No armored vehicle to draw attention, only an easy-pickin's Ford F1, key under the driver's side of the bench seat.

Banker Phillips didn't regard the strongbox as objectionably heavy, considering its contents. Personals, he called them. Loosely tossed inside the hasped box were a few dozen early-minted US coins and about as many stamped on Confederate silver. Underneath were thirteen small Confederate gold bars laid side by side. They served as a collective paperweight for a folded single sheet of fine parchment and the very real wealth it represented. Instructions on the sheet, hand-printed decades earlier as if by a calligrapher, directed the seeker to the much larger hidden treasure. Tucked alongside the map was a polished key wrapped in brown oilcloth.

Against a light February rain young Edwin Shiller, hunched over in the alley and marking time by shifting from one foot to the other, waited. He had no plan to coldcock the guard; he had no plan at all. But being on the hefty side, he easily overpowered the smaller Jimmyboy by planting a fist squarely on top of the little man's head. Jimmyboy crumpled and Edwin caught him up and sat him behind the bank's back door. When the prominent banker appeared through the doorway lugging the strongbox, Edwin, realizing the magic touch of his fist, thumped the man and marveled at how his legs too wobbled and gave out. The box crashed to the pavement, coins and bars jangling inside. Edwin let it lie while he dragged the not-so stately Banker Phillips over to join his dozing guard. He hoisted the box and set it in the cab and was about to drive off when he looked again at his two casualties propped against the wall under the eave. He collected the canvas from the truck bed, shook off the rainwater and covered the men, careful to tuck the tarp under their chins. Back in the cab and its fragrance of newness, Edwin methodically started the motor, set it in gear, found the windshield wiper knob, and pleasantly drove away with bounty beyond the dreams of anyone in the impoverished town of Shaw's Bow.

Not an hour after Edwin had greeted the banker and his guard in the alley, he sealed the chest of coins and gold, map and key excepted. Standing pleased, he watched it vanish under a tangle of willow roots in a small pond on the rural parcel owned by his brother, JT.

Edwin was toweling off in his tiny house, admiring the map and key lying on his sagging twin bed, when he heard the parade of constabulary vehicles careen up his drive, the restraint of stealth abandoned by an agent in charge. Edwin wrapped the two articles in his damp towel and crammed the wad up the chimney flue, figuring no one would chance to light a fire in his soon-to-be vacant bungalow next to his brother's.

Buttoning his only clean shirt, he waited patiently for the sharp rapping at his front door. Counting to three, he opened it to stare into the twin blued-steel barrels of a shotgun, unusually long from his defenseless perspective, and revolvers trained over his upper torso. Hair still damp and a few drops moistening his face, he offered no resistance and was led away to the fanfare of officers congratulating themselves on a splendid arrest. Of the law enforcement representatives local, state and federal, not one man took notice of Edwin's knuckles stained with soot.

There was no question Edwin was the malefactor, not when both victims described him tipping his hat and bidding a genial good morning before putting them out. And not when he returned the banker's new pickup in noontime daylight to its previous spot in the alley. Edwin didn't deny a bit of it and was accordingly bussed away, his unparoled life managed in a chain of federal prisons.

Despite backroom cruelty to do the enemy proud, Edwin revealed nothing of the strongbox's location. His answer to every agent's coercion: "My momma and daddy brought me up respectin' the law, least wise, most of it. So, Mr Lawman, I'm right sorry for what you call my noncooperation. I'm doin' the best I can. But it looks like I'm to claim residency of your hospitality, forever without end, amen." The last phrase he threw in to feel somewhat intellectual if not religious. It was about all he remembered from old Mr Fitchert's Sunday School class.

They didn't find Edwin's treasure, nor his map and key. Agents gave up their search, indignant the chest would be kept secret despite their finest attempts at persuasion, but no less satisfied with the capture of their criminal.

Banker Phillips, reluctant to disclose specifics of the box's contents without self-incrimination, managed his way to immediate bankruptcy. Reverting to his first name, Simon, he backed a borrowed truck to his front door to load belongings of yesteryear and his perplexed but faithful wife, and disappeared to Arizona's burgeoning courts of aluminum siding.

All told, a fortune had been effectively mediated from one to another. With cheerful use of his natural strength, in only minutes Edwin Shiller made a pauper of the banker with the promise of conferring enormous wealth upon the elder brother he adored.

JT Shiller visited his younger brother every month to whichever facility Edwin was carted to next. From dwindling personal financial resources he attempted to grease countless wheels, but his most earnest pleas for Edwin's release were snubbed at the highest levels. Kid brother had become a pariah to local lawmen, lawyers and legislators, and moralistic fodder for preachers across denominational lines.

Not even JT knew the location of his brother's discovered gain, and began to doubt it did exist. On a sunny September day JT, in threadbare but matching coat and trousers, drove over for his monthly visit to the medium security facility. Strolling the perimeter of the visitor's patio away from listening ears, Edwin put a hand to his mouth. He quickly and quietly said, "My chimney," while faking a respectable sneeze. JT passed the younger Shiller a work bandana and said, "Bless you, brother." For that small act of kindness he was richly rewarded.

The next day during a late summer thunderstorm, JT located the map and key in the chimney flue of Edwin's tiny cottage, empty and unmolested for close to three years. He disregarded the strongbox resting at the bottom of his pond in order to procure the greater wealth.

The map's directions, finely written in paragraph form, described landmarks locally known and little changed. JT chose a day when the weather was pleasant for strolling and greeting passers-by in Shaw's Bow. Parking diagonally near the end of Lee & Grant Street, he donned the fedora he routinely wore for what he called his constitutional. With effort he relaxed his pace from overly eager to mildly motivated. JT was a calm young man by nature, but that day his patience was hard-pressed for the surprise on the other side of the door described in the map as the final destination.

An ordinary closet door it was, off to the side of a dirty washroom marked Coloreds in the furthest part at the back of an ancient empty warehouse handed down to the former Banker Phillips. JT shook his head passing the washroom door. *Not one man with color, not one without. All of us kin, every last one.*

The lock obeyed with only minor resistance, and the closet door opened on hinges idled for years but still quiet. The space inside was deeper than he expected. He'd brought no flashlight so he felt his way back with short steps and arms outstretched. His hands touched the unfinished wall before his foot tapped a loosened floorboard. Curious, JT knelt at the board and with little difficulty lifted it away. Underneath was a layer of dirt, decomposed leaves and—he suspected but didn't want to know—hardened feces. Thinking he ought to return with light, his greed got the better of him and he began sifting through the filth in the darkness.

A good eight inches deep he reached a layer of fitted cobblestones. Excitement peaking, he manhandled the smooth bricks out of the hole. His craving for discovery was rewarded when his fingers touched a rough wooden crate. Scooping out more dirt and whatever, he dragged the sealed container out of the closet into what little light the high smoked windows of the old building allowed. With relative ease he yanked away the top waxed-over slats to find a toddler's blanket. Lifting that away, he squinted down at the glorious end of his rainbow.

Stacks of US currency, all of it good and very legal tender.

Packets of fifties and hundreds lined the top four rows, a small fortune alone. But the waterproofed crate was deep. Under those upper layers of smaller notes—chump change—were bundles, at least twenty layers deep, of currency bearing the image of Grover Cleveland. One-thousand-dollar bills were still circulating in those days, until their discontinuance much later by the Federal Reserve System, about the time the United States also took custody of the moon.

In the abandoned warehouse, JT commandeered his fortune. It took only a child's fistful of thousands to purchase the old building as well as the parcel of land next to his farm house, "to help the economy." By the late 1950s the new land baron had acquired possession of about half the town, and the community's depression was long lifted. He dispensed hundred dollar bills here and there, on occasions determined special by his own calendar, to appreciative nieces, nephews, and anyone else he regarded as deserving. During the nineteen-eighties and nineties he sold most of the crisp Clevelands to collectors for two and three times their face value. He lit one note to the most expensive Cuban cigar to be had, just because he could, though he didn't much like cigars.

JT raised few suspicions. No one associated him with his brother's theft or punishment. He'd gradually established himself as a principled leader in the community, so it seemed right the man's influence and affluence should grow.

Jimmyboy Wheeler the bank guard had an inkling early on of larger treasure but kept his thoughts to himself. Being somewhat resourceful and himself bitten by covetousness, he weaseled his way into the Shiller dynasty by marrying the least attractive niece in order to set up shop close to JT, whom he suspected as the brains behind what he called the caper. But JT hadn't gone to school just to eat his lunch. One Sunday morning on the steps between the twin Doric columns of The First Baptist Church, JT privately voiced casual concern for Jimmy-boy's future welfare and personal safety. The little man, quick on the uptake, drove by night with his young bride and little one to resettle somewhere deep in Canada.

For years rumors of the strongbox's existence made its way quietly among the most senior relatives of the two Shiller brothers. Those select few swore to Edwin's allegiance in the unspoken hope that they, like JT, might become shareholders in a very limited partnership. But the brothers cared little about rumors, no matter gossip's resemblance to reality.

One

2002

IN THE THIRD SUMMER OF THE NEW MILLENNIUM, Brooke Potter crossed into her thirteenth year, and anyone with an eye to behold could see she was becoming an uncommon beauty.

Though not one without flaw. The natural maturity of her left leg had cut short its growth prior to that of its twin by a quarter inch. A sad complement to her appeal, she was burdened with the affliction of a gimpy gait becoming pronounced whenever she grew anxious.

Brooke had another problem; her worst fault, according to her mother.

Quite unintentionally, in a pond one summer evening she uncovered the family secret. A violation deserving swift and lasting reprisal.

The extended Shiller family had gathered for their annual Fourth of July barbecue at JT Shiller's, Brooke's great uncle and family patriarch on her mother's side. JT owned the most square-mile sections in the county. Some years earlier he had covertly blocked his year-round creek to increase the size of a small pond to a worthwhile private lake, which he still called the pond. The first year's planting of bass and crappie kept a steady source of freshwater sport for himself and his favorite relatives—which included them all—and invitation-only derbies whenever he felt the urge to show off.

Thoroughly convinced of the soundness of his heritage, JT traced his direct lineage to JC Shaw for whom the town, Shaw's Bow, was named at its founding back in 1785.

JT Shiller was an anomaly of his generation. He didn't march the boulevard with the early civil righters, but he never allowed a deprecating word to cross his lips. His home had only one door to welcome all who entered. He encouraged everyone he met, whatever their skin tone or belief, to be the best they could and reach their highest capacity. When the mayor asked how plans were going for the Shiller clan's annual reunion, he corrected the politico. "Friend, we don't do clan. We're kin, every last one of us, are we not?" JT Shiller was everyone's favorite neighbor. Favorite churchman. Voted, if they did that sort of thing, all-round favorite in the county.

Strangely, JT wasn't above the law, and he moved effortlessly under every radar. Officials, elected or hired, uniformed or coat-buttoned, were content to leave him alone, so long as he remained undetected and gave liberally to their politics and wishes.

Unmarried and progenitor of none to his recollection, he treated his nieces and nephews with special courtesy. Finding each one's particular aptitude, he coached the more gifted who would soon enough be entrusted with mantles of responsibility for the Shiller inheritance.

JT Shiller's great niece, Brooke, held the most promise.

The weather on the day of July Fourth had been unseasonably cool, but not so chilly as to keep Brooke and her cousins out of JT's pond. In fact, they hardly let their feet touch land except for trooping out of the water when lunch was set out, and then supper. Toward sunset JT lit the bonfire at the shore and the older folks pulled their collection of lawn chairs around in a semicircle. The youthfuls, as JT dubbed them, gravitated to the dessert table, then on over to the far field where the eldest nephew, Barlow, and the other older boys were sorting through bags of fireworks procured by JT from across the state line and beyond.

Brooke didn't leave the water, appreciating the solitude. Not needing dessert after the huge feast, and not much of a sweets kid anyway, she located the constant warm current at the end of the pond under the large weeping willow's tendrils touching the surface. Lazily treading the dark water just above her shoulders, she idly pushed her toes off the soft bottom as she listened to the bonfire crackling under the dusk sky. Invisible to those on shore, she loved being quiet, hidden, alone, buoyant. The sounds from the campfire floated across: occasional laughter over an old story, an uncle adding a few more wood scraps to the blaze and the embers spitting their way skyward.

Suddenly voices stilled, as if secrets were disclosed. Brooke's toe nudged something firm. It didn't give like the muddy bottom. Thinking it was nothing more than a large stone, she concentrated on picking up stray words above the hissing of pitch from a green pine branch. Then things got very quiet, and everyone turned toward her hiding place. She knew they couldn't see her in the gathering darkness with the firelight's glare before them. So why were they all staring her way?

She heard one of her aunts say, "It's still there, isn't it, JT?"

The woman, Brooke thought it might have been Aunt Claire, was immediately shushed by the rest. One of the uncles, it had to be Claire's husband Clair, said in no uncertain terms, "That blasted thing's gonna have to be moved before any of them kids wander across it. You know it, I know it. Eddie done it a decent burial. Question is, who's gonna give it the resurrection without the locals finding out?"

The adults were silent a long while. The warm current tailed off giving Brooke a chill.

"JT, darlin', what is it y'alls are hidin' down there?" The question came from Sheena, Brooke's younger aunt imported by marriage. Everybody knew and didn't need to proclaim Sheena the family scatterbrain. She was awarded fair recompense, however, with a frame fashioned in dramatic proportions most women envied, while every man gazed in awe when she took deep breaths.

More shushing, then Sheena's husband Reeve was none too kind. "More words like that, sweetness, and you might just find yourself down there too."

Brooke had never heard the hint of a threat from anyone in her family. If her kin had their fault, it was being too nice to each other. But there it was. Sheena had been served notice. And Sheena shut right up.

Two of the aunts tried to cover for Reeve. "He didn't mean it, dear, you know he didn't mean it."

After a silence that engulfed even the campfire's crackling, Brooke, now shivering but afraid to move, heard JT himself. He began to chuckle. More silence. Brooke's tension sought release. The warmth she introduced to the cold water brought momentary relief.

"You might as well know it all, Sheena my dear. We've got no secrets here, now do we?" The way JT said it made Brooke glad she was hidden in the water, and sure that Aunt Sheena had entered a danger zone. Then without prologue, eighty-year-old JT Shiller turned the key and unlocked the family diary.

That July Fourth night under the willow, phrases drifted to Brooke like, "Mostly silver, maybe some bullion"; "Confederate gold, you say"; "Paper'd have rotted long ago"; "Don't know for sure, it's still Eddie's".

Poor Sheena just didn't get it. Always a half bubble off plumb, she said too loudly, "Let's go for it right now. See if it's really there."

Oddly, no one muzzled her. Brooke saw them stand as a group, look around to be sure all the youth were across the far field dazzled by the aerial displays of mortars, barrages and whistles as if war had resumed against the North. The adults slowly and deliberately made their way to the pond's edge.

Sheena's boldness grew. "Where is it, JT? I'm goin' in."

Again, no argument.

"Under the inner branches of the willow." JT was barely audible. "Keep stepping around. You'll find it down there."

Sheena, who was never one of Brooke's favorites because she was a poser, removed her sundress. The women gasped, the men gawped. Once they saw the bathing suit underneath, the women clucked their tongues, the men chuckled, and her husband Reeve swore, "Sheena, one of these days…"

Sheena waded into the pond and quickly pushed her way along the shallows, then deeper toward the old willow. Brooke did her best to hide among the entwined roots and was about to duck underwater when Sheena's foot struck hers.

Sheena's scream shook off a few dozen willow leaves. Whispering, Brooke begged her not to tell. But Sheena, who never thought much of Brooke either, yelled out, "Here's another one of your little treasures hidin' here all by her lonesome."

Thirteen-year-old Brooke Potter was driven out of the pond, limping uncontrollably. The congregation of grandparents, uncles and aunts, even Aunt Claire, and led by JT Shiller himself, encircled her as if she were a prisoner of war. Her mother—JT's favorite niece—joined in the party. Her father silently drifted off to the side, forsaking his only child. Shivering from cold and disbelief, Brooke was interrogated, humiliated, pushed around by a few.

Confused, alone, she didn't understand her sin. Staying in the water after the other kids had left? Skipping dessert? Maybe Aunt Claire could be a little miffed if a wedge of her apple pie might have been one left behind, but she'd keep her head about her.

What, then? Brooke had only wanted to be by herself for awhile. Her foot touched a rock. Nothing more. It was a rock, wasn't it?

She became the outcast simply because she stumbled upon an old family secret. A sunken treasure of some sort, she understood them to say. She perplexed long afterward over the family's rage, trying to give rationale to their behavior. But reason had no place in their system. Only power, control, censure, blame.

JT Shiller's extended family held high standing in the community. Each member was required to play the part well of proper Southern deportment, with an underlying seething reserved for anyone perceived to endanger their supremacy. Brooke became their closest and favorite threat. The night she chanced upon Edwin's treasure became the family's opportunity to shatter her gift of loveliness, to immerse her in self-contempt. She wasn't good enough, they told her. Didn't belong, they said. Never would.

Why they had turned on one of their own made perfect sense: to maintain power and control. To keep the family secret a secret. To assert that no one was exempt from reprisal.

All the same, she was compelled to parade her remarkable beauty as the family trophy, a hard payment for her unintended discovery.

The citizenry of Shaw's Bow held her in admiration. She possessed a certain grace, no matter her limp. As Brooke matured, townsfolk stopped and stared when she walked by. Ordinary people they were, unfamiliar with the dynamics of ancestral dysfunction, having not peeked into closets of powerful families reared on disease.

Imprisoned in her mother's family, Brooke was kept under constant scrutiny. They convinced the regal swan that she had become the ugliest of ducklings. Early on, Brooke learned that her only practical, and therefore appropriate, responses to her family's torment were contrition and shame.

A couple of years into her prescribed confinement, her cousin Barlow thought to exercise his overeager prowess over Brooke. Her mother, a Shiller through and through, saw it coming. Her single demonstrated act of a mama's protection was employed that one moment when she cornered the lad and threatened his masculinity in no uncertain terms if he so much as looked at her daughter again the way she'd just caught him eyeing her.

Abandoned by those closest—mother, cousins, daddy— Brooke learned to hide her feelings of disgrace behind knowledge from books, and later her mastery of self-defense for protection and to compensate for her uneven step.

The night of her high school graduation, family and friends gathered for her party in JT's immense living room. They loitered around, impatiently sipping punch and nibbling cashews, reciting small talk about crops, fishing lures and shotgun reloads. Not even the homecoming queen of three years straight deserved to keep her relatives from their dinner. The nine-foot-high grandfather clock struck its bass notes announcing the late hour, when suddenly one of her cousins with less aptitude bolted into the house crying the queen was gone. That night Brooke's mother read the note on the kitchen table. *Let me be and I won't tell. Don't and you'll all go to jail, not just Uncle Edwin.*

The family council reviewed the issue and decided to give her leave, if that's what she wanted. But JT Shiller, the chieftain regarded for his moral standing, wondered if he'd done right by the lovely girl with promise, after all.

Two

Three years ago

AN UNINTENDED FIND IN HIS TWENTY-NINTH YEAR, Bryan Cord chanced upon his first true love. The girls he'd known could all be grouped into casual affairs. And he couldn't claim much success there.

But his first true love was different. Surprisingly different. His own boat. Not his dad's or Uncle Steve's. Just his name on the registration. She belonged to Bryan Chandler Cord.

When he first saw her at the Seattle docks, he was immediately star-struck. So what more appropriate name to give her? *Starstruck*. He possessed the lady of his dreams. And she owned him. And it was all good.

Cord made her his because he wanted her and he had the plastic. His job paid better than he supposed he probably deserved, but he was a natural at connecting the right corporation with the right software. While his colleagues in the sales force could claim decent monthly sales, Cord's greater outcome came by actively listening to the buyer's IT head. He took time to determine that person's language and personality—they weren't all geeks—and ask the right questions. He studied people not computers. His clients believed he cared more about them as individuals than as consumers. Bottom line, he made his company a lot of dollars, and for that he was remunerated a lot of dollars. Even during economic hiccups, he was in such demand it wasn't unusual for him to hand off contracts. His teammates believed he pretty much walked on water.

On a Sunday evening in November at the local pub with his work team, he offhandedly mentioned he might like to look at boats. Some of his friends took it upon themselves to help him search for the perfect vessel. Some insisted on sail, one suggested he restore an old tug. Office chatter often drifted to the latest collective viewpoints on "Cord's craft." One cold day in January, one of the self-assured women on his staff had had enough of what she called endless speculation. She packed Cord into her Miata and sped him to the floating boat show on Seattle's Lake Union.

Yachts of every size and description sat proudly in their slips, many of them within easy reach of his spending limit. It wasn't long before a new blue-and-white 37-foot Formula Performance Cruiser caught his eye. Stylish but not showy. Reserved but not bashful.

The yacht's broker, dressed in the attire of a yacht salesman not an owner, welcomed them aboard and began to enumerate the boat's highlights. Cord and the girl left him to his monologue and went below. It took only a few moments sitting in the cabin's conversation nook with his pretty coworker to recognize obvious benefits to owning that particular boat. Back on deck, the broker's patience and off-hand mention of a healthy boat-show discount were handsomely compensated when Cord told him, "I guess I'll take it."

"Yes sir. Of course, sir." The broker lost no time concluding Cord hailed from roots of nobility.

Cord reached into a front cargo pant pocket for his wallet and slipped out one of his platinum cards.

"Maybe this could do," he suggested.

Not following Cord's intent to immediately purchase the boat, the broker took the card and said, "We do have some excellent payment options to make it easy on the budget." Then with a wave of the card he asked, "Would you like to place a deposit to hold her—the vessel, that is—while you make other arrangements?" The guy actually winked at Cord's co-worker. "Or we can create a doable plan right here."

"Would it be okay to pay for it now?" Cord asked.

The broker's jaw dropped. "You mean now? Like, all?" Realizing an immediate commission, he quickly recovered. Straightening his navy sport coat and tucking a light blue polyester shirt into tan Dockers, he enthused, "Yes. Of course, yes. Fine. Yes."

The girl, unable to stifle a muffled laugh, turned away to feign inspection of the numerous instruments and gauges at the helm. The following Saturday the sun peeked out from behind winter clouds, so she joined Cord on *Starstruck's* voyage from Lake Union through the Chittenden Locks and north in Puget Sound to a small marina close to Cord's apartment in Port Strand.

While the boat proved worthy of Cord's appreciation, his passenger that day was somewhat less than a delight. The girl for all her spirit and passion at work was resistant to even his slightest curiosity. Not that she rebuffed him. She seemed to genuinely appreciate his friendship, giving him heartfelt attention. Strange girl, he thought. Amusing, confident, easy to be with, nice to look at. What was with her? He guessed it a few weeks later when he overheard her make some reference to God, as if she knew him. From then on Cord kept her at arm's length with superficial conversation.

Cord never figured he'd fall in love with a boat, but he was charmed by every avenue *Starstruck* opened—on the water, in the marina to new friends, other relationships. Sure, she developed the usual quirks expected, even required, of a boat. The pervasive aroma of salt and sea embedded in her upholstery and everything else porous, frequent in-water maintenance, periodic haul-outs, unforeseen repairs. But she didn't argue or question his judgment or loyalty, and she was at the ready to comply with his every desire. *Starstruck* had stolen his affection, taken him for a ride, all the while aiming to please. He was her master; she gave him power and fulfillment. And peace.

Three

Almost two years ago

BROOKE POTTER COULDN'T BELIEVE SHE was being dragged through the main entrance of a building whose name she wouldn't have associated with a church. Interesting labels newer centers of religion were given: Elevation, Soma, Synergy, Flood, Mosaic, Radius. As if they were concealing their identity.

Scanning the room for a close exit, Brooke had definite doubts about the whole idea of being in a house of God, not to mention the company of the guy pulling her along. He'd seemed okay when he checked out books at the library where she worked. But tonight he proved to be underwhelming. As a vendor of his newborn religion he was a yawn. His message about life-change enthralled him alone. She thought it trite. Without doubt, he was quickly becoming forgettable.

CHURCH. WEIRDLY NAMED, AND about the last place Bryan Cord expected to visit, let alone spot someone interesting. A friend of Cord's thought he needed God so bribed him into coming to a community thing.

"Dinner's on me," the friend had said. Sure enough, spaghetti. Mounds of it. Carbs to satisfy. Even a few brewskis on ice. Cord remembered hearing that churchy people weren't allowed to soak a few suds. He decided to hang around.

On a Saturday night in June in a multi-purpose room sectioned with round tables and institutional chairs, two captives of their respective hosts stood looking over uninviting donations to the potluck. Whether they were attracted to one another or drawn out of desperation to the neutrality of the dessert table, Brooke Potter and Bryan Cord found momentary refuge, there with squares of hardened fudge.

Brooke's five-foot-eight allowed her to look most men in the eye. That night she rather liked tilting her head to meet Cord's. They were light brown, emphasized by his deep tan. She guessed he stood a couple over six. Nice.

"Come here often?" he asked.

"That's your best?" she asked.

He shrugged. "Bryan."

"Brooke," she shrugged back.

She liked him. He seemed shy, but held a quiet confidence. He had the look of a Bond, without the cruelty. When she told him that a few weeks later, his reply was pleasantly modest. "I did drive my uncle's Aston Martin once. He still doesn't know that."

"Nice tan," she said moving away from the table.

He actually looked self-conscious. "Out of a bottle," he shrugged again.

She knew it wasn't true, but she went for his self-effacing humor. Cleverly reserved.

At that moment her chaperone playing the part of body-guard walked up to the table and said he needed to get her home. Brooke hated being treated like a child. Cord found the little frown alluring.

"Hope to see you again?" He offered it as a question.

She liked that too. Not pushy like the dullard grabbing her hand and conducting her toward the door.

Cord lifted a hand to wave and she smiled back, her deep blue eyes actually twinkling. Ponytail loosely pulled back—strawberry blond. Interesting walk—bit of a limp.

While he watched, his host came alongside and reminded him of the requisite sit-down for some kind of talk. The young preacher with topknot and tight jeans talked about God with undeserved authority, throwing in street language to convince only himself he was edgy therefore cool. Cord excused himself from his host and aimed for the exit, thinking about the girl with the limp.

YOU LIKE BOATING?" He called two days after the church thing.

He must have gotten her cell number that night—she didn't know how.

"Yes," her simple reply.

It was sufficient.

Their first date. Where else but his powerboat, *Starstruck*, on a warm evening in a small cove tucked in a hidden island somewhere secret among the San Juan Islands of Washington's northwest coast. After a splendid dinner of Cord's creation, they relaxed in the cockpit over small glasses of port, talking till late. She posed the most surprising questions. And it went both ways, revealing much about themselves, their dreams.

"When did you discover your leadership strengths?" She actually asked that. Cord later blamed it on too much port, but couldn't resist his response. It just came out differently than he planned.

"If I told you," he said in mock seriousness, "I'd have to kiss you. I mean, I'd have to…to, uh-h…"

She acknowledged it was the perfect Freudian slip. That, and the self-conscious smile of his. Brilliant. With her chin resting on her hand and her eyes dancing in the candlelight, she stared deep into his, and her voice became sensually breathy. "So tell me."

Conversation gave way to passion. With more than a few weekend romps on the boat, Bryan and Brooke knew they fit well in just about every way. They spent the remainder of the summer's weekends exploring the San Juans. They liked the same music—mellow. Seafood the same way—out of the water and onto the grill, drenched in drawn butter. The same movies—she was into intrigue and he appreciated romance. That summer they began to seize every moment and couldn't get enough of each other.

Cord had never before met a woman who completely captivated him. Early on over nachos in *Starstruck's* cabin, Brooke caught him unawares by asking if his boat's twin power plants might not generate more horsepower if they were fit with custom exhaust manifolds and beefier ignition systems. And if he wanted to get serious about muscle, losing those stock trannies for something bulletproof.

"Physically stunning, and a dazzling mind," said Cord. He toasted her with a chip loaded with cheese before setting it in her mouth.

Brooke crunched the chip and bobbed her head. "Shucks, Bryan."

"You do know a lot about a lot," he said, forgetting his nachos.

"I've actually read some of those books people check out at my library." She crossed her eyes. "Some I've read twice."

He'd loved her humor. Feeling a casual ease with her he said, "I'm a slow reader. Always have been."

"There's nothing wrong with that, is there? The question isn't how fast you read, but why. And, of course, the takeaway."

"I'm a pretty simple guy, Brooke. I read a book because someone suggests I'd like it. If it doesn't grab me, I close it and move on. Why do I read? Because the book keeps my attention. No deep answer there."

"Can I rephrase your 'why' answer?"

Cord took a chip for himself. "You amaze me."

"Reading fills life's darkest cavities with flashes of light. And with every glimmer you find a little more hope. Monday, Tuesday, Wednesday, any day of the week."

He stared at her, the chip still in his mouth. "You're too good to be true." He almost whispered it. "And, I've never heard anyone say Wednesday with three syllables."

They reminisced often about their first meeting, in a church of all places. But neither had any inclination to dwell on the aspects of religious systems, or anything other than getting together. Their intimate conversations in quiet inlets ranged from banter—*in high school I was just another creep; in college I turned into a real jerk.* To profound honesty—*sometimes it seems like there's this presence after me; I don't want it to be God, if there is one.* From personal regrets to hopes for a future that would allow an escape from the past.

Cord offhandedly asked, "When you look into the future, what are your dreams?"

Her answer caught him off guard.

"Dreams?" she said pensively. "As in hoping for a better something around the corner instead of coming face to face with the twin of the monster already chasing me? I'm still try-ing to wake up from a nightmare."

He didn't take that trail with her, not because he was in-sensitive, which he could be. But he wasn't quick enough to change gears to serious reflection. She didn't bring up her dreams again, and he having other things on his mind, forgot he'd asked.

Then that September night. They'd only met the beginning of summer, but it seemed they'd known and been known for years. He gave her the ring. No prelude, no tongue-tied will-you-marry-me, no compulsory discussion. He quietly dropped the sparkler in his palm, motioned it toward her and asked, "So, you think you might wear this?"

It was all so perfect, and unlike her teen years, a fairy-tale.

Two weeks later they were informally wed on the boat in the presence of a few select friends, one of them securing a provisional license to perform the civil rite. The ceremony was blessedly quick.

"Okay, so like, I pronounce you two married. Now seal it!"

After the kiss, not the shortest on the books, the wedding couple popped open the almond champagne—a case of twelve proved sufficient for their crew—and tossed the one-shot preacher overboard to show their appreciation for the tax ben-efits of marriage. With just enough bubbly to assuage any doubts about their matrimonial plunge, Cord headed *Starstruck* back to the dock to drop off their friends. He slipped a wad of hundreds to the marrying buddy for his trouble and some new clothes, then with his bride of three hours immediately sped back out to a predetermined honeymoon cove.

Bryan and Brooke Cord. Alone again, at last. And legal, like it mattered. Their merriment continued in earnest on the boat, which they appropriately nicknamed *Passionate*. They didn't come up for air for four days. Life together was flawless.

Mrs Bryan Cord. Something her mother would say. No, her grandmother. Brooke wished she had known her dad's mom, Gramz, better. But Lakeview, Ohio was a long way from anyplace Brooke happened to be.

Gramz possessed a depth mingled with mirth. Always on the lookout for life's adventure, despite the risks, or the dangers. Forever seeing the positives in life and people. Without fail she told Brooke she was praying for her, whatever that meant. And for Brooke's high-pepper-quotient personality, and Brooke knew what that meant.

Gramz would take her preacher to coffee during the week to pick his brain, even argue the poor man down. Then she spent Sunday mornings, when the weather was good for a stroll, hanging out with kindred spirits around a table at Keene's Koffee, talking over long brunches about the God her preacher followed. The Rev, Gramz called him, asked her—once only—why she didn't darken the door of the church. She explained her worsening peripheral vision kept her balance wobbly. Besides, she could be a brighter light for Jesus seated at a table for six than stumbling into a church row. Every Sunday thereafter the Rev drove her to Keene's on his way to preach. What was it about Gramz that Brooke loved? Something deep inside.

Brooke and Bryan flourished together. A uniquely real couple, surprising their friends who thought it unlikely. Open dialogue became their standard communication. Old faults, which had been countless, were discussed and released. New mistakes with each other, minor and major, were dealt with and let go. Like when Brooke washed and dried Cord's only wool suit. Significant shrinkage. But suits were out for him anyway so he gave it to the kid next door for a middle school play of Sherlock Holmes in knickers.

Brooke and Bryan Cord were new people. With each other. For each other.

Four

CORD'S PHONE RANG OUT THE UNIQUE TONE.

"Yeah, babe," he answered.

"I'm leaving from work. I could go for dinner out to-night," said Brooke. "You look like you could use some nourishing restaurant food too."

"I know that tone in your voice. Come home, take off your shoes—and anything else. I took the afternoon off. Dinner's covered tonight. Specialty of the house. My finest."

Brooke. One of the most beautiful women in Cord's world. Okay, *the* most. Was it wrong to be taken in by beauty when it went so far beyond skin deep? How else to describe the woman of his life: incredibly brilliant, piercingly astute, caring, gentle—when she wasn't kickboxing and formidable when she was.

She walked through the back door, tired but exquisite.

"I put it together, all from scratch," said Cord, sliding a pizza from the local shop into the oven. "Lots of cheese, four kinds. Sun-dried tomatoes, 'shrooms, kale, no onions."

"I see. But no anchovies?" Brooke made a face as she said it.

"Want me to take it back?" He turned on the oven. "Broil or bake, which one?"

"It'll cook either way. I'll pour the wine. Have you a preference?" She slipped off a pair of heels.

"How about that chianti on the bottom shelf. Let's be ordinary tonight."

Finishing the partial bottle of wine and leaving two pizza slices for Cord's breakfast—provoking another grimace from Brooke—they took their iPhones into the small living room, which she called the parlor.

Antique Oriental silk and Tibetan wool rugs covered the original hardwood floor of their Craftsman-style cottage, and a cluster of early seascapes by a favorite Newport Beach artist graced one wall. An expensive sofa the saleswoman termed a chesterfield with matching stuffed chair and a scarred coffee table handed down from Cord's great grandmother filled the room. Off to the side stood a small round table with a working black rotary phone.

The couple scanned Facebook posts.

"I rarely look at this anymore," she said. "So much trivia. I don't care what Emma wore last night to dinner. She posted a photo of the latest guy she's calling her favorite person ever."

"She the one who didn't show for the wedding?"

"That's her. Her previous pet human of all time needed…oh, no."

Cord looked up from his screen. "Something wrong?"

She didn't answer.

"B?"

Her attention remained fixed on her phone.

"Brooke? You there?" He thought he saw her shiver. "What is it, babe?"

She tapped the phone off. "Nothing. It's nothing, really."

"Pretty big nothing. Tell me."

She set her phone on the side table. Cord waited.

"If you must know," she said, "my mother's family is holding a reunion. I'm invited. We are. At one of my aunt's." Her attempt at a smile inverted to a frown.

"Awesome. In Kentucky?" A west coast boy, Cord had only flown over anything east of Las Vegas for business.

"Yes. But no, I don't think so," she said.

"Sure, it'll be cool. When is it?"

"It's their annual Fourth of July party, but this time they're insisting everyone must be there."

Cord had wanted to finally meet the family, and told her if they were anything like her they must be amazing.

She countered, "Let's spend that weekend on *Starstruck*. Let it live up to the name we gave it last summer on our honeymoon. *Passionate*. Take the entire week. Just us. Anything we want."

Unlike the Brooke he knew, she threw up roadblocks until he pressed for an answer.

"I've told you I don't have good memories of my childhood. Can we leave it at that?" Her voice was tight, her eyes burning.

Cord, trying to be helpful, proposed, "It might be what you need. You know, revisit, climb that hill of the past and see that the demon isn't so bad after all. I'll be with you the whole time."

She relented, tapped the phone and accepted the invitation.

Uncharted

THE FLIGHT FROM SEATTLE to Chicago's O'Hare triggered anxiety in her that Cord had never seen. It only increased on the hop into Lexington's Blue Grass Municipal. They picked up the rental and took the road south for Shaw's Bow. He figured the drive through Daniel Boone National Forest would relax her. He figured wrong.

The closer they got to her Aunt Gretchen's farm east of town, the more Brooke's agitation grew.

"You want to talk, B?"

"No. It's just that I haven't seen the family since high school. I've changed; I doubt they have." To herself she whispered, "I hate this place. Nothing good ever happened here."

"Can I help? I'm here, babe."

"No! Just let me be." First time he heard her snap at him. "And don't call me that."

"I always call you that."

"Never again. You hear?" He detected an accent he hadn't noticed before.

Brooke made it a brief appearance. After a few hugs to younger cousins, she made her way to Aunt Gretchen's kitchen to avoid the rest of her relatives.

Cord naively gravitated toward the food tables. The most tantalizing home-style cuisine he'd ever seen up close, extending further than any appetite could crave, each dish with a benefactor and a story. Ribs donated by the Wheelers over 'cross the dale in Mervston; the finest cuts of venison dressed out by three or four of the family hunters; squab raised, reamed and roasted by the Peters twins; huge platters of deviled eggs designed by Cousin Arbutus; a pyramid of corn on the cob just picked and barely blanched from Uncle Mylo's patch; and various other culinary delights worthy of at least honorable mention. And it had to be set out before the desserts because not even at Aunt Gretchen's was there room for the entire feast to appear in total glory all at one time.

Cord tried to mingle with the good-oles, but got no further than the outer periphery. He didn't know to come prepared, and Brooke hadn't clued him in. Wearing cargo shorts not jeans, sneakers not boots, no socks, and a tee shirt from one of last year's triathlons, he admitted to the recognized senior figure, JT Shiller himself, that he didn't own, much less carry, a piece, or drive anything built in America. Meanwhile Brooke kept her distance from every group and spoke only briefly with a neighbor she remembered from childhood. Not another person, and positively not any in her immediate family. No one saw her double over in pain behind a kitchen counter, clutching her stomach.

Cord had just bitten into the juiciest pork rib of his life when he noticed Brooke giving Aunt Gretchen a barely sociable embrace, and signaling to him they were leaving, right now. Aunt Gretchen began to pack a lunch for their return to Lexington. Cord was about to express his appreciation when Brooke firmly declined.

In the car she began to shake.

Four miles up the road skirting the town Cord pulled into a turnout overlooking a narrow finger of a large lake and shut off the engine. "Time to talk, Brooke. You don't need to carry this yourself."

They parked in that turnout for more than two hours. A state trooper cruising his stretch of the road slowed down twice. That afternoon Brooke Gretchen Potter Cord began to reveal and relive the darkest part of her twenty-eight years she had kept secret since she was thirteen.

"Brooke, you said you've changed since you left here. Maybe they've changed too, for the better. Do you need to give them a chance? They seemed to enjoy each other, and I felt welcome, sort of. And the food was great. Is it time to let go of the memories, the feelings? So they don't keep hurting you."

Brooke stared at him in disbelief. Did he not get it? Had he joined the other side—over pork ribs and deviled eggs? She had banked her trust in this man. Could she still?

Puzzled, Cord phoned in the cancellation of their one-night stay at the Hampton, drove straight to the airport, turned in the car, and bribed the airline reservation clerk for a last-minute shuttle to a forgettable airport. Then, for an extra lot of dollars and tolerating a you-know-I'm-really-not-supposed-to-be-doing-this lecture, booked onto the last flight to Dubuque, from there to Denver in middle seats at opposite ends of the cabin on an airline better named Obscurity, and on to Seatac in Frontier's first class.

Outside the terminal very early in the Pacific Northwest morning dampness, Cord hailed a sleepy cabbie for the airport Hilton.

"Booked much solid," the reply in broken English. "You okay Marriott? Could be room left. Is close."

"Fine. Do it."

At the Marriott off Independence Avenue, a just-as-sleepy hotel counterman enduring the last hours of graveyard sold them the Presidential, claiming it was the last room he had. In the huge suite they took off their outer clothing, stripped the king bed of its duvet, collapsed and didn't wake until the cleaning girl barged in late that morning.

Parting with the last of Cord's cash to steal another hour, and a *gracias, señorita*, they each showered, Brooke in slow motion. It took a fair bit of convincing, but she agreed to stop for a late lunch in the hotel's coffee shop to nibble around the edges of a small salad. Finding her Honda in a rental lot, Cord took her keys and got behind the wheel. They drove the three hours north in silence.

CORD COULDN'T FIGURE IT OUT. The pieces didn't fit together. One week everything was fine, a good life, great marriage. *So, we take one little weekend hop to the other side of the country and it all collapses right in front of me.* Overnight she shut the door, literally. No dinners together, no evening conversations in the parlor, not even surface how-was-your-day. Certainly no sleeping together. Nothing. She locked herself in the bedroom. Actually locked the door. Sure, he could have wrenched the knob and walked in, but hearing that button click told him she was inside and he wasn't allowed. The only time he saw her was when she stole into the kitchen to nuke her own dinner then bolt back to her fortress.

Cord was baffled. On the occasions he could catch a glimpse of her, he saw a sadness in Brooke not there before. Less than a year into their marriage her emotions began to lead them both into mine shafts of gloom neither could escape.

None of their friends had any illusions their marriage was made in heaven, or even near the second star to the right, because these two were pretty earthy. But those close to them saw the beginning of something that everyone—drinking buds, his anyway, and her three friends—agreed was a decent match.

In their first months together she couldn't deny his honesty. "Brooke," without warning he'd solemnly misquote in a deep voice an old Superman movie, "I'll never lie to you." She'd reply as Lois Lane, "Then what color are my panties." He couldn't answer, of course she wouldn't tell, and they'd quickly find the bed. Well, at least that was something.

At one time she liked his name. Bryan. Even loved saying it. Bryan Cord. Brooke and Bryan. Only a month into dating and they were inseparable, known to friends as B&Bry, as if they were one.

But that was then.

Quirks that once charmed mysteriously became annoying habits. Verbal exchanges grew short and sharp. The boat, formerly for frolic, slept alone in its slip for weeks, then months. Their small cottage overlooking the water became a nighttime jail to escape during their workdays. The California king, once the playground, developed a three-foot DMZ down the middle. Cord declared her side North Korea and settled for the couch.

Now, a year and a half after the wedding, she thought of him only as…him. Both had brought junk into the relationship. She admitted the baggage scale tilted more against her, but he wasn't above analysis.

She grew to hate him, surprisingly fast. He became the target for a loathing stored deep within and hidden well, until now. He was crowding her with his presence. She needed out.

But she still wanted to believe him. A few months earlier a friend had loaned her a novel about someone meeting God in a faraway mountain cabin, or something like that. It was an arduous read, and the movie, though lauded by her colleagues, stretched too long for her taste. But one thing she remembered was that God, or someone characterized as God, said the more a person loves another, the more that person will trust the other. Brooke thought she probably did love Cord early on, more than she'd loved anyone. But that was a few eons ago. Nowadays she despised him. Trust? Not a hope.

But neither had cheated on the other. Well, she knew she

could have. And he argued he hadn't.

No one expected to see the dream of their marriage flip to a nightmare. And it hadn't taken two years from I do.

Uncharted

Five

Look, I've tried to make this work. You know I have."

Cord kept his back to her, his focus on stuffing the sports bag with the first clothes he could grab from his side of the closet.

Their wedding night. So long ago. The entirety of their short marriage only sixteen months, the latter part interminable. Already a punishing marathon.

"There's no pleasing you," he said. "It's never enough with you. So okay, you've got what you want." He turned to face his wife. "I won't do this anymore, B."

She stood in the doorway, leaning against the jamb, arms crossed, glaring. "It's Brooke."

Bryan Cord had never thought a voice could produce immediate climate change inside four walls. He went back to stowing the items he'd need for work. He wanted out. Out of the house, the war zone they'd once called their haven. Away from her disapproval.

"Do what you want," she said. "You haven't tried and you know it. You haven't given us anymore than fleeting attention since you climbed out of bed after the honeymoon."

Bed? Cord knew his retort would level her. He played out the scene in his mind. His words would sting, she'd turn away crumbling, begin to cry—more like a little girl than a woman, leave the room, slam the door of their single bathroom, stay there for hours. Silence, except for her relentless sniffling. He hated the way she blew her nose. Like a ship in distress.

He wouldn't fight her again. He settled for, "I don't remember it that way."

He yanked the bag shut, nearly tearing the zipper, and grabbed the handles. Enough clothing to get him through the next five or six days. He'd sleep on the boat. Away from the arguments, the hostility. Away from B…Brooke.

She thought his passive reply an indicator of the small victory due her and pursued more emotional high ground.

"You've never been one for debate."

He couldn't compete with her mind. Or her vocabulary—a walking thesaurus. He didn't answer. Give her the win.

He was about to leave when she said, "Your hat."

He snagged his favorite cap off the floor in the corner of what had been his side. He pushed it on his head and made for the door.

She held fast to the threshold and begrudged him only space to sidestep past. He pressed against the opposite jamb to avoid brushing against her. Her touch made his skin crawl.

Funny, it didn't used to.

But that was then.

At the backdoor he called over his shoulder, "You know where I'll be."

From inside the bedroom, "I care?"

She knew he wouldn't close the door.

Opting for the motorcycle over his restored classic 1973 Volvo 1800ES, Cord strapped the sports bag onto his new Triumph Thunderbird and pressed the starter. He could have wheelied out the driveway, but he had nothing to prove. He wasn't angry. He was fed up.

His helmet. On the drier in the back porch. Forget it. He needed the freshness of the night wind against his face. He reversed his cap and unhurriedly pulled onto the dark Port Strand residential street and turned the bike toward the marina. The hiss of the tires sluicing the wet pavement and the fragrance of the northwest winter relaxed his tension a bit. For the first time in too long he felt a hint of release.

Brooke waited in the bedroom for the motorcycle's exhaust to fade to quiet. No tears this time. No sniffling. She never sniffled. She didn't do a lot of things he said she did. She hated his accusations.

She walked to the backdoor, still in heels, and with finality closed it. She loved the sound of the dead bolt sliding home. Why did it feel so right to have him gone? She had absolutely no desire to hear that bike again. No wish for him to return. No need of him, at all.

She turned off the parlor lights and made very sure the porch light was out, the welcome mat hidden away.

Who was that one guy from that church? Walking into the empty bedroom and kicking off her heels Brooke tried to recall the fellow's name. Was he really that bad? Certainly not any worse than how her husband turned out.

Her husband. The word repulsed her. And yet…

Her thoughts were always on Cord. She used to love him for the unpretentious magnetism he held. Now she loathed any reminders of him.

In the bathroom she briskly and sloppily brushed her teeth, using her towel for her face and wiping the sink with his. Opening the bottom drawer of the dresser she chose her beige nightshirt, the one down to her ankles. The one he detested. She climbed into the huge bed, all hers, positioned herself squarely in the DMZ and waved her arms and legs as if making a snow angel.

Alone. Finally and wonderfully alone.

Six

DAMP. DARK.

The coating of fog over the marina matched his mood.

Cord stepped onto his boat's swim platform, glancing at the name on the transom. *Starstruck*. Whose idea was it to use the name *Passionate*? No surprise, for their ardent weekends together.

He knew his marriage was more than an extended fling. He'd loved Brooke, deeply loved his wife.

His wife. The first few months the title had a strange ring. When the market checkout girl called her Mrs. Cord, Bryan had to stop himself from looking over his shoulder for his mom.

He shook the thoughts from his mind, opened the marine canvas sun-bridge cover and brushed away the raindrops pooled on the tarp. Tossing his sports bag on the cockpit's L-shaped dinette and zipping back down the cover, he took the two-step ladder down into the cabin. Turning on the lights and activating the digital climate control, he scanned the boat's interior and nodded. Home.

Starstruck was his haven from conflict. Even on the stormiest days, his safety. If divorce was on the horizon, he'd give up anything. Except the boat. Brooke could have all the furniture, the ninety-inch OLED Ultra HD TV, whatever she wanted. Okay, the cottage too; the parlor didn't suit him anyway. He'd even donate a kidney. But not his boat. Or the car. Nor for that matter, his comic collection. There were some things the man must contest.

And come to think of it, the name of the boat, as of now, would return to *Starstruck* not *Passionate*. Although, Cord considered, passion just might become the narrative of future pursuits in her venue.

Inside the spacious cabin, he went through the floppy case of Blu-ray disks and settled on the re-mastered *The Great Escape* as the first of a double feature. After this evening's argument, the title seemed appropriate. He opened a galley cupboard for popcorn and nuked the first of two packages. While it was popping he pulled a Newcastle brown and Black Toad dark from the fridge. Good to see there were three more of each. He wasn't planning on sleeping much without the soothing effects of a little—or a lot—of brew. He didn't care when he'd wake up in the morning, but for the consideration of his work colleagues he should call in sick. Better do it now before popping the second bag.

Or tomorrow.

He dumped his cell in a drawer under the chart table, opened his first bottle and took a fair pull as the second bag began to pop. With the remote he clicked on the wall-mounted 43" borderless TV. He had every intention of getting lost in a world of drama played out by long-dead actors to chase away intruding thoughts of B…Brooke.

The screen came to life with the opening credits. Cord stripped to his black boxers, pulled on a favorite sweatshirt and threw aside the duvet. The popcorn was hot, the beer cold. He lay back on the bed, adjusted the wireless headphones and sank deep into three soft pillows, drinking and munching.

He took a peek at the boat's chronometer. Only 9:20. She wouldn't be asleep yet.

He hadn't noticed the lights on in the boat moored next to *Starstruck*. The older man peeked from behind the curtains of his motoryacht to see who had walked down the finger wharf shared by the two boats. Satisfied it was *Starstruck's* owner, the man let the curtains fall back into place, smiled warmly at his wife perusing a copy of *Masters Track & Field News*, and resumed his examination of a navigational chart.

Uncharted

Seven

THE OLDER COUPLE IN THE MOTOR YACHT alongside *Starstruck* appreciated a full night's sleep. Travis and Carly Edgerton shared a comfortable though not spacious queen bed. Early on they had staked out their own territories, Travis generally annexing more than his allotment. Carly, content with her thin slice along the bed's edge, was grateful his rhythmic snoring wasn't measured in decibels. A friend had described the cruelty of her husband's sleep apnea, holding her own breath until he finally exhaled. Tortuous.

While other couples worked toward a modicum of accord and were slow to rise above arguing the finer details of husband-wife duties and restrictions, Travis and Carly took hold of and nurtured a unity of joy. Ample disagreements came along, to be sure. They both had their eccentricities, saying they were strengths a bit overcooked. Travis frankly admitted his might be more numerous and bothersome. Carly revised that to infuriating. But without fail, they came around to being all for each other, loyalty cultivating their camaraderie.

Married many more years than either had been single, the Edgertons grew to savor life, and life together. Relational storms—one of them recent—they accepted. Not all had the potential to capsize their union. But some could. Such was life. So the two stood alert with each other over their marriage, protecting the treasure they called *us*. Despite irritations, traumas, and disappointments—and in part because of them—they grew together into matrimonial completeness that allowed them to claim one another as best friend, soulmate, sole lover.

Dr Travis Edgerton, his hair closing in on silver and still requiring monthly trims, stood himself straight at not quite five-ten. Carly, her five-five frame superbly athletic, grudgingly came to grips with a one-size larger figure. She submitted to thrice-yearly spaghetti-curl perms of her graying mane, insisting she was still mostly blonde.

Together they shared life. They were all about pursuing its adventures and surprises, walking side-by-side into whatever might await them. Just the two of them, on their own again.

Empty nest syndrome—the resultant loneliness of parents when their young adult children discover life beyond the family fence. Some of their friends waved tearful goodbyes to progeny and spent too many hours reliving the old days of kids home and under foot, as if those earlier times should forever remain the culmination of family blessedness. Life revolving around Little League, ballet, and my-child-is-cooler-than-yours bumper billboards, was understood to represent familial well-being.

The two Edgerton children, Susan and Scott, did their compulsory lessons in music, she the keyboard, he mismatched on cello and not quite figuring out how to hold the thing. But they loved sports. Both earned full-ride scholarships, their universities actually giving good money, all four years no less, for

Suzie to maintain a civilized seventy-eight on the links, and for Scott to run fast. Whether either excelled wasn't an issue to Mom and Dad. Rather, how much they valued the experiences—that's what counted. Of course, Scott's preliminary bid for a spot on the US Olympic team in the 200-meter dash wasn't all that disappointing.

Some family units in the local church culture followed interpersonal gurus. They loaded up on the latest parenting books and talking head DVDs—often for zilch as their kids, not yet out of middle school, kept secrets from their parents.

Not so the Edgerton family. Togetherness meant fun, and Travis made sure of it. He, usually without forewarning, created wonder. As a young family, they huddled overnights inside a living room fort constructed of dining room chairs, blankets and couch cushions to watch a string of cartoon videos he picked up at the library.

One winter night Travis lit a campfire in the center of the room, windows wide open for ventilation. Though he said he'd been careful to protect the carpet from the propane-heated lava rocks, the next morning he trudged into the rug vendor's, hiding a smirk with Carly happily leading the way to buy the 8x11 Persian she'd been eyeing for years and now needed to cover the two-foot scorch circle.

The safety of a family's fun and laughter often led to honest conversations. They didn't look for opportunities to create object lessons, but let them happen. And happen they would. One night at the dinner table Suzie, then nine, asked her parents if they had been virgins before marrying. Quite a family discussion followed well into the night.

The Edgertons were a boating family for as long as the kids could remember. As they grew into adolescence, they were treated to weekends on the water with other water-loving families. Those expeditions by and by brought Travis and Carly a daughter-in-law. One clear summer day Scott, in his middle teens, gazed for the first time upon the emergent beauty of the girl two years his junior on the boat sharing their slip. Sparing the details, the inevitable development of her young form progressed and his interest advanced. In his eyes Amber became the prettiest and classiest girl in Port Strand, with a proclivity for bringing happiness to the people she loved. Daughter Susan married her young college golf coach. The Edgerton offspring treated the folks to grandchildren, Scott and Amber offering twin boys now eleven, Suzie and Jayden adding a girl four years later, the apple of everyone's eye.

Travis and Carly, barely crossing over into their sixties—an age their grandkids couldn't imagine functional—looked and felt younger. A good ten years younger, they claimed. Possibly fifteen. Both contended with medications, but they were able to ward off the effects of slowing down by seizing life all the more—with a little moderation. One large mug of coffee, half real half decaf because it seemed a reasonable compromise to their physician's counsel to cut back on caffeine. Daily exercise on the track when the Northwest sun spoke up—they still competed in masters track events. Workouts in the neighborhood weight room with the midmorning group when the weather turned pigheaded.

Travis and Carly had always been drawn to the water. But it was only a couple of years ago when they decided to live on it full time. Calling it a pre senior-moment decision, they announced to their kids they'd rent out the townhouse to a nephew, sell their beloved wooden Chris-Craft, and move onto a 47-foot Bayliner, a northwest native they could purchase for less than you'd expect. Good grief, said Carly—her very words—it's got almost as much floor space as the townhouse.

And a washer/dryer stack. Even has a hallway, Travis added. Tell me the last time you saw a boat with a hallway.

The kids offered their acceptance; little else they could do. Their parents found ways to create adventure. Living aboard a yacht seemed safer than skydiving, as if either would try skydiving. Well, Mom still might. The grandkids thought the move was cool, and the nephew who'd be renting the townhouse was already planning a redesign.

How long they'd live aboard? Probably four or five years, or ten. With the nephew contributing a modest rent to cover their monthly moorage, it'd be an easy financial trade-off. Perhaps one summer they'd take their powered home up the Inside Passage to Alaska. Hundreds of boaters followed those breadcrumbs every year.

The grandkids were always eager for an overnight at Grandma's and the Doc's. Travis had retired early from his position as professor in leadership studies at a local university. Now that he and Carly were fulltime liveaboards, the youngsters awarded him the moniker, Cap. Sometimes they reverted to Doc, the name they grew up calling him. Carly was Grandma—Commander when she was at the helm. Whether moored in the slip or out on Puget Sound, Cap and the Commander grasped the wheel of life.

This night, the grandparents were alone, serene in their stateroom. The ship's chronometer silently announced an hour yet too early for the Creator to consent to the sun's rising from its nocturnal dash past lands Far Eastern. Travis entertained dreams of coffee, albeit half decaf. Carly, finally able to drift beyond her husband's cadenced snoring, dreamed of nothing.

Uncharted

Eight

I<small>T WASN'T GOOD</small>. T<small>HE BED WAS BIG</small>, it was comfortable. But it was all wrong.

Brooke Potter Cord reached for her cell on the side table and touched the home button to light the display. A little after 2:30 AM. She had dozed a couple of hours, but was now fully awake.

And angry.

Bryan Cord had simply walked out the door and escaped her rage. She deserved a good argument, but he took a coward's way out. Typical. When it came to a quarrel, there was no way he could stand up to her barrage of verbiage. Except when he attacked her where it hurt. He had discovered her weak spots, the ones where she could build no defense. It took no more than a couple of key words and she'd wither. She knew he could have said more, but he never pursued the attack. He just shut down and crawled away to what she called his emotional crypt. She hated him for that. The more she chewed on the memories, the more she loathed everything about him.

In the darkness she replayed scenes of their marriage. A continuous loop of romance, disappointment, frustration, anger, tears, fighting. More romance, more disappointment, more anger, more fighting. The memories made her stomach churn. What was so wrong about them to sour their love so quickly, completely? Why did the bad far outweigh any good? She caught herself asking why she was so angry.

There had been no affair, he insisted. The girl was just a colleague at work. On his team, he said. The same girl with him when he bought the boat. Brooke met her at the pre wedding party Cord's team had arranged for them. She seemed genuine then, so Brooke didn't consider her a threat. But over the last year her name came up more than it should have. Meredith Mayhew. Meredith said this, Meredith sealed that deal. Meredith, Meredith.

Nor had Meredith kept her opinions to herself. She even pretended to be religious, talking about a faith. Relationship with the Lord, she called it. Fancy maneuvering, Meredith Mayhem.

Then the bikini. When Brooke chanced upon one of foreign origin in the boat's head, colors she'd not be caught dead wearing, Cord claimed it belonged to one of her own friends. *I'll never lie to you, Brooke.*

"One of my friends?" she muttered to herself, alone in her king bed. Brooke felt like she had no friends. Okay, perhaps Emma did leave it; it was something she'd wear, even sober.

But that didn't excuse Cord from bending too close over Meredith at her monitor when Brooke just happened to drop in at his office for the ski jacket she'd forgotten. Oh, they both pleaded innocence. Just getting a better look, he said. At what? Did they think she was blind, and stupid? *I'll never lie to you, Brooke.*

Was Brooke so flawed that he was already looking for another playmate?

Her mind wouldn't stop creating the scenes of the last half year of turbulence. Her anger spiraled. She wanted revenge.

She looked at the cell again. 4:53. She didn't remember dozing. The Northwest's winter darkness would only grudgingly give way to a diffused twilight, but not for another three hours. She'd get no more sleep, so why should he be given the luxury? She threw the covers off and stormed into the dressing room to change. Pulling on her jeans she reran his last words. *You know where I'll be.* Well, that's where she was going. He could pretend that boat was his little castle on the water, but the walls were about to be breached. Early morning or not, she couldn't wait to have it out. And if he had company, so much the better. Brooke was aching to break up a party of two.

Her anger off the chart, she suddenly cocked her arm back and threw a fist against the wall.

"Ow!"

No drywall construction in this 1920s cottage, the walls were made of old wood lathe and inch-thick plaster. She rubbed her right hand. Nothing broken, and she felt a satisfaction in the tension release against a wall that did indeed give. She admired four shoulder-height knuckle imprints.

Charging to the garage she jumped into Cord's Volvo ES, slammed the door—he hated the doors slammed—shoved the manual gear shift in reverse and peeled out of the garage. She almost skinned the right fender against the garage door frame and wished she had. Cord loved this car. He loved the boat. He loved everything shiny and just so. Okay, she was going to show him how easily his toys could be hurt. Still in the driveway, she mashed the brakes, threw the stick into first and jerked the car back into the garage, this time aiming the right fender for the garage door's steel track. The scrape of metal against metal, long and squealing—a sweet sound. The neighbors were sure to hear it. She jammed back into reverse and the car growled out of the garage a second time, a strip of door trim clattering on the concrete. Brooke savored that sound too.

On the damp street the rear tires spun before they grabbed, and the ES fishtailed slightly. Keeping the accelerator to the carpet and grinding gears, Brooke blew through the stop sign at the end of the block.

Nine

D<small>ON'T</small> *EVEN* <small>PRETEND YOU'RE ASLEEP!</small> We're going to talk. Right now!"

The voice pierced through the nightmare, sounding like someone Bryan Cord didn't want to know.

But he wasn't dreaming, and the clamor only got louder. And it was still dark. Shaking his head to clear out the ruins of a thick sleep, he placed the voice's source somewhere near the galley, too close to him. Even in his half-stupor, he was amazed that the woman's blast of verbal assault had gained such penetrating attributes.

"B?" he croaked. Three beers and two bags of dry popcorn four hours earlier had clogged his throat. "What're you…?" His hands fumbled around the pillows for his cell phone and couldn't find it. "What time's it?" He spied the digital clock on the opposite bulkhead: 5:27.

"I don't *even* care what time it is, or who's with you. Get out of that bed!" She placed heavy emphasis on *even* when her anger reached the upper register.

"What are you talking about? There's nobody here." He snapped on an overhead light. "See for yourself. Just me. Now you." Then muttering, "I don't *even* think I'm here. Great, now I'm saying it. This has got to be a nightmare." Forgetting the cell, he searched among the duvet folds for his sweatpants.

"You're trying to find humor? You know that won't happen." Her voice rose a full octave in only two sentences. Not since a Navy air show had he felt such aural distress.

"Keep it down. You'll wake the old folks next door."

"I don't *even* care who's listening or how much they hear." Her statements were punctuated rather efficiently by expletives.

Cord stumbled his way into the salon, still pulling on his sweats.

Brooke peered past him. "Where is she!"

He looked at her as if she had burned a circuit. "She who? What are you doing here?"

"You know who. Your bimbo at work." Another expletive, and still screaming.

"Huh? Bimbo? You mean Meredith? Why would she be here? And she's no bimbo, What's with you, Brooke?"

She strode past him and scanned the stateroom. Seeing nothing more than the empties and some popcorn kernels on the floor she walked back out. Without a word she stared at him hard.

They stood facing each other until he raised his eyebrows in confusion and sighed deeply. "You want to sit down?"

"I'm fine standing."

"Okay, stand. At least you've stopped screaming."

"I've *what?*"

"Brooke, you're…" He didn't finish the sentence. "You want something hot to drink?" He stepped toward the galley to start the stove. The propane burner popped to life.

Still glaring at him, she sat down at the far edge of the settee. "Black tea."

"You like herbal."

"I said black."

The kettle was slower than the microwave, but the water stayed hot longer. While it warmed over the hiss of the burner, Cord opened a galley cupboard and pulled out a small basket of assorted tea bags. He picked two Darjeeling blacks and dropped one each in the mugs perpetually set on the black granite countertop. He couldn't find anything else to busy himself under her glower, so rather than pace the small floor area or fidget with nonessentials, he planted his feet with the counter between himself and the woman he'd once loved but now suspected might be deranged. He noticed she was rubbing her bruised right hand and didn't want to know more.

"So…" he spoke tentatively, his shoulders scrunched, hands in his pockets. He had trouble bringing his eyes to meet hers, so piercing and fiery blue even under the cabin's muted lighting.

Brooke read the tells of his discomfort and rendered them as evidence of guilt. Her anger was fierce, and she loved examining what she interpreted to be his shame. She reveled in the heavy silence between them.

Cord wanted to take another stab at carving a pathway toward his bride, but at the notion of her being his bride his brows furrowed and the corners of his mouth tightened. To Brooke it came across as a smirk. Perhaps unintentional, but there it was plastered on his face.

Before another volley could cross her lips, the teakettle began to intrude, offering its buffer of a screech, not completely dissimilar, Cord appraised, to hers.

He turned about in the galley and poured the hot water, then placed a steaming mug on the coffee table before her. When she didn't move toward it, he found a spoon and a small jar of honey and set them near her. As he went back for his own mug she guardedly picked up the spoon.

He eased himself toward the opposite edge of the couch and took a sip of his tea. Much too hot. He held the mug in both hands, cold from tension. She stirred hers, not allowing the spoon to touch the edge of the cup.

Unable to think of anything she might accept as courtesy, he simply asked, "What can I say?"

"You can tell the truth." Without taking her eye off him, she put the spoon on the table, the sound of it emphasizing her impatience.

He scrunched his shoulders again, his default tell.

"What truth? Do you want me to make up something so you can hate me more? Sure, I can tell you I've been fooling around with Meredith, or anyone else you'd like to name. But none of it would be true. B, I…" He saw her right eyebrow arch. "Brooke, I don't know what you want from me. Confession? For what? Tell me. I need you to tell me." He still couldn't understand how he'd become the bad guy.

"No! You tell me the truth! You pride yourself in your honesty. Well, be honest with me! Bryan! Right now!"

A chain of profanities flew from one to the other, neither in their agitation able to form complete sentences quickly enough without the use of street vocabulary.

Getting nowhere with argument, Cord tried switching hats and taking the intimate tack he'd seen in one of their chick flicks.

"You're the one I wanted to marry. Not her." He thought introducing a hint of levity might be a nice touch. "Besides, she wouldn't have had me. She's so…so religious."

"Oh, so you're saying I was second on your list?"

So much for levity.

"Or third? How many women did you have to go through before you finally got me to climb onto your boat?"

There was only so much of her indictment he could tolerate.

"Where is this going, Brooke?" His voice became menacing. "You want out? Is that it? Okay, we'll end it. Here and now."

Never one to back off, through gritted teeth she said, "Yes, I want out! What was your first clue?"

Cord looked away and shook his head. Brooke read it as derision.

"You think you're so wonderful, don't you? Go ahead. Shake your head as if I'm just another storm to pass through before you can escape back to your private little life. I've never meant anything to you from the beginning, have I? Well, have I?"

His limit of endurance reached, he returned her glare with a smoldering that caused his brown eyes to darken. He spoke slowly with finality. "I won't argue with you anymore. You turn everything that isn't right about us into some kind of attempt of mine to hurt you. That isn't how it is with me."

Something inside Brooke broke loose, and out rushed a deluge. Cord couldn't get a word in. On and on she droned. And when she made a full circuit of her diatribe enumerating his faults, she set her internal playback to Repeat to run through the entire litany yet another time, and then 'round again for more. In her adrenaline onslaught she didn't read the telltales of his mounting tension.

Cord began to pace behind the galley counter attempting to form a small retort, but her barrage of words wouldn't stop tumbling out. After her third lap he had his fill of insult and stepped out from his space toward her. She interpreted his approach as aggression and raised her arms in defense. He stopped, still a distance from her. His words spewed out in a low growl.

"Would you please shut! Up! I heard you the first time."

They glared at each other.

He had more.

"You don't quit. You bury people. I'm not the enemy. You don't know who your real enemy is. You're an attack dog."

He tried to hold back the next salvo, but it'd been stored away too long.

"You're impossible to reason with. You need help."

No turning back now. She wouldn't be stopped. The gale-force fury she'd held in check since her youth was unleashed without containment. Her scream was guttural.

He turned his back to her and expected her fist to the back of his head. He turned again to face her, only to see her rushing up the ladder through the doorway. He stared after her, reflexively rubbing his head, imagining a small knot growing.

THE OLDER COUPLE in the yacht next to them heard it all. Crescendoing voices mounting higher, threats quickening, tea-kettle screaming. They hadn't known Brooke well in the three years the boats had been slipmates. But it took only a few moments to recognize that despite her exceptional beauty and lightness of speech she carried and fueled a heavy heart.

Brooke stormed out of the cabin to the cockpit and into the predawn light. Turning back to face Cord still inside, she lashed out at him, her voice choking with the emotion of long-suppressed pain.

From behind her window, Carly Edgerton heard the sound of deepest anguish. Brooke's words were nearly unintelligible for her sobbing. In the early mist, the couple could only watch between closed curtains.

Brooke spun around, her eyes wild, searching for an object to attack. Choosing the one closest to her, she ripped off *Starstruck's* navy blue sun-bridge cover in one tremendous grab and yank. Travis was surprised at the strength generated by her fury as she effortlessly wrenched the entire canvas away. The staccato pops of the snaps severing from their anchors sounded like machine gun fire.

She turned back to the cabin to blast a legion of obscenities that made little sense when grouped together. Then, still alone in the now roofless cockpit, she wadded the cover and with both arms heaved the entire mass—canvas and Isinglass windows—out into the water. The girl was unstoppable. Turning once more to face her adversary in hiding, she issued one final torrent of invective, then hoisted the lounge cushions off their seats and pitched them in, one after the other, until all were overboard. She leaped over the boat's gunwale onto the finger wharf separating the two boats. Travis and Carly backed away from their window, not sure they couldn't be seen. Brooke in her unrestrained rage took no notice. Sobbing loudly and clutching her stomach, she ran with a pronounced limp to the main dock, up the gangway and to the injured Volvo 1800ES.

All was silent, no movement on either boat.

"She was certainly using her outdoor voice," noted Travis.

"A lot of hurt in that girl," said Carly. "I hope she finds help." She went to the galley. "I might as well start the coffee."

After ten long minutes, Cord stepped topside to survey the damage. With a boat hook he began to retrieve the mess of canvas mostly submerged. Everything else had already drifted too far from his reach.

Travis emerged from his cabin. Foregoing his customary cheerful greeting he silently lowered his tender and rowed to pick up the cushions floating away with the bay's outgoing tide.

"Looks like that's all of them," he said a half hour later, handing up the last of the cushions. "Anything heavy you might be missing, the diver will find on the bottom when he scrubs my hull next week."

Cord took the cushions and stacked them against the soaked canvas he'd draped over his boat's stern to dry out. "Sorry to wake you so early. Didn't see that one coming."

"Not a problem. We were asleep anyway."

Ten

NINE IN THE MORNING.

Bryan Cord had tried for a few more winks after thanking his neighbor for the help, but with too many tosses and turns, it was hopeless.

Better call the office. Does angry and disgusted qualify for a sick day?

He pulled his cell from the chart table drawer where he'd left it the night before, swiped and waited for his admin's succinct message.

"Hey, you know the drill. Talk to me. *Ciao.*"

"Won't be in today, Molly. Tell Mitch to go ahead with his sales plan. It'll make us more than my earlier idea. We'll debrief when I'm back. Monday, I guess. What's today—Friday? Thanks, Mol."

He dropped the device back in the drawer and made his way into the head.

Resigned to an empty day, he threw on a sweatshirt and ventured out to the sun-bridge to reattach the still-damp canvas Brooke had ripped off. He stretched the main piece across the top of the canopy frame, and a large stainless steel tube that had unhinged in the fracas came clattering down, bringing half the scaffolding to topple with it, leaving the rest dangling. The commotion seemed endless.

With a guttural oath he was taught in his youth by a friend who knew Turkish, Cord abandoned the clutter, snapped on his life vest and stepped over the mess to his inflatable. An hour's row in the morning chill wouldn't make the scaffolding magically reassemble, but it might ease his mind.

He was about to set off when he heard, "Come aboard for coffee when you get back. Sun's out; cockpit will be warm."

His neighbor, Professor Travis Edgerton, poked his head out the door. The old guy had always been cordial to him; helpful too. Even so, Cord tried to beg off.

"I probably ought to run a few errands."

"Nonsense. They can wait. We'll have a fresh pot on. Besides, you owe us for the untimely imitation of a middle school marching band just now."

"Sorry, sir. Seems to be a habit with me lately."

"Breakfast too, if Carly has her way. Don't be long," he said over his shoulder. At the door he turned and called after Cord, "Don't call me Sir. Makes me feel old."

Travis and Carly set the table for three in their enclosed rear cockpit. The little space heater brought a cozy warmth.

"What's for breakfast?" he asked. "Omelet? I think he'd like that. We still have any of your cinnamon rolls?"

"As you wish, master. And the second pot's brewing as you speak."

In her running togs, Carly Edgerton displayed her athleticism. Having just bid her fifties adieu, she raced in local fun runs, still always one of the early finishers with women half her age. Four or five times a year she and Travis entered national masters track and field events, and saved up for travel to biennial world meets. In competition Carly preferred fifteen-hundred meters, but she could be talked into teaming up in the sixteen-hundred relay. Travis stuck to sprinting, his hundred-meter times in the high elevens, faster than a decade ago and better than most of the youth he worked with. The great thing about the hundred, he'd boast, you don't have time to wear yourself out. They both volunteered to coach the high school track team.

Cord rowed hard toward the marina's breakwater and continued into the middle of the empty channel. He paused to watch the sun take possession of the cloudless sky. Stunning.

But it was time to get back to the coffee he had second thoughts about accepting. Oh well.

He secured the dinghy then jumped aboard *Starstruck* to brush his teeth to get rid of last night's lagers. Slipping on a clean pullover fleece, he hopped onto the finger wharf between his boat and the Edgertons' *Soulmate*.

"Hello? Permission to come aboard."

Travis met him with a mug of steaming coffee and motioned him over. "You like it black or with additives?"

Cord took the proffered mug. "Black today. I need the jolt."

"Figured you might. Take a seat, why don't you. Sun's great, isn't it? Breakfast coming up."

"But…"

Travis left to help his wife bring out three plates, each covered with an omelet of three eggs folded over jack cheese, mushrooms, fresh basil and sliced tomatoes. Carly's gourmet creation was dressed in a mild dill-yogurt sauce and crowned with a small wreath of cilantro. The table was also graced with a platter of warm cinnamon rolls and a small dish of Moroccan olives.

Cord followed the Edgertons' lead. They didn't dig right in but took their time sipping their coffees while looking out beyond the small marina toward the channel. A huge container ship made its way to take on cargo a few miles to the east.

"Care for hot sauce?" asked Travis, taking off the cap and passing the small bottle. "Myself, I need to go light this morning. Last night's chili has outstayed its welcome."

Cord intended to sprinkle only a few drops of Tabasco on his omelet, but a small stream settled in the middle. "Yikes. Like I said, I need the jolt." He spread the sauce around with a fork.

Travis picked up a couple of olives and spoke, seemingly to no one at the table. "Thank you for great food, for great boats, great neighbors. You are good." He savored the black olives, one at a time, and set the pits on the edge of his plate.

Who was he talking to just then? Was it a prayer of some kind? Bizarre. Cord chose not to ask, but dove into his extra hot omelet. And it was surprisingly perfect.

"Thanks. This is cool. I mean hot. 1 mean…"

"Glad you like it," said Carly. She and her husband were old enough to be his parents. He had reached a degree of ease with the doc across the aisle, but in the three years their boats shared the same wharf he'd never addressed Mrs Doc by name.

As if reading his mind, she said, "Bryan, call me Carly. I know your friends call you Cord. Which do you prefer from us?"

"Don't worry," Travis piped up. "She's straight forward with someone she sees having potential for being a friend. Looks like you passed the test."

Cord's characteristic lopsided smile crept across his face. He felt a bit awkward, but he liked this older couple; it was easy to take to them.

"Bryan," he answered. "Or Cord. Or Chan. That's what my mom calls me sometimes. My middle name is Chandler, her maiden name. She and my dad shortened it to Chan—for laughs, I guess. After Charlie Chan, some old movie series they liked."

"We know the Charlie Chan movies," said Travis. "Actually before our time, but we've watched every one of them. Same era as Laurel and Hardy."

"I'm not familiar with them either," said Cord.

"Travis reminds me of Stan Laurel," said Carly. "That goofy look when he wants a chuckle. Works too, every time. Maybe you've heard me call him Stanley."

When Travis smiled his entire countenance lit up. Laugh lines had once dominated the contours of his face because he'd grown to relish the ordinary moments of living. But in the last few years worry furrows grew deeper. His young granddaughter often tried to smooth them away with her little palms, but they always reappeared. "Don't worry, Doc, it'll be fine," she mimicked grownups. He thanked her and challenged her to rock-paper-scissors. "Best of three." "No, five," she said and scrunched her face in concentration. His furrows relaxed, and the leftward crook of his nose—the result of a twenties event he didn't discuss—grew less conspicuous. These days the stories of life still contained their own punch lines, and Travis loved telling them, though now with a melancholy from banking some of life's distresses.

As happens in conversations, there was a pause at the table signaling a directional change. They were all aware of it. Cord felt a foreboding. He knew the aspects of his life were about to be dissected.

"You doing all right?" asked Travis.

There it was. And probably the precursor to, How about keeping a lid on the midnight noise.

Cord was quick to apologize.

"No need, Bryan," said Carly. "I hope you know that. We're only concerned for you and Brooke." She seemed genuine.

"I guess you...," Cord paused a moment, "you noticed we haven't been doing all that great lately."

"Difficult to miss," said Travis.

"Looks like the whole thing's over. Good while it lasted. A lot of it anyway."

"Is that what you want?" asked Carly.

Cord wasn't ready for the question. The lady had spirit.

"To be over so quickly? No. But I don't want what we've got. Who needs more fighting?"

Travis remembered a GK Chesterton quote about marriage being an adventure, like going to war. He kept it to himself.

"How did you and Brooke meet?" Carly persisted, but Cord was all right with it. For now. He told them about their first evening at the church.

"Church?" asked Travis.

"First and last time." Cord wasn't aware of his smirk.

Carly wanted to know about their relationship. For some reason, Cord liked her sincerity and wasn't repelled by her probing. He dropped a morsel to see if they'd feed on him like predators, or care about him as they seemed to so far.

"She was the most incredible woman I'd ever met. Everything about her. But overnight she became somebody else.

How could I know I'd lose her? The friends we knew, 'no love like our love they'd say. Then love slipped through my fingers, somewhere along the way.' My mom and dad used to listen to those lyrics. I don't know who sang them.

"Nat King Cole," said Travis. "'I should forget, but with the loneliness of night I start remembering everything. She's gone, and yet there's still a feeling deep inside that she will always be …'"

Carly finished the line, "'Part…of…me.'" Her alto voice floated on the air like silk.

"Do you want her back?" Travis pulled no punches himself.

Cord sat brooding on the question while his host topped off the three mugs. It was a fair question, one he'd been asking himself. He had no answer, and told them.

Then he said, "You'd have to ask her too."

Curious thoughts flooded his mind. What if they did ask her? What if Brooke could talk honestly with someone who wouldn't try to force upon her points of view not her own? But were these people as real as they seemed? They prayed, openly. What was that about? They didn't seem like the religious door-to-door kind with their books and pamphlets. *Is there an agenda I'm not cluing in on? What am I getting myself into?*

Carly was quick to interpret Cord's inspection of his fork. "I hope we haven't overstepped."

"Try an olive or two." chimed in Travis, ready to lighten the mood.

Cord lifted a single olive out of the dish and set it in his mouth. Not too salty but a strong natural taste.

"Yikes," he said again.

"I like them when they talk back," said Travis.

"This one yelled," said Cord, and took a sip of coffee. "No, you haven't overstepped at all." He set the mug down and rubbed his forehead, thinking.

"Actually, I appreciate the openness. To be honest, I'm not sure it can work."

Eleven

CORD CAME HOME TO *STARSTRUCK* EVERY NIGHT after work, almost a week now since he moved out of the cottage. Once more he was captivated by her charm and her quiet. On board it was easier to put his dismantled marriage on hold and focus on work.

He'd formed a capable cohort of sales talent, and when unleashed it became a unit of power envied in the workplace. But in the last month or so the team began to show signs of fracture.

The epicenter of conflict was the newest hire, Signa Thomsen. Cord, ignoring the dictum, Hire slow fire fast, had grabbed her up on the spot. In short order he began to have doubts. She was a good worker, but not a fit. Two of her coworkers had made several attempts to bring her into the team. But she didn't recognize indicators of kindness, filtering each person through her grid of blame for unstated past personal grievances. Cord came to admit he couldn't stand the woman himself.

One of the team referred to her as Napoleon and the name stuck. Feeling her presence before seeing her approach, a few quietly slipped a hand inside a shirt. When she'd leave the office her usual twenty minutes early each day, they would hum France's national anthem. Signa Thomsen was Danish.

Then just last night the lid blew off. The team met for the monthly get-together at their favorite pub. Signa grudgingly tagged along. During a moment of vulnerability over a third Irish on the rocks the woman next to her lamented the loss of a breast to cancer. Signa, indignant at the woman's need for truth telling, blurted, "And I caused that?"

All conversation ceased and every eye fastened on her. Signa began to clue in to the chasm between herself and the others. Standing alone at the end of the bar she knew she was found wanting. No, needing. She lowered her barriers of locked-away resentments and admitted to the woman who had quickly created distance from her, "I'm not an okay person, am I?"

Their silence and stares grew heavy and Ms Citadel-of-Power fled the scene. Someone began to hum France's anthem, others joined in the chorus, one singing in French. In that vicious moment Cord watched his team rupture. He let Signa run, set down his own half-full plate and silently walked out, making his way back to his sanctuary—*Starstruck*.

AFTER A LONG NIGHT of internal wrestling over what he labeled his own ineffective team leadership, not to mention endless corporate demands and the craziness of his life, he reached the only conclusion he thought reasonable. He picked up the keys to his disfigured 1800ES, which Brooke had hired someone to drop off at the marina. Cord drove to work in the early rain and typed up the handwritten letter he'd crafted between 4 and 5 AM. Without his usual "Hey Marko" greeting, he handed it to his boss. Effective immediately Cord was finished with it. All of it.

Marcus Elkin kept his feet crossed on his desk and glanced indifferently at the single sheet.

"Gotta give two weeks' notice, buddy," Elkin took a long sip of his lukewarm coffee. "Or you're docked all your vacation, and probably your manhood."

"Can't go on, Marcus."

Elkin set the mug down and toyed with a pen, twirling it around each finger of his right hand. "Saw this in a movie once. Good dexterity, don't you think?" He didn't expect a reply. When the pen reached his index finger he spun it to point at Cord. "I'm giving you a two-week break, effective now with pay. Make it three. I'll work with your team. I heard about last night at the pub." He left his desk. "Sit down. Don't move."

Cord's boss cleared his morning with his administrator, Molly, came back and scooped his old hooded ski jacket from the floor in the corner. "Let's go."

"Where?"

"You're taking me out on your boat. You've never invited me. This is the day, kiddo."

"Not sure about this, Marcus. Not to mention it's raining."

"Tough. It'll clear." He waved Cord's letter before stuffing it in a front pocket. "We'll talk about this. Other things too. You drive. Oh, and I know what you're thinking. So let's just see if I turn out to be the body part you're calling me right now."

Cord was a good six inches taller than the other man, and didn't know how many years younger. He had to catch up with him.

77

"Marcus?" he said to his boss' back.

"Tell me."

"You're right."

"I'm not your leader for nothing. Had breakfast? We'll stop by Rosa's on the way."

"Mexican for breakfast? Make it Harry's. Coffee's better."

"You paying?"

"Rosa's then."

Twelve

Ramon and Rosa Cortez met while working in the convent next to Oaxaca's *Catedral* in southern Mexico. He was the gardener, she the maid whom *las hermanas* kept on out of pity. Joined in marriage by one of the *padres*, they shared a tiny apartment in the poorest part of the congested city. One evening before falling asleep Ramon confided to his young bride a longing to taste life beyond urban noise. She, welcoming adventure, told him she could pack quickly.

The next morning Ramon hastily finished weeding the courtyard gardens and Rosa moved like lightning in her cleaning. Without the approval of *la madre superiora* but accepting her sympathetic consent, they left that evening on the all-night bus north for Puebla, a suitcase between them. There they were dumped with a mass of migrant families being rustled into semi-trailers with wooden benches that would eventually cart them off to the produce fields of Vicente Guerrero on the Baja peninsula.

The work was hard, living conditions deplorable. There was little leniency in *el jefe*, but he wasn't cruel, and he left Rosa alone.

After each crop's harvest, the company of families were paid in *pesos* then loaded again into the semis for other fields and more squalid living. Ramon had different vistas in mind. The evening before their next payday Ramon and Rosa huddled together around a wood fire just outside their cardboard walls.

"I have a plan, *mi chica*."

"I'm listening. I always listen."

"I'm grateful to *El Señor* that you listen, and so attentively."

"The older women say it is the shortcoming of my youth, one I will outgrow soon enough."

"I hope you never do."

"What is this plan that keeps us from sleep on our fine ragged blankets on someone else's ground?"

"We speak the same language, you and I, *mi novia*. If we continue in our servitude we will always for the rest of our days sleep on someone else's defiled earth."

"My interest is awakened, but my eyelids are heavy. Tell me more, *querido*, but tell me with few words."

"Sometimes you ask too much, *Rosita mía*. In short, it is this. Tomorrow we will be paid. A pittance for certain, but real *dinero* no less. We will leave the labor of the fields, and *adiós* we will bid our friends. We will make our way to the ocean shore and find a small sailboat."

"*¿Perdón?* I must have dozed into a dream. What did you say about leaving our friends? And something about a boat?"

"We will provision the craft and sail to America."

"Sail? Who taught you to sail? You have seen no body of water bigger than a stream from inside our work bus. And where will we find your *craft*? Will it simply lie on the sands eager to be taken? And taken it must be, for we have no money to buy your *craft*. And how do you know where to sail?"

"America is north, *querida*. We will sail north."

"So, as simple as that."

"No, but more adventurous. I promise you that, *mi vida*."

"*Más loco*."

"Then we will be crazy together, you and I."

"*Sí. Dos vagabundos locos*."

Throughout that night the flame of a daring spirit began to glimmer in Rosa. While others in the compound slept, Ramon and his wife whispered and giggled their happiness in a shared vision, reckless though it had to be, and in their daring to chart a course far beyond imagination.

It took a few days less than a month, but in a stolen sixteen-foot sailboat with a tiny cabin—*one day, Rosa, we will repay the owner, with high interest*—they silently drifted into California's Newport Bay in the darkness of a foggy night.

Gliding past huge waterfront mansions with every light blazing, Ramon whispered, "We must be in America."

They nuzzled in between two private docks on Balboa Island and beached the boat in front of a high-end residence with an architecture and expanse resembling a hotel.

"I hope the guests do not peer out of their windows," said a worried Rosa taking Ramon's hand and jumping to the sand.

Leaving the boat on the narrow beach, they changed into clothing they also stole from an unwatched laundry drier in the two-block town—*I am not sure we will be able to repay for these*—and crossed the bridge to the mainland to walk north.

California's laws on illegals were lenient and the Hispanic community welcoming. Ramon and Rosa hid within the protection of a large Guatemalan family in Costa Mesa, initially finding odd jobs. They both developed a skill in cooking, their dishes expressive of their native Oaxaca grabbing the attention of the neighborhood. The young twosome were hired as cooks in a famous Mexican restaurant on Pacific Coast Highway, issued green cards, and made more money than they imagined possible. When eligible, they followed the advice of their manager, who took motherly charge over their welfare, and obtained US citizenship.

Ramon was a man of dreams. One night before falling asleep in their own rented apartment, he whispered to his wife, "I think I would like to open our own restaurant."

"Oh? And have you been sipping *pulque* again?"

"It was *mezcal*, but I did not swallow the worm."

"Tell me your plan, *mí soñador grande*, but in few words so I may spend the entire night dreaming crazy dreams you put in my head."

"Would you like to visit Seattle, in the top of the country?"

"Have you already quit our jobs?"

"We will tomorrow."

"*Más loco.*"

"Always crazy together."

The manager kept them in employment until she could organize a proper send-off. A hat was passed among the two dozen employees, and the proceeds were matched by the manager herself, then doubled at her insistence by the head office. A busboy with few aspirations but plenty of promise volunteered to drive their goods in his pickup to meet them the following week on the north side of Seattle. He packed his own possessions in shopping bags and crammed them behind the seat. Resting beside him was his treasure: a flamenco guitar played by his grandfather, but looking like it'd been thrown away.

The morning after the company's send-off a matured, confident and prosperous duo surnamed Cortez chose the long way to the Pacific Northwest. Detouring their four-year-old Saturn Outlook SUV south across the Mexican border, they made for the village where they had stolen the sailboat for their voyage to freedom.

Imaginative stories steeped in the mystery of the boat's sudden disappearance eight years earlier were embellished over time. One stop at the cantina by the ocean was all it took to discover who had owned the boat.

"There is the one you want." The barkeep nodded toward the beach. "*El hombre* just there at the shore. He does nothing but sit. You ask him about his boat and you will not escape." He went back to wiping out empty glasses with his apron. Ramon thanked him and was at the door when the proprietor called after him. "*Amigo*, you want to laugh? Ask him about *los piratas* with their *pistolas* to his head to seize that old tub."

They saw the fifties man sitting atop a large rock staring off into only he knew what.

Ramon approached him. "*Permiso, señor.*"

"*¿Sí?*" said the weathered man, not taking his gaze from the horizon.

"I believe I have something of yours. That is, I did."

"*¿Qué es mío?*"

That day Ramon and Rosa Cortez repaid a debt, and then some, turning the man's loss into his wildest dream come true. At the setting of the sun he stood at the helm of his own older but very worthy thirty-one-foot Catalina sail with a small Diesel inboard. Ramon and Rosa Cortez closed the books on their single overdue bill.

Thirteen

ONE OF MY FAVORITE HANGOUTS."

Marcus Elkin led the way and Bryan Cord followed his boss into the tiny restaurant.

Rosa's. Unintentionally separating the storefront offices of a one-horse doctor and a street lawyer on old town Water Street off the main thoroughfare, the Mexican eatery claimed no awards for its nondescript façade. But inside bright greens, reds, yellows and blues revealed the heritage and personality of the two proprietors. One entire wall was muraled to render the tranquility of a rural Mexican village square. Over the counter hung posters of Aztec and Mayan ruins, photos autographed by a flamenco guitarist and a legendary bullfighter, and one framed US fifty-dollar bill. *In America we must think big*, insisted Rosa's husband Ramon. Authentic Mexican folk music at a discreet volume was accompanied by the cook's voice from his side of the pass-through.

"*¡Hermano* Markos!*" shouted the owner from behind the counter.

"*¿Qué pasó*, Ramon?"

Uncharted

"*¡Bien, bien, amigo!*"

The owner escorted Cord and his boss to a corner bare wood table. Two straight-back chairs noisily bumped across the dark tiled floor as the guests seated themselves.

Cord reached for the half-page menu tucked between bottles of hot sauce next to a small stack of napkins. Elkin pulled the menu from his hand and set it back. "No need for this. You're having Rosa's Special."

Cord was about to take issue with being told what to eat when Ramon Cortez set before them an outsized platter of warm tortilla chips and two bowls of double roasted salsa. He went back for two glass bottles of ice-cold Coca-Cola and a dish of sliced limes.

"Coke for breakfast?" observed Cord taking a chip.

"Better than the coffee," muttered Elkin.

"You received quite a welcome." Cord squeezed a lime into his drink.

"Comes from an incident a couple of years ago. Ramon used to call me *Señor*, same as he addresses others. Always a friendly greeting."

"How did that change to Brother Markoo?"

"Well, this one day at lunchtime I'm waiting for my order and drooling over the aromas coming from the kitchen. So, these two big guys find their way to a table close-by and order Rosa's Special. Best tamale-burrito combo anywhere. I mean anywhere! And the double refried beans—can't wait! But the two complain about their meal and get louder until they're just this side of insulting. Dockworkers too, so I'm not about to tangle with them."

"You apparently said something."

"I simply offered to buy their meals. They asked why. Because the food's that good. What I wanted to say was they

86

were holding up my order. One of them frowns but takes another small taste, says it isn't all that bad after all. The other one does the same, apologizes to Ramon. They finish, order two more to take out, drop down a big tip and try to pay for mine. Ramon says he's got mine."

"All that from 'I'll buy yours'?"

"Funniest thing. From *dos puercos* to *mis amigos* in under ten minutes. Now they're regulars. And of course, having big appetites they and other shipbuilders keep Rosa's doing a fine business."

"You've got a knack, Marcus."

Elkin tossed a hand in dismissal. "Wish I could say the knack, as you call it, was effective in all areas."

Cord crunched a chip loaded with salsa. "You didn't bring me here for the nourishment. What am I supposed to do? Last night my work team degenerated to mob status. All against one; one who crashed and self-destructed."

He aimed to squeeze another lime into his coke and sent a spray across the table. Wiping it with a napkin, Cord asked, "What is it about the women in my life? Signa has the talent to be a leader, but won't play nice in a bigger sandbox. She seems to be chased by something, someone, she can't escape, or won't release. The woman is a black hole of emotional need nothing can fill." He grunted. "Like someone else I know."

Cord heard his boss say, "Seems I've got blind spots myself, especially when it comes to women. Batting oh for three in marriage." He filled a large chip with salsa and used it as a pointer for emphasis. "What I'm saying is, Bryan bud, I hope you can steer clear of the landmines I've stepped on for the last too many years. Dig into some wisdom, you know?"

Cord shook his head and his smirk was lopsided. "I'm a little beyond that. I detoured wisdom six or eight steps back."

"Hope I don't pry too much, and don't tell me if I am, 'cause I'm paying the tab here. But the real concern isn't Signa. It's Brooke." Elkin crunched the chip. "Isn't it?"

"Yes. And you're prying."

"You want me to back off a little?"

"A little? As in, until later when we're on the boat and I become your captive audient in my own space? You might as well plunge in now since I don't have a choice either way." Cord dunked another chip in the salsa. "And to think it's my boat, and I'm the captain."

Ramon walked up and set down two enormous plates, each concealed by one perfectly cooked tamale, a burrito the size of a tree trunk, and refried beans barely contained by the rim. He parked a covered dish of hot flour tortillas and three more bottles of cola between them.

"Enjoy, *compadres*. *Que Diós tus bendiga*. Blessings, *amigos*. I will join you shortly."

They plunged into their meals, Elkin heaping extra salsa on his burrito and beans. Neither of them spoke while they dined on the culinary delight Elkin christened the Benediction of Mexico, downing Coca-Cola bottled in Ensenada.

Cord eased up from his overstuffed burrito and tilted his head toward the singing coming from the kitchen. "The cook's got a decent voice," he said, wiping his mouth with a sizable napkin.

"Name's Paco," said Elkin, still eating. "He's been here as long as the owners. Moved up from California with them. Quite an accomplished guitarist. Most afternoons after closing he'll get down on some serious flamenco. People crowd into this tiny room. Gives a concert every Thanksgiving at the Scout Hall. That's his stack of CDs by the cash register. Kid's incredible."

Back to eating, Cord asked, "What did Ramon mean, he'll join us?"

"He takes a quick time-out when I come in. Part of the friendship. It's good for us both. Sometimes Rosa stops by too."

Cord forked off a large bite of tamale, the corn flour perfectly seasoned. "Got to say this is one of the best I've tasted. How long did you say they've been open?"

Ramon brought over another chair and clapped Elkin on the shoulder. "How goes it, *hermano*? *Hola*, Bryan." He emphasized the Y in Bryan as if it should be pronounced with a tilde. "Long time no see, *amigo*."

"Ramon," asked Elkin, "how long have you and Rosa been operating in this hole in the wall?"

"Twelve years almost," said the native Oaxacan, taking one of the soft drinks for himself. Seated he was nearly eye level to the men; standing he barely cleared five-three.

"All good years, right?" Elkin almost laughed saying it.

"*¡Caray, hombre!* You think we are made of stone?"

"How did you get through the hard times?"

"You suggest the difficult years somehow gracefully disappear with age or experience? There is nothing graceful about it, *amigo*. The effort to advance is just that—great effort. And sometimes only to stand your ground, even if it is rented. Rosa and I weather our adventures together, though she likes to say we are both *un poco loco*."

Ramon took one of their chips and loaded it with Rosa's double roasted salsa. "And possibly we are, it could be. We have *mucho* laughter together to keep going. It is our daily vitamin. But tell me, *amigos*, you do not work at your office today?"

Elkin spoke for them. "Bryan here is taking me out in his boat. We'll have our leadership meeting on the water."

"*¡Ay qué bueno!* One day I should like to return to the water." Ramon spoke wistfully and was about to offer a part of his past when Rosa walked over and put her hand on her husband's shoulder.

"Another time, *querido*. Our seven tables fill sooner than expected."

Ramon looked around the room, stood and shifted his chair back to the adjoining table. "*Sí*, another time, my friends. Enjoy your boat. One day I will join you there."

"Not without me," said Rosa. "A month together in a small sailboat far from land was enough many years ago. But these days I would like to share more adventure with you on the waters of our middle years."

Ramon wrapped his arm around his tiny wife, he a full head taller. "Tonight we will dream wonderful dreams together again. It will be our own leadership meeting."

"But not until our customers are satisfied," she said guiding him to another table.

Cord and his boss cleaned their plates and let the huge breakfasts settle while slowly sipping the last of their drinks. Elkin paid, not bothering with a card but leaving two twenties on the table. Before they reached the door Rosa gave him a large bag containing two sturdy take-out dishes covered with foil.

"The salt air will bring much appetite," she said before welcoming the next customers walking in.

Cord lingered back to set down another twenty.

Fourteen

A LIBRARIAN? YOU'RE JOKING.

The same reaction from everyone Brooke met. Especially guys. Eyeballs bug out, mouth drops open.

Why so surprised? She loved knowledge. Thrived on it. But to smaller minds beauty and brains couldn't share the same person. One guy bragged about his former flings being long on talent and short on intellect. "Speaking of blocks of wood," he'd said, "I dated a girl like that. Didn't matter. Chicks shouldn't be thinkers."

Twit.

Brooke Cord took daily refuge in the quiet comfort of silent old friends who always enlightened and seldom disappointed. She loved her library, calling it the 'liberry' with her workmates, her childhood pronunciation when she first walked through the single door of her hometown's reading room. At six years old she'd stood enchanted by the room's shelves of children's books, popular fiction and periodicals catering to a rural readership. Even then the fragrance of learning filled her senses. Books became her life and she grew accustomed to hiding in pleasant worlds as she traveled through their pages. A degree in library science allowed her fulltime wellbeing inside their shelter.

Today, between lending books and replacing volumes exactly so in their spaces, she stole too many moments reflecting on her aloneness. Solitude hadn't been all she'd promised herself. Her disquiet rose from the loss of the one man she'd believed worthy of more devotion than her books.

Seclusion prevailed as well over her later afternoons at the gym, perfecting the kickboxing moves she'd begun in high school. Distancing herself from the young mothers hoping to gain control of their widening thighs on stairs and bikes going nowhere, Brooke introverted herself in her ear-budded world of Handel and Schubert during free-weight workouts and training at the punching bag. Only once she paused her playlist to overhear their conversation. She wondered how they, intellects manifestly challenged, satisfied themselves with so many single-syllable expressions to prattle on about so little. She swore if she heard 'me n' her' one more time, she'd scream. Throwing her kicks high and hard to the angry progressions of Wagner also kept her aloof of every man ogling her.

Except for one luckless fellow. Thinking himself a trailblazer of the superior gender, he summoned her to spar, which he presumed would be good-natured while validating his dominance. Brooke demurred, truthfully forewarning him he might know more than he. His scoff was irksome, so with a sigh she stepped aside for him to choose his place on the mat. Dancing like a marionette he invited her to take her best shot. She gave it sixty percent and laid the stud out. Afterward men still gazed, but from guarded distance.

But Brooke's nights alone were unexpectedly dull, her microwaved meals mechanically gobbled while she stared at

Wheel Of Fortune to throw off the silence. A game show, justified only by a curiosity in Vanna's latest gown. *That's something not even my grandmother would be caught dead watching!*

Brooke felt deeply flawed. A limp from a shorter leg, barely noticeable and consciously hidden, became pronounced with fatigue or anxiety. Except for that single imperfection she appeared unspoiled. Her family had named her the gimpy queen. She despised both labels.

During her early high school years she vowed to become a librarian, for the love of learning, and to hide within the silence of antiquity. Her library, like all assemblies of books, was set apart to give asylum from the stress of living. Her limp was indiscernible as she ambled among the stacks. Her books were her haven, and they didn't argue back or draw attention to her flaws, physical or emotional.

She picked up a periodical forgotten on a table, opened to the article, "Forever Marriages: What Makes Them Stick?"

Forever? She snickered to herself, strictly holding to the code of library silence.

She reflected on the concept of being married an entire lifetime. An incarceration where the only change of pace in an eternity of banality and boredom would be learning to cope with multiple annoyances of the same person. *A lifetime? Not my marriage!* A year plus too much was plenty!

She was about to replace the magazine on its stand, but curiosity pressed her to give the article a scan. At her desk behind the high counter she read the first words, "How do they make it last?" and tried to keep her mind from wandering to Bryan Cord, her none-too-soon ex-husband. The four-page article made bold assertions, mostly to sell the magazine, she concluded.

Uncharted

"Tough marriages don't mean tough people." *Whatever that means.*

"The longer the marriage, the better the sex." *Was this written by a nun?*

She flipped to the front cover. "Inspired: One Marriage Under God." *Obviously for religious women.*

Turning back to the article, she read, "Marriage is just another word for blessed." *People actually believe this?*

Careless thesis, marriage being workable to last one's duration of life. The authors must have been Brides of the Church after all.

Mindless pablum. Why can't religionists just come out and face the reality that couples don't play nice? Brooke was convinced that marriage eventually deadened individual uniqueness and destroyed reasonable trust in relationships.

She allowed that hers was a jaundiced view of married life. She was through with Cord, but not done with him. Something in her wanted to square off on him in a round on the mat, a round she'd condense to one or two moves.

What had he done to ignite her wrath? Or had it been the family of her youth? Never mind, Cord was the one standing in her path and he wore the target. *What I want*, she declared to herself, *is to be left very alone.*

She turned the pages too fast, the breeze fanning her face to cool her irritation. With finality she closed the magazine and walked it to its proper place on the shelf.

But she couldn't dismiss the article's title, "Forever Marriages". Forever with Cord? A slow death.

Why do I hate him? What was his failure?
Does he give me a thought?

Fifteen

Sunshine burst through the clouds for a welcoming pre-spring day as Cord drove his boss Marcus Elkin the few blocks to the marina. He habitually searched for parking lot end spaces to protect his classic 1973 Volvo 1800ES from swinging doors. Like his other possessions, he babied his car.

Three years earlier, he'd been channel surfing and stumbled on an episode of the ancient TV series, *The Saint*. The car stole the show for Cord; he couldn't get it out of his mind. A month later, out for a Sunday motorcycle ride on an open road east of suburbia, Cord caught a glimpse of a deep blue 1800ES going the opposite direction. Now a rarity, any ES on the road was pristine and worthy of double-takes. A fast U-turn and quick acceleration brought him alongside the car.

"Nice car,'" he yelled over the road noise.

"Thanks," the driver called back.

"Mind if I see it up close?"

"Coffee shop next signal."

The retired couple from a few cities over were the car's original owners, having purchased it new as a wedding gift.

They acknowledged to Cord they *might* be willing to part with their treasure to someone who knew the deeper meaning of care and pride. Cord flashed his most winning smile and proposed, on the spot, three times their asking. Two weeks later the ES was his.

Today, with the car's scarred right side from Brooke's joust with the garage door track and an upcoming appointment with the body shop, Cord casually squeezed into a middle parking space closer to the marina dock. But he made sure his boss Elkin eased the passenger door shut. Slamming the door of a masterpiece, even injured, wasn't tolerated.

A short walk through the gate to *Starstruck's* slip, a turn of the ignitions and the marine engines immediately rumbled to life. While they idled, Cord untied two of the three dock lines, bow and mid. He loosened the stern line and handed the bitter end to Elkin standing by at the transom. As Cord folded back the canvas bimini cover, his neighbor in the yacht next to *Starstruck* walked out of his cabin holding a mug of steaming coffee.

"Morning, Doc. Coffee good?" Cord asked over his boat's quiet exhausts.

"A good one indeed." Travis took a sip from the mug. "Taking time off from work?"

"This might prove to be more of a workday than in the office. Doc, my boss Marcus Elkin. Marco, Doc Edgerton."

With the essentials of dockside pleasantries fulfilled, Cord eased out of the slip while his boss released the stern line.

"Where to, Cap'n?" asked Elkin as he settled into the portside mate's bench.

"Might was well aim for Saddlebag Island. We'll have the cove to ourselves on a weekday."

Outside the small marina Cord pushed the throttles forward and the boat climbed up on step to glide along the broad channel leaving hardly a wake. He gave the massive cargo ships at anchor a wide berth, observing Homeland Security's demand to stay 500 feet from ferries and other commercial vessels. Ten minutes later he activated the electric windlass to drop anchor in fourteen feet of water and dig into a mud bed lined with eelgrass.

"Tons of crabs here for the taking during open season," said Cord. He motioned to a small cockpit refrigerator aft of the helm. "Care for a drink? I've got plenty."

"Still filled on breakfast. That was like eating at a trough. And Rosa gave us even more for lunch! I'll find something to drink later."

There was no breeze and not much of a tidal change so the boat swung little on its anchor tether. The bow pointed north out of the cove, the eastern mainland to starboard. The sun cast its glow warming their backs.

Marcus Elkin, a driver-type who got things done, wasn't one to mince words. Without preamble he launched into his first in a series of questions which he referred to as Queries for Cord.

"Seems more like a return to your personal inquisition when you hired me," said Cord.

"This one's rougher, pal. Wish I could put it another way, but the subject matter comes under the heading, You don't need to lose your wife. The question isn't how to get her back but fundamentally, do you want to be the husband of Brooke—what's her middle name?"

"Gretchen."

"Pretty. Brooke Gretchen Cord."

"As you said earlier, this coming from a guy who collects marriage certificates."

"Three. And in my case, three too many," admitted Elkin. "I doubt there will be a fourth. My exes pray there won't."

Cord diverted the focus to Elkin's relationships. "What made the unions, if I can call them that, go bad?"

Elkin accepted the detour. "You want to know? The first one made it to four years, but was all about me. She was my sidecar, nothing more. The second one was a chain reaction to the first. A Fedex marriage: rush the package home, unwrap it, keep it in bed. As for my third, I'm still not sure. Ask her and I think she'd tell you, three strikes in the sixth inning, game over. Tickets should have never hit the kiosk."

"Meaning?"

"She couldn't find much love from used material that had been preformed and cast off by others before her. Interesting though, the last one, Michelle, wanted to make it work. The woman really tried. We lasted fourteen years. But like I said, she didn't have much to work with. So just to be plain here, I'm no candidate for matrimony mentor. But I don't think your marriage to Brooke needs to end like my three."

"You obviously see something neither of us sees in each other, or ourselves."

"You and Brooke started with something deeper than a momentary sizzling passion."

"We had that too." Cord's mind began to drift back to nights just last summer. So long ago.

"No doubt you did. You made an attractive couple. But there was something else you both offered. You wanted the best for each other; you protected each other with good words."

"Good words? I guess—early on."

"It wasn't so in my relationships. We kept hitting dry spells, mostly marital, but personal too, and our verbal skills dried up. Couldn't find an oasis in our deserts."

Cord had to ask, "Dry spell. What did that look like?"

"We liked and admired each other, okay? Possibly even loved. But the marriage dehydrated. I don't mean just sexually. What we had in our first years faded, then vanished. We both knew it. Even talked about it. Was it just a season of life? We didn't know."

"Which marriage are you talking about? Do I need a scorecard?"

"The last one. Michelle."

"Dehydrated marriage," mused Cord. "A fitting picture. Not even two years and our marriage is more like scorched. I don't know how things degraded so fast from superb to severe. We ended up calling each other by name only when we were fighting. Threw in a few descriptive titles too."

"That's not unusual, I suppose. I remember how we used to love saying each other's name—just to say it. Toward the end I only heard *Marcus!* when she wanted to get my attention because she needed something from the fridge or when making some other demand. She only heard her name from me when I was upset with her. You know how parents call their kids by their full name when they're mad at them. Used to be I'd say hers just for the pleasure of saying it. Michelle Annalee Elkin. At the end, I couldn't stand the taste of the sound."

"Brooke says my name and makes it sound like she's throwing up."

"Your marriage is young, Cord, not long enough to learn how to navigate relational rough spots. It's all still new for you both."

"What are you saying? That we haven't heard our death knell?"

"You may have. But I think you've both got more going than you recognize."

"Why such an interest in rescuing my marriage?"

"Because I see yours as not only salvageable, but a relationship that's got lifelong potential."

"You looking for something in my marriage to Brooke you didn't get in your three?"

"I don't think that's it. Maybe some. I've only talked with Brooke a few times, but each time I've been impressed with her reality. No presumption, no mask, just honest simplicity. Someplace in there might even be a loving heart."

"You're joking, right? C'mon, Marcus, you're trying to slip a storybook cover over a nightmare. Baggage, man. She's got it. Her family fed on only two emotions—passivity and anger, under the umbrella of concealment. You want to know her defaults? Blame and payback."

"Her past considered then, should it be a surprise she'd dump any less of a load on her relationships?"

"Anyway," said Cord wanting to route the conversation back to less treacherous ground, "I thought this outing was intended to be about what we do with Signa Thomsen after last night's disaster at the pub. Or do you really have a not-so ulterior motive here? Other than taking your own three-hour tour."

"You found me out." Marcus nodded, looking across the water to the distant mainland. "Looks peaceful out there, doesn't it? But in each of those houses on the shore and up on the hillsides, they're all dealing with the shortcomings of their relationships, the bleakness of their futures. And some of them will simply give up. So yes, I do have an underlying motive.

You're too valuable to lose. And, I'm thinking so is Brooke. Signa's issues are minimal compared to yours right now."

"Cheap shot. Thank you."

Ignoring the slight, Marcus said, "Signa's also replaceable. Sorry to be harsh. At this time, to put it bluntly, you're not. So, pardon me, but it's time to pry some more. You don't mind. Do you."

It was stated more as a rule of engagement. But Cord didn't mind. For some reason he felt a growing affinity for his nervy boss. He asked, "Where do you want me to begin?"

"I figure you know."

Cord took a deep breath, held it. When he exhaled he said, "I can trust you, right?"

Elkin's nod was slow, solemn. "You have before."

"I'm not used to talking this way about my wife with other people. Only my boat neighbors, and that was last week."

"That's actually refreshing. Most people can't stop complaining about a spouse to others."

"Never needed to."

"She's been that perfect?" asked Elkin.

"Not just that. It's how I was brought up. Not that my family hid our junk. We just never felt the need to set it out for display."

"Shows me I've been right about you all along."

"How's that?"

"Good roots."

Uncharted

Sixteen

THAT WAS THE TURNING POINT? A FIZZLED family get-together?" asked Elkin after listening to Cord's abridged account of attending Brooke's family Fourth of July gathering, her rocketing anxiety, and their long talk at the turnout on the way back to the airport. Elkin opened *Starstruck's* bar fridge for a flavored water.

"Seemed to be," said Cord. "From then on she began to freeze over. Couldn't get any conversation from her. We entered a state of marital détente."

"Interesting way to put it. Did the trauma also have to do with the memory of a childhood molestation of some sort? An older brother? Uncle?" He opened his bottle and sipped.

"That's the crazy thing. Not really. Yeah, guys in high school tried to hit on her; one look and you know why. The closest thing to assault was when one unfortunate kid tried to grab a kiss during the lunch hour when all the students were watching. She clocked him, and while he was down kicked him hard enough to break two ribs. Two football linemen had to pull her away."

"Lot of anger there."

"I've discovered."

"There might be more hidden than she's telling. Or re-members. In time she may, if it's important."

"Her family made a point of putting her on display, but there was none of the violation you'd expect. And I asked."

"You asked her, point-blank?"

"Yes. One night just after the reunion when she still acknowledged my voice. 'Brooke, did someone abuse you?'"

"She said…"

"Her eyes grew so large, those gorgeous eyes. 'What! Why would anyone do that? I'd never let them. No, Cord, that isn't it at all.' Calling me Cord was her signal she trusted me. Then. I haven't heard that from her for months."

"She told you the offense?"

"The skeleton hangs quietly in the family closet."

"That's got to be grist for nightmares."

"Brooke was subjected to a family-wide clampdown. She was just a young girl who had no defenses."

"I don't want to pry."

"You say that a lot, don't you? And yes, you do want to know all the details. I did. Anyone would."

Seventeen

CORD TOLD THE FULLER STORY, AS HE UNDERSTOOD it, of Brooke's tormented youth, her recompense for uncovering the Shiller treasure.

"What became of the booty?" Elkin leaned back against *Starstruck's* cockpit cushions, absently watching a tugboat on its way to chaperone a cargo ship into the harbor.

"She doesn't know. She assumed it was scooped out of the mud and divided among the older members of the family, JT of course taking the bulk and adding to his estate."

"So, help me understand this." The tug chugged away out of view. "I'm not tying in how Brooke became the family felon. Wouldn't the man in prison—uncle, wasn't he? Wouldn't he do?"

"This is where you need to turn off the logic switch. Here's the dynamic. Her family needed someone to injure. It came down to meanness."

"Tell me again what she did that was so wrong?"

"That's just it. Only one thing, but it was a huge thing for them. She happened upon Edwin's treasure box. She actually did them a favor, giving them newfound wealth. But finding the chest wasn't the issue. It was exposing JT's deceit. The prized beauty revealed the monarch's secret."

"That's it?"

"You're not tracking, Marcus. I didn't either. The key here is that it was the family's secret. The bond that held them together. And it became the family's identity. Crazy, I know."

"Beyond crazy. The family was bound together by, what, a lie."

"Now you're getting it. A lie, and the prospect of many pots of gold. So instead of hating JT, they turned their wrath on Brooke. She was expendable, his generosity wasn't. They hammered the belief into her that she was the one to blame for upsetting their uncomfortable balance, and made sure she'd hate herself for it."

"You make her sound like she descended from heaven and fell into hell. You're not overstating?"

"Think about it," said Cord. "What if you believed all your life you were garbage, when all along you were a show-stopper?"

"The opposite actually happened to me." Elkin attempted a smile. "Then I looked in the mirror and couldn't argue."

"But what if the mirror lied? Or what if it didn't lie, but you couldn't permit yourself to see yourself as you really were?"

"Sorry, I shouldn't have joked. I understand all too well why believing a lie about yourself is so disabling."

"I didn't see any disconnect until her family reunion. After that I began to see pieces of the puzzle, and a few started to fit. But—."

"But you had no idea what to do with the picture coming into focus." said Elkin. "You didn't like it and you couldn't fix it."

"Exactly. You've been there?"

"My second marriage."

"So what did you do?"

"Couldn't do a thing. Wasn't permitted in that space. Why do you think I call her the middle child?"

"Brooke hates calling them her people or her kin. You know what pulled the lever for her?"

"I'm not following. Say that in a different way."

"What convinced her that she was the alien were the undertones of being adopted."

"I had no idea she was. When did she find out?"

"Oh, she knew all along. Her dad, the family outsider, told her when she was four or five. The way he told her, out of gratitude that she'd be his daughter, made her glad to be adopted. But her mother—kinfolk came first for her—never owned up to it. Brooke couldn't understand why she was never close to the woman. Her dad was her protection during the early years, then he backed off too, kept to himself. She thought she'd made him mad for something she'd done. But he was just overpowered by his wife—they must have divorced—and her people. Brooke was better than all of them. In every way."

"Then what was it about her being adopted?"

"It hit her one day during her junior year in high school. She finally clued in that no matter how hard she tried, she couldn't make the others accept her. Add to that, she was the one who opened the door to the family secret. That's when she started to distance herself from everyone around her. Parents, relatives, school friends—most of them were related anyway.

She dug a relational hole she filled with resentment as payback. Of course, she couldn't tell them because they were too powerful, even if she was the homecoming queen and the county's darling. So she stuffed her anger, which turned to molten rage. And guess who now stands in fury's path?"

"But you didn't initially see any of that in her because she'd had years to put on another face."

"And it was so good, and always beautiful. Man, you've never seen anyone so pretty just waking up in the morning. All I saw was poise, sincerity, pleasure, even playfulness. And enough vulnerability to assure me she was the real thing. But she'd been walking through life holding back tears."

Elkin sat pensive, lightly rubbing his forehead. "The poor kid. Such a heavy load to carry."

Cord didn't say anything for a long while. Then, "Going to that reunion tipped her over the edge."

Elkin asked, curious, "What about the uncle who stole the strongbox. Edwin."

"I Googled him. Still languishing in a cell, a lifetime from the hint of parole. And his crime was only stealing a box of money. And from what I could read, no one knows how much or even what he actually took. Comes down to his being one of those guys people love to hate."

"The Howard Cosell of the prison system."

"Who?"

"Before your time, but I remember as a kid watching Monday Night Football with my older sister and her boyfriend—I got to wear his letterman's jacket during the games. Cosell and Dandy Don. They made MNF an experience. Argued the entire game. Gifford sometimes couldn't call the play for their bickering."

Cord was glad for the comic relief from his boss. "The names I don't know, but I get the bickering."

"As did I," said Elkin. "The books I'd read on conflict in the workplace didn't help in the home. Not because they were wrong; I just didn't want to play by the rules. One of them said, 'You don't have to attend every argument you're invited into.' So where's the fun in not striking back?"

Cord caught Elkin's dexterity at segueing from buried treasure and family censure to his agenda. Here they were alone at an isolated island, and his boss changed hats on him, assuming the role of life coach. The man wasn't going to allow another treasure to remain buried.

Cord went with it. "Brooke and I didn't have that problem," he chanced. "We avoided argument to keep the peace. Until we tanked."

"Keep the peace? You know the difference between peacekeeping and peacemaking?"

"You're eager to tell me, right? We've got the time, if this is part of the workday. You hungry yet? I could go for some of that Mexican lunch."

Elkin reached across for the bags of food and set Rosa's still warm soft tacos on the cockpit table along with slices of lime and tubs of salsa.

Cord opened the cockpit fridge for drinks. "Got coke, cherry coke, root beer, cream soda. Or a stout if you want."

"Make it cream soda. Haven't had one of those since I was a kid. No more beer for me. One of the reasons my marriage licenses have become wallpaper. I tell you I'm in AA?"

"Never knew that about you. Is it helping?"

"Too late for my marriages. But I'm better for the meetings."

"'Hi, I'm Bryan, and I'm a jerk.' Something like that?" Cord set the drinks and glasses with ice on the table and was about to pop open his coke when Elkin began to speak.

"Thanks, God, for food, for Cord. Show him what he needs to know."

Cord was stunned. Why hadn't he noticed praying people before? First Doc Edgerton, now his boss. And neither of them fit the stereotypes he'd seen portrayed across the media.

"What did you just do?"

"You mean what I just said? Most folks call it praying. I thought it might be nice to talk to God. Didn't disturb you, did it? I mean, it's your boat and all."

"No no. Until a couple of days ago I hadn't seen anything like that up close. You met my neighbor, Travis. And you guys actually talk to God? I never took you for one of those people."

"I don't think I am, but if saying a quick thank-you marks me, I'm good with it."

"When did you start?"

"Praying or drinking?"

Cord looked away and sighed loudly. "Marcus, Marcus."

Elkin smiled back. "One of the women in AA told me it might be good to talk to God. 'On my own?' I looked at her the same way you're looking at me. Possum at the Freightliner. 'Give it a try,' she said. I did. Still do. Funny thing, it seems to help."

"With what?"

"Life in general, I'd say. I'm no churchgoer, so I can't tell you about any religious accouterments. But I feel better for it. I don't know, maybe I just talk to myself."

"Probably more likely. But if it helps keep peace better, I ought to try talking more to myself."

"Oh, right, the difference between keeping and making peace. You want to hear?"

Cord opened the bags and spread the Mexican food on the table. "I'm still on your clock, *Señor* Elkin."

"*Gracias*." Elkin poured his soda into a glass and slurped the foam. He took a soft taco, spooned on additional salsa and refried beans and added a squeeze of sliced lime.

"Peacekeeping," he began as he handed the taco to Cord, "is what most families do, most companies too. We recognize there's a problem, but refuse to address the core issue so it does a low simmer. But we tell ourselves everything is fine. We hate the other guys, but we smile a lot, holding the tension just under the surface. We call it keeping the peace."

"Pretty much describes most of my last year."

"Then there's peacemaking. That's the difficult one because of one crucial element. Know what it is?"

Cord took a drink, keeping his eyes on his boss over the rim of the glass.

"Good, you're all ears," said Elkin. "Intentionality, my friend. Plain and simple. Peacekeeping allows conflict to remain, even entertains it." He picked up a taco and took a bite. With his mouth full he said, "The stance of the peacemaker, or peace builder—much different. Face the issues head-on, in the open. The peacemaker's goal is to bring harmony into an environment where there is none. Talk about self-sacrifice, that's it right there."

"More like suicide if I were to attempt that with Brooke. I'd be handing her a loaded .45 and she'd empty the clip. Then she'd scream at me for my blood on the wall."

"The peacemaker takes all the risk. Deliberately picking the low cards when you need to, because you see the bigger picture."

"So she can use the same cards to my disadvantage."

"Seems like iron sharpening bread, doesn't it? One slashes the other and boasts in the triumph. You want to make headway with Brooke? First step, stop fighting back."

Cord took a second taco and silently chewed, a small grin forming as he entertained heaving Elkin overboard into the cold water of the tiny uninhabited island that wouldn't be visited until the next warm weekend.

"I know what you're thinking," said Elkin. "And yes, I would be missed. I've got a four o'clock with my third ex and her lawyer. So instead of tossing me overboard here, you'll get more pleasure feeding me to the sharks at four."

"It was a thought."

Elkin went for broke. "Cord, I'm not convinced you and Brooke are on the Titanic."

"So we're not arranging the deck chairs as it sinks, right? Just about every seminar speaker uses that stale word picture."

"More accurately, the two of you are alone on one of the lifeboats. You dragged her out of the freezing water, almost falling in yourself. So you're both in the boat and need each other's body warmth to stay alive. But you're arguing about who sits where, who should take lookout and who rows. And you've got one oar between you."

"Pretty accurate, until last week. The boat went under."

"Pop quiz. You come into my office and you're troubled over something going on at work. What's the first thing I say? I mean the very first thing?"

"'Sit down or pace as much as you want, however you process best.'"

"After that."

"I'm not sure."

"Of course you know. I always say it. Help…"

"…me understand."

"Exactly. Help me understand. The three most important words in peacemaking. A matter of simply allowing the other person—Brooke—to speak and get her hurt out on the table."

"I'd have to block out two days just to let her vent. It would be safer to open a barrel of radiation. With no hazmat suit."

"Two days? I've given you three weeks. With pay. Seems to me, this is your opportunity.

"More like a last gasp."

"Take the risk, pal. You want her back? Go after her."

Hadn't Doc Edgerton said the same thing over breakfast the week before?

"She'd see right through it," said Cord. "Probably call you and scream, 'You put him up to it, didn't you, Elkin? Didn't you? Didn't you!'" Cord's volume grew and he began to sound like his estranged wife.

He caught himself. "Good thing no one else heard that."

"Help me understand."

Cord got it. He was suddenly disarmed. But would Brooke be receptive? Or would she use all her powers to level him? At least he could retreat to his boat at night.

Then it struck him. He was afraid of his wife. Honestly afraid. When she went on her rants, he couldn't match her barrages.

"You think she'll want to understand me?" he asked his boss.

"No guarantee, is there? Comes down to this, Cordless. Is she worth it?"

"Was your third wife?"

"That was a rabbit punch."

"Help me understand."

"I do, Cord."

"I know you do. The road ahead is a big unknown. What if Brooke and I should get back together? That's a long shot, I know. But what if?"

Elkin took off his sunglasses and rubbed the sides against his temples. "Let me toss this out. What do you want?"

Cord grunted. "I can't answer that alone. How can I take us where she doesn't want to go?"

Elkin set his shades on the counter. "I'm with you. But isn't the question going to be answered first by you before it can be answered by both of you?"

"She's got to answer the same question. I don't think she will."

"You don't know what's going on in her mind. But you. What is it *you* want?"

"I wouldn't want her like she's been the last few months. But if I could choose, I'd want her as she was when we were happy. Not that I'm trying to go backward in time, but we did have something good. Very good."

"Okay, before you look at steps to get to where you call good, let me ask again. What is it you really want?"

"I just told you."

"Tell me again."

Cord sighed. "You're asking me to spell it out, is that it? So you can hear my words."

"Not for me, my friend. It's all for you. And it could be for Brooke."

Cord waited a long time to answer, for the lump in his throat to soften. "All I want," his voice hoarse, "is to tell Brooke how much I want to love her, and for her to give me more time to show her I mean it." He looked Elkin in the eyes. "There. I said it."

Elkin kept quiet.

Cord added, "That's what I want." Then, "Isn't that what you want with Michelle?"

Elkin was startled, put on the spot. "Excuse me?"

"Don't tell me you didn't see that coming. Isn't that what you want too? To still be your wife's husband?"

Elkin rubbed his hands together, interlaced his fingers and grimaced. "Another rabbit punch."

Cord's uneven smile grew. "Yeah. My friend."

Uncharted

Eighteen

Brooke admitted to moments of loneliness, but took delight in the safety of quietness—sharing her house, her bed, her life, with no one. The TV stayed off longer despite Vanna's wardrobe and Alex Trebek's switch from glasses to contact lenses to glasses. She was especially glad—thankful, if there were someone other than herself to whom thanks might be due—to be rid of Bryan Cord. His habits, his voice, his presence.

Cord stuck close to *Starstruck*. Now into his third day of his boss Elkin's imposed furlough, and the tenth day away from Brooke, he labored to fill his time with meaningless tasks. Set and reset the mooring lines, check a completely dry bilge for the hint of moisture, call for a voice check on a perfectly functional VHF radio, review last year's fishing regulations. His meals were no less mind-numbing. Stroll over to the marina coffee shop for a sandwich and listen to old salts discussing cuprous oxide levels and epoxies of bottom paint, or stay aboard and open a can of soup in peace. Order pizza one night, drive to the Asian buffet on another where he'd find a back corner table to gorge himself on teriyaki and mediocre sushi, away from the other lonely singles. Stop at a Red Box for a rental because the marina supplied inadequate wifi for streaming and he was tired of his collection of DVDs. Having no schedule to keep or projects to complete, every night he fell asleep bored and exhausted.

Elkin might be right about meeting with Brooke to listen to her. But Cord dreaded calling. And he couldn't come up with a neutral place. It'd have to be in a public setting where she'd be less likely to shriek at him. Cord was still running on fear. Afraid of the woman he'd said he loved—a lifetime ago.

He waited another day before he brought her number to his cell's screen. He stared at it until the phone blacked. He set the phone down and reached for an opened bag of oven-baked potato chips. With a second handful he looked over at the phone again. *Can't use it with greasy hands.* He got off the settee and washed his hands in the head, blew his nose, checked his two-day beard, straightened his cap. *I should brush my teeth again*, an hour after the first time.

Ten minutes later he picked up the phone and spoke.

"Call, uh…"

The phone spoke back, "Didn't catch that, Cord. Tell me who you want to call."

He paused too long, deliberating.

"Today, big guy?"

He'd have to tone down the phone's personality. He didn't need another feisty female.

"Call Brooke."

"Calling Brooke."

Ringing.

She probably won't answer. Hope not.

Still ringing.

Brooke. Not B. Call her Brooke.

On the fifth ring she answered.

"What!"

Great beginning.

Too flustered for a preliminary Hi Brooke, he simply said, "Can we talk?"

"Why!"

Help me understand.

"I want to hear your side of things." *Dumb. Really, really dumb.*

"My side? As if yours is tenable? Who put you up to this? Elkin did, didn't he? I'm not one of your office gamers."

"Brooke"—*actually got that one right*—"I just want to talk with you. Not to you, not at you. Can we?" *Good line, Cord. Where did that come from? Might even work.*

"What's the point, Bryan?"

She asked a question. Said my name like it was a bad taste, but she didn't throw up. Is this working?

With nothing to lose, he entered the depths. "Can I pick you up and we go for coffee? Wherever you want."

"Not in the ES."

"You can come over for me if that's better. I'm at the marina."

"I know where you are. When?"

When? Now what do I do?

"Whatever works for you. I mean, whenever you're available. Whenever you can."

Cord heard a loud, impatient sigh, then, "Two hours. Be in the parking lot. I'm not stepping on that boat."

"I'll be at the gate."

She made him wait an extra thirty minutes in the rain. *It's only a drizzle*, she justified her delay as she finished toweling off and put on her most eye-catching jeans and sweater combo. Not quite sure if she was dressing for him or herself, she took extra time to apply her minimal make-up. Appraising herself in the mirror, she saw a woman who looked like someone she wanted to be.

Driving extra slowly through the parking lot she saw Cord standing alone, cap backward, hands in his jacket pockets. She pulled up and he tried to open the passenger door to get in. It was locked. She took her time to touch the unlock button.

Getting seated he said, "Thanks for meeting with me." Her fragrance, not powerful, always right, filled his senses. He chanced to steal a glance at her. Flawless. Breathtaking. *Why does she have to go and do that to me?*

Struggling to bring his mind back to his purpose for meeting, he asked if she'd had lunch. No. Would she like to try Mexican? No. How about George's Grotto by the water? No. Family Farm away from town? No.

Out of suggestions and exasperated, he was ready to call the whole thing off when she said, "Let's walk on the ferry to Weekes Harbor."

"Sure, if you'd like. Of course."

"Don't think I want to do this. I feel more protected with a trained crew watching for irregular behavior."

He was about to say he'd be the one needing protection, but he held off. The hour-long cruise might be a neutral setting after all. Plus there was a decent coffee shop close to the landing on the other side.

He paid for parking and their walk-on tickets and they were the last to board the two-ten sailing. They took a corner portside booth at the window, both relieved there was an affixed table between them. While the ferry coursed its way through the San Juan Islands, every ten minutes one of the male crew strolled the large passenger cabin with a wary eye for articles left unattended. His pace slowed every time he passed them to admire the indoor scenery facing his direction.

Cord couldn't take his eyes off her either. She was still his wife.

"You look great," he said.

"Thank you."

"Have you been okay?"

No answer.

"I've been given three weeks off."

More silence.

Tread carefully. How do I get from here to Help Me Understand?

With no comment to bridge the chasm, he unconsciously shrugged and said, "I guess I'll just begin."

Brooke didn't move, nor did her demeanor soften. Why make it easy? He wanted to meet; okay, so talk. *But you'd better be careful, hotshot. I may have walked onto this tub with you, but no one says I need to leave the same way.*

"The only reason," Cord began, "I wanted to see you was to ask if you'd let me…" Regrettably, he paused.

She jumped right in. "What. What do you want from me? Whatever it is, I don't believe you."

Fumbling for words he tried to continue. "…if you'd let me try to understand what you're feeling."

Then he found the words.

"What do I need to hear, Brooke?" *Simple, to the point. Peacemaking. Got it.*

Her stoicism was daunting. He couldn't think of a follow-up, so he sat waiting.

She sighed softly through her nostrils, a sign she was slowly lowering her guard.

"You don't mean it, do you?" If she were to drop her defense, she wouldn't hurry.

He didn't move a muscle, but began to breathe through his mouth, his indicator of discomfort. His pent-up tension gave him a metallic taste so he snapped it shut. He could think of nothing to say except, "Yes."

She turned toward the window. The ferry was slipping by one of the smaller islands. A fishing boat sped by, its two occupants in yellow slickers. After an eternity for Cord, Brooke turned back to him.

"You do mean it?"

"I really… Yes."

The door was open. Would she walk through?

She chose to drive a semi.

"You're not the same man I married. The way we started, it was all wrong. I wish you'd never called me."

He tried to reply, but could form no words.

Nor did she give him time. Instead she leveled him.

"You need to go your way, I'll go mine. I'm better off on my own. I've got a lawyer, you get yours."

He felt like he'd stepped on a landmine. He didn't hear her next words, but later recalled they were devoid of emotion. The woman, his wife, sat across from him. Striking. Composed. Detached. He was looking right at her, but she wasn't there. Only a likeness.

"I suppose," she was saying, "you'd like to find another place to sit."

No hint there. He stood, tried to say something, but she had already turned away and was looking out the window. He'd been dismissed.

She felt an acute stab in her upper abdomen, but hid her grimace.

It was a long return trip to the mainland. They stayed on opposite ends of the ship, she at starboard, he looking out a port window. The wandering crewman increased his rounds to every five minutes. The ferry docked, she walked to her car, trying not to hold her stomach. Cord called for a cab.

She pulled her Honda into the garage, taking up both spaces. Inside the cottage, she slipped on the ankle-length beige cotton nightgown Cord hated, threw a TV dinner in the microwave, poured a tumbler of Chardonnay—she didn't care whether it was a dinner match, finished them both quickly, and went to bed early, luxuriating again in her ownership of the center. She refused to acknowledge her tears.

CORD PAID THE CABBIE at the marina gate, almost forgetting a tip, and walked down the steep gangway at low tide to his boat. Once aboard, he got into his old sweats, nuked a bag of popcorn and took two brews from the fridge. He sat silently at the cabin's table munching and sipping, sometimes guzzling, wishing he had thrown Marcus Elkin overboard in that small cove.

Help me understand? It might work in a controlled office. People on the team play nice or they're ushered to the street. But a marriage stuffed with emotions, devoid of civility, on its way to extinction? He wasn't shown the street. More like the Dumpster. *Peacemaking? Thanks for nothing, Marcus.*

Starstruck's cabin lights shone until Two AM. Cord's neighbors kept an eye out.

Uncharted

Nineteen

Pacific Northwest winter squalls.

The sounds, fragrance, motion of the marina while hunkered down in a thirty-knot gale. Raindrops bursting against *Staarstruck's* rooftop, the dull ring of nearby sailboat riggings slapping their masts. They soothed his spirit.

Provided she was secure in her slip.

Tonight, anchored alone in a tiny hidden cove miles from the marina, she took head-on buffeting winds gusting to twenty knots.

"Well, you wanted to get away, didn't you?" Cord shouted to himself above the noise while he bungee-wrapped a flapping section of the cockpit canvas at the stern. Cross-pour rain pelted his face, his cotton sweatpants soaked mostly on his right side. A strong blast whipped his cap off. He tried to snag it without losing his balance, but it sailed out over the two-foot chop, plopped on the water and was swallowed by a cresting wave.

Too cold and angry to utter more than a single curse, he hastily wrapped the canvas around the scaffolding, and made his way below.

In the warm cabin, he dried his hair on a bath towel—he could faintly smell her fragrance—and kicked off his wet clothes.

"Take a week off from people. Find a little hideaway for time to look at life." He augmented his self-talk with expletives. "Might have been a good idea to check the weather first. Maybe?!"

He left the wet things on the teak floor and reached for the last half of his third stout of the night. He downed that in gulps, and popped open a fourth bottle, flipping the cap in the general direction of the galley sink. Earlier, while sober but expecting to be more than a couple sheets to the wind, he let out extra anchor chain for a seven-to-one scope of ground tackle to depth. With a hundred and ten feet of heavy chain in sixteen feet of water, he assumed the hook would glue itself to the bay's floor.

Cord had every intention of filling an empty stomach with alcohol now, and he didn't care about later. He deserved to drown his melancholy, and—tomorrow's hangover a given—he wouldn't be deprived the experience.

He opened one of two bottles of Macallan single malt, gifts from a client. He never did go for the hard stuff, but tonight was going to be different. He deserved to get good and hammered, stinking drunk. He poured four or five fingers—he didn't count—into a pewter stein, sipped a little.

And stopped. No matter how much he tried, or how expensive the drink, he couldn't get past the taste of eighteen-year old paint thinner. And such a big bottle, with another to go with it. He was about to empty the opened one down the

126

drain and let the marine life beneath absorb it. He remembered one of the old-salt liveaboards—had to be Maury—telling him to revive a boat's fresh water tank with a fifth of whisky once a year, or more often as desired, which would suit Maury's taste. Well, a quart and a half ought to wake up *Starstruck's* water tank all the more. Pouring both bottles into the tank's opening, Cord would rely on his supply of stout, and a dram—or more—of another interesting bottle in the pantry to escort him to oblivion.

After the fourth dark beer, a few trips to the head, a half bottle of a red wine that tasted not too bad, then a too-large glass of a sweet cinnamon tasting whisky labeled Fireball, he felt himself relaxing more than a little, except for being tossed by the waves rising to three feet in a wind measuring forty. He stretched out on the bed and let his stomach do the walking.

A scraping sound radiated through the taut anchor chain. Had to be the anchor shifting.

It dragged a few feet then grabbed again into the gravel floor.

Convinced he'd earlier set the anchor well, in his inebriated state he didn't think anything of it and lay still on the bed wishing the wind would cease. He recalled some story he'd heard about Jesus telling a storm to stop. He wished he could be Jesus right now.

The chain dragged and grabbed. Cord, presuming the anchor finally found it's home, went back to dwelling on the sloshing of his gut.

He heard it again, this time longer and louder. The plow-style anchor released its grip and followed the boat with the wind, digging a ninety-foot furrow in the gravel like it was preparing to plant corn.

Cord muttered something he supposed Jesus wouldn't have said and dragged his legs over the side of the bed, his feet somehow finding the floor. Holding onto anything secure he could grab, he swayed his way aft to the short ladder up to the cockpit. He missed the first step and tried again. With both hands firmly on the side holds he lunged upward and landed on his knees on the deck. Raising himself up to the helm he was about to start the engines to move away from the shore, now much closer.

At that moment the anchor found a bed of clay and burrowed its tines deep, solid. The sudden jerk on the chain threw Cord back into the chair.

He held steady to watch if the boat would too. Though *Starstruck* bobbed and weaved in the three-foot waves, she remained secure, and still a safe distance from a reef no longer submerged at low tide.

Starstruck bounced and staggered all night. Cord's stomach sought quiet from its own storm within, its contents having made course adjustments no longer flowing with his tide. By the next morning the boat's holding tank had nearly filled from his multiple trips to the head. Interesting how a porcelain toilet bowl had become the closest of friends during his hours of need, that realization made in a lucid moment almost meditative.

MORNING. THE NEW DAY gave some respite from the storm, and the boat juked less on its anchor tether. Winds had abated to a modest eight knots and the sun broke out. But Cord stayed put on his bed, hiding from rays that pierced through the portholes and skimmed across the walls to the deepest reaches of his throbbing head. The thought of breakfast became an agony. That large fireball had tipped him over.

Had the seas been flat calm he'd have had no problem holding it, so he said. He'd have even gone for more in the morning, claiming something about the sun crossing the yardarm as the appropriate time for the day's christening. But last night's alcohol consumed in a washing machine had taken him out. His Uncle Steve would have called him polluted, schnockered. But he'd have understood, yes he would.

An arm across his forehead, Cord woke again, opened an eye and peeked at the chronometer. Five-thirty and dark. He'd slept the day away and was glad of it. Headache mostly gone. A little hungrier.

And the boat rocked less.

He carefully rolled off the bed and made it without mishap into the head. Splashing his face he noticed a slight foaming and mildly sweet fragrance of the water out of the tap. He'd thank old Maury later.

He looked at himself in the mirror. Like he'd been in a fight and the other guy landed a couple. But Cord wasn't a fighter, so he scrunched his shoulders and asked, "Tell me again why I'm here?" Talking to himself seemed right.

"She ditched me. Get a lawyer, I've got mine she said. Okay, so I didn't expect another go at the marriage, but not divorce so soon. Do I even know a lawyer she doesn't? What about that kid down the hall? Out of law school. Her guy would have him for lunch. Or is it a woman? Probably just like B...Brooke. Might as well raise the white flag. Give up the ship." He patted the bulkhead next to the vanity. "No, not you, old girl. Better than a wife. Just you and me." He looked around. "Kind of hungry. Need a cold one. Drank the last. Got to be another somewhere. Cockpit fridge."

He rooted out one more dark ale. The last.

"Elkin asked if I want her back. So did the doc. Do I? Good question. Not a good question. Can't get past the lawyer. Divorce could be nasty. Or maybe not." He stared at the beer, decided against it and put the bottle in the fridge.

"Never wanted anyone else. Just her. Even with the limp. Hardly notice it. Great body. I do notice that. What is it about her I want most? Everything."

He pried open a can of mushroom soup. The substance pulled itself into a pan. He added a tin of Vienna sausages and stood at the stove waiting for the contents to heat. Taking the pan off the stove, then plopping himself down at the table, he clutched a tablespoon and ate from the pan.

"Specifically? Why do I want her? She knows how to converse. Oh yeah, sometimes too lively, but there's no boredom with her. Sitting across the dining room table, looking into her eyes, hearing her voice. Who else pronounces February with two Rs? And the front room—she calls it the parlor. Just good talking, because talking together is good with her." He halved a sausage with the spoon and ate both pieces.

"Do I love her? Okay, so the way I've gone about love comes out pretty feeble, like I'm not trying. So then, what's she looking for?" He looked off into space.

"I have no idea."

He finished his improvised dinner, persuading himself his marriage too was finished, unfixable.

Still hungry, he sliced an apple and slathered the wedges with peanut butter. His sweet tooth called and he was quick to answer by downing a large Hershey's, following up with globs of more peanut butter topped with honey in a coffee mug. He nuked it for ten seconds, mixed the elements together and slowly ate the concoction, mopping the inside of the mug with his fingers and licking them clean. Thinking he might want coffee in the morning he threw a mess of grounds and probably enough water into the maker. At seven-thirty he called it a day and went back to sleep. But not before considering that he might still love his wife.

MORNING TWILIGHT DIDN'T SHOW UP all that early in the Northwest winter. Cord climbed out of bed and took three steps without losing his balance. The ocean was flat calm. He turned on the coffeemaker. He couldn't say why, but he wanted to see the sun rise. Throwing on his ski jacket he went topside just as the sun broke above the water. He wiped the moisture off the bench seat and settled down with an oversized mug of steaming coffee. Exceptionally strong today.

Just another sunrise, it seemed at first. But today's was unique. Brighter colors, downright awe-inspiring. The sun's rays bounced off the water to illumine *Starstruck* and the forest along the shore behind. Couldn't beat the view from where Cord sat. Nothing between him and the vividness that he didn't know why he called glorious. No one around to spoil its purity.

Or to enjoy it with him.

He wondered if God liked the colors of a sunrise. Probably not much more than an indifferent bystander—if he was out there. How'd God come into his thoughts? Cord had been too busy in life to notice the handprint of a Creator. He figured Brooke was too angry to admit there might be a handprint.

He needed physical activity. Setting the coffee aside he dropped the dinghy in the water for a row around the bay. He pushed off from *Starstruck* and put his back to the oars. Watching the small wake he was creating behind in the still lagoon, he didn't care where he rowed, or where his musings took him.

Uncharted

Marriage. Cord's parents were proponents of the custom until his dad's death forced widowhood upon his mom. She'd always consider herself a married woman, eternally linked with the husband she knew, she loved. More than loved. Cherished. Those two were devoted to each other. *Too bad it didn't transfer to your son, Mom. Dad, wherever you are.*

Cord's neighbors, Travis and Carly in the yacht next to *Starstruck,* seemed to wear marriage well. He could hear Carly saying, *Bryan, marriage isn't a problem to solve, as if we're always on our guard against outside energies, or each other. We hang out together because we like to. Work, play, talk, make love, argue. This isn't a search for perfection, or even normalcy. Let me say it again—married life, and I mean when we're in it for the long haul, can be just plain messy. And we're fine with that. Do I get angry with him? At times, very. Because we're that close. No one else gets all of me. We take care to smooth our rough edges because we're in this for life. It's called real time marriage.*

His boss Elkin could claim no more than a string of relational failures. But that didn't stop him from taking a swing at explaining healthy marital conflict. *Cordless, the bigger the conflict, the costlier. I'll tell you, when it gets really bad is when your words take her back into the hostilities of childhood. One minute she cries in terror, the next she attacks. And you clam up and run for it. Neither knows how to argue without threatening or shaming the other. Making up, if you can get there, is seeing how you can stay standing, holding your ground without resorting to aggression, because you're trying to get on the same side. Knowing what I know now, I wish I could start over.*

Then the little Mexican couple who owned the restaurant. He hardly knew them, but those two were always together— and they liked it. *Amigo, like good seasoning, we put the right effort, just enough into this life. Good spices, not too fiery. Sweet not sugary. We find things keeping us laughing together. Marriage, it is not our—how is it?—assignment project to complete. We are happy the most when we are together. Does not* Él Señor *enjoy our laughter? Our contentment?*

God seemed to show up when those people spoke. Everything about God talk seemed a language to itself.

What would God say about marriage? Any real interest in it? Did he grieve someone's loss, or hold it against the ones who lost?

But here's the reality, for whoever's listening out there—there's no more us.

He backed off from hard rowing and idled his way over submerged rocks to an adjacent finger bay. Drifting close to shore he lazily dipped the oars in to keep a slow forward movement, gunkholing along the water's edge, meandering in the shallows. He watched a small crab zip for cover under a kelp frond on the ocean's floor.

What's Brooke's take on the Ground of All Being other than looking up who coined the phrase? Any interest at all in someone bigger? Or who that might be? Moot issue though. She wouldn't come to the discussion table. Gave her seat to the lawyer.

Time to move on, Cord.

OUTDOORS AND ALONE—he'd especially needed the last three days after the storm had sped by. Granted, no new revelations, but a sense of personal regrouping. And in some sense, he felt being watched over. By whom? Not much interested in pursuing more useless thoughts about God, he chalked up a good feeling to a week of actual rest.

He waited till dusk to think about heading home. Taking his time to warm the engines and raise the anchor, motoring back to port in the dark brought fitting closure to his retreat from his discontent. The seascape took on a new quality by night. Crawling at four knots not racing at thirty, *Starstruck's* twin engines murmured their pleasure idling in peace, without stress. Cord read the marker lights—*red, right, return*—to guide him home and steer him clear of submerged rocks—what old salts referred to as unintended aids to navigation. The winter night staged a near blackout so he kept his eyes peeled for floating debris and the running lights of other past-curfew craft and occasional nighttime tugs towing mountainous barges.

All too soon the red and green harbor lights blinked their welcome. Gliding past the jetty, Cord's leisure craft—aptly called—slipped over water instantly relaxed from rippled to glass.

The craft knew her way home, and she communicated to her master matters that those unfamiliar with boats and their waters would not hear. To Cord, this final interaction was reason to prolong the close of the day into the darkness of night. Ever so slowly the captain escorted his lady down the last fairway to her slip, methodically securing her dock lines. Just before quitting the engines, he stood at her helm to take lingering delight in the hum and fragrance of the vessel that time and again provided the environment in which he recovered his sense of self, away from land.

He turned off the engines and sat back down. Total stillness. In a sense, it seemed his perspective was changing.

I'm back. Am I better?

He'd withdrawn from the world for a week, and it'd left him alone. He'd done some thinking, but he wouldn't have won a prize for level of depth.

So I'm not a deep thinker, okay?

But he examined things he hadn't before.

Relationships—how mystifying, and at the same time necessary to life. Not commodities to exchange, but gems holding their own fire.

Brooke's vocabulary must have rubbed off on me.

And speaking of fire, Brooke certainly had it, that much he knew. But more like a diamond than hot flames. *Well, flames too.* Cord chuckled at his own wit.

The facets of another person—how does one peer into the depths? Had he ever tried? *Thought I had.* Possibly more than he knew. Knowing and being known: at the same time satisfying and exhausting.

Who knows me? Is being known good? Who does Brooke know? Can she? She's absorbed in her own stuff.

Then it struck him, for as long as he'd been around her—an eternity covering fewer than two years—she'd never relaxed. Behind her perfect face she was a woman on edge. And after that family reunion her edge got sharper. How could he have helped?

"You're joking, right?" His voice confirmed his thoughts, but he held it to a murmur so the folks next door wouldn't hear.

"Life was good. Very good. Then we go for a short visit with her people, and she blindsides me."

What would he do now, if he could? Nothing anymore, she'd made sure of it. Besides, he was no match for her intellect, or her wrath.

Okay, enough! He tried to switch off his thinking, the product of his brain back from vacation.

The question exploded before him, *Do I still care?*

The answer burst out, "I really do."

But did she? Could she?

More thoughts crowded in, throwing him off.

"Who's this about? Her? Me? Maybe I should keep it all about me, and move on."

Silently, the truth struck.

No one else compares to Brooke. B.

Cord went below and brewed some late night coffee. He wanted to do more thinking.

Twenty

IT HAD NEVER OCCURRED TO BROOKE THAT SHE could be loved because she was a lovable person. Her normal response was straightforward dismissal because she believed the comment to be directed toward her physical appearance alone. She'd never yet seen anyone conceal the thorough head-to-hips scan. What others may have called love she labeled libido.

Lovable? That one mystified her. All her life she was viewed and paraded as the trophy. But she could think of no one who'd adored her for the person she was and wanted to become.

What was a lovable person? Or, what could *lovable* look like? In her library were plenty of references to define the word, but none went beyond the surface. Fetching, endearing, delightful, winsome. They all fell short of what she longed to be said to her. She couldn't put words to the craving, but suspected if it should be satisfied it might give her life.

She avoided looking at her likeness in the mirror. She always had, and couldn't see what others said they saw. A few seconds were plenty, to make sure she looked right to fill the part people demanded. She couldn't discern anyone behind the eyes staring back, except those of a broken little girl lugging a backpack of grief.

Yes, Cord came the closest to honoring her. Honoring. The word seemed to hold meaning for her. He'd admired her, somehow making her feel worthy of being cherished, that she deserved to belong. No one else had the kindness to direct words like those toward her. For that matter, few owned a vocabulary adequate for descriptive words of more than two syllables.

Unconsciously shaking her head, Brooke shelved her introspections into a back corner of her mind and refocused on the book cart before her, placing her silent friends neatly in their respective places.

Cord told her many times she was too good to be true.

"That," she said aloud to herself, "was then."

"Excuse me?"

She was startled by the patron whispering next to her.

"Yes. How may I help you," she said, forcing herself into the present.

"I'm looking for a book on marriage. One that might give some answers to difficult questions." The woman looked to be about Brooke's age.

"You and I both." A slip of the tongue. Abandoning the attempt at a witty recovery, Brooke walked her over to the correct aisle. "On the left about halfway." She had no intention of getting any closer to the books. She was thanked and made tracks to her desk behind the central counter.

The woman slowly went about reading titles on the books' spines. One, *Intimate Allies*, caught her eye. Catchy. Fascinating idea. A half hour later she brought a small armload of books to the counter. Brooke was alone and grudgingly moved from her desk to help the woman scan them for withdrawal.

"Find everything?" Brooke asked, not honestly caring. Passing the woman's card and books under the barcode reader, her eye paused on the title of the top book.

Allies. Not a hope. Not my experience. Could that even be possible? Seemed to her that a person would need to be at least somewhat likable to become an ally. Or lovable.

The realization struck her hard. Intimacy—she was through with it. Finished hoping for any relationships requiring closeness. Finished believing. Finished trusting. No going back.

Barely able to suppress tears, she slid the books across the counter to the woman and managed a tight-lipped grimace falling short of a smile.

Uncharted

Twenty-One

Back in the slip for one fitful night of sleep, and already bored. Tired of TV dinners, canned soups, Asian buffet. Sick of popcorn and rented movies. Might as well face the day, and let tonight's dinner take care of itself.

"Welcome home. Good trip?"

Cord looked up from washing the salt off *Starstruck's* hull and tossed a wave in Travis Edgerton's direction. "For the most part. Back for supplies. Ran out of beer. I'm thinking of heading out for a couple more days. Not sure yet."

"Quite a storm a few nights ago. You obviously made it through."

"It's nice to claim it a past experience. Not one I'd want to repeat." Cord shut off the water hose. "Mind if I ask you something? What's your secret?"

He was surprised at his own question. *What am I doing asking him anything?*

"Not sure I follow."

"I guess I should explain. I had to do a lot of thinking out there this week. Maybe too much thinking. Definitely too much beer."

Travis shook his head doubtfully. "Neither one good on rough waters."

"Doc, I'm on my way to a divorce and I'm not sure why. I was sure I loved her. I've never had an ex before, thought I had a wife. Not sure I want either now. I just spent six days away from obligations and people. But not from thoughts of her. You. You and Carly. You're different. What's with you two?"

"You like meatloaf?"

"What?"

"Meatloaf. Dinner tonight. Join us."

Cord didn't want to endure another evening alone with his thoughts and tiresome menu.

"Thanks, Doc. I'd go for that."

"Good! I'm pretty sure it's meatloaf. You like lima beans? I love limas."

Travis caught Cord's hesitation. "Okay, then. We'll have Brussels sprouts. Just joking. Make it peas. Or, no veggies. Come aboard at six."

CORD SNAGGED A CABERNET he had forgotten about in *Starstruck's* small cooler, and stepped across the finger wharf separating the two boats. He knocked on the side of *Soulmate*'s cabin before stepping aboard.

"Thought this might go with dinner." He handed the bottle to Travis.

Travis inspected the wine label. "My my. This must be an expensive wine. The bottle has a cork."

"You find enormous value in mediocrity," Carly called from the galley.

"I've always considered it a beautiful thing."

"You wouldn't mind if we used wine glasses tonight instead of coffee mugs?"

Travis wasn't choosy in how he drank his wine. Or coffee or beer. "Not at all. That way we can study the wine's legs to determine alcohol content. I'll set the bottle on the counter to let it breathe. You think ten seconds ought to do it?"

Carly laughed and kept a remark to herself.

"Saw it in a movie," said Travis, glad to get a rise from her. "Guess you nodded off then."

Seated in the cabin's dinette, they hadn't taken two sips when Travis said to Carly, "Cord asked me an interesting question this morning."

"Oh?" She set down her glass. "Tell me, Bryan."

Cord found himself on the spot. But it had been at his own request. And he was strangely comfortable with it.

"I asked the Doc, and I'd like to know, what's your secret?"

The subject was on the table, no taking it back.

"Not that difficult to answer," said Travis.

"But not without a few stories to go with it," Carly interjected. "Sure you're ready for them?"

Without waiting for Cord to answer, Travis began. "During our early years we read a number of books on how to assemble a good marriage, as if snapping Legos together. There were a few helpful hints, but many more demands."

"So, did you build your marriage on good genes?"

"Not us," Carly was shaking her head. "Every relationship is unique. Sometimes wonderfully, but painfully too. Marriage is not a neat package. Why try to make it tidy? All the really fine things in life have never been orderly, or sedate." She poured more wine into each long-stemmed goblet.

"I was just thinking the same thing a few days ago out on the water," said Cord. "Stormy. That was us."

"Personalities are different, so are the mixes," said Carly, pouring a little extra into Travis' glass. "Parentage, experiences, family background, no family background, styles of communication. I could go on but you get the picture, don't you?"

"Beginning to."

"What we learned, and continue to confirm, is that someone else's observations, even when they're bestsellers, are simply meant to be helps, not universal laws."

"But that's how some are presented." Travis jumped back in, carefully setting his glass on the table. "Sorry to climb all over this, but most of those books and the gospel-like reverence they're rendered have been an irritation. I've watched countless couples try to take surefire steps to success only to end up more miserable than they were. Follow the my-size-will-fit-you rules, and sure as there's deep water you'll end up in therapy. You want to know why?"

"I think he's about to hear it anyway," said Carly, sipping her wine.

"Actually, I'd like to know," said Cord, reaching toward the dish of Moroccan olives always on the table, then thinking better of it. "My parents claimed no recipes for having a good marriage, they just seemed to make it happen together. Until my dad died a couple of years ago."

"I'm sorry, Bryan," said Carly. Sincerity. Compassion. Had she experienced the loss of a parent?

Travis stretched his arms over his head. "All I'm saying is, people don't need to make marriage so tough. You've heard it called hard work, right?"

"No, I hadn't read that warning on the label," said Cord. "But it's sure true from where I've been the last year. Isn't love supposed to be all you need?"

Travis sat upright.

"Don't start again, Trav," said Carly. "You don't need to get back on the speaker's circuit."

"Just one thing," said Travis.

"Just one? Promise? Even with an audience? Bryan, you heard him. You're the witness."

Cord didn't quite know if they were joking, but their body language was casual and their smiles genuine. The ribbing had to be part of their relational shtick. Lately he'd been observing couples, and each seemed to have a corporate persona they presented to their friends. Some, as if they were business professionals or lived in a Facebook world, gave outward displays of *espirit de corps* to hide shortcomings and failures. This couple in front of him seemed to be as honest in private—their boat only five feet from his—as they were in public. Their playful banter revealed who they were together. What was it about them?

"Marriage isn't hard work," said Travis. "You know what it really is?"

"You're asking me?"

"Marriage is discovery, and coming at it with healthy perspective."

"Just words to me, Doc. You'll have to clear it up."

"He's right, Trav. Bring it out of the classroom."

Travis took up his wine for a long sip. He held the glass to the light to study the wine's legs. "So then, look at it this way," he said, putting the glass down. "Two completely different people. One is said to be comfortable on Venus, the other happy in his exploration somewhere beyond Andromeda. And they join together, creating a tenuous oneness that's nonetheless a unity God calls worthy of his attention. By the way, I hope you're okay with my including God in the mix. He's quite important to us."

Not waiting for Cord's response, Travis said, "But as I was saying about the hard work of marriage. I don't know if it's as hard as it is intricate. And like Carly has said, messy."

"If a marriage relationship were characterized mainly as demanding," Carly took up, "why would we try it on and think it might fit for a lifetime with that anchor to drag along?"

"I say change the paradigm," said Travis, Cord ping-ponging from one to the other. "Where do we find the enjoyment of each other's friendship? What's it like to become quiet shelter for each other? Or put in another way, where's the fun of marriage?"

Cord stared absently at the bowl of olives. Hadn't he and Brooke been good to each other, safe for each other? In the beginning they were ready to rush to the other's defense at the hint of trouble—not that there was any difficulty Brooke couldn't take on herself. Loyalty quickly formed and appeared to be growing. There was no challenge so great that each wouldn't face for the other. As for the fun part...

"We had all that," he said. "The makings of a long marriage. I don't know if it could have lasted a lifetime. Who can predict that? But a long time, I thought." More images of the fun part came to mind and he smiled.

"Sure, we lobbed an occasional barb at each other, but it was part of the love, I guess you'd call it. We stopped short of insult, at first. Hey, I knew if I went too far she could take me out with one punch. Then it changed. She changed. I did too."

Cord lifted his glass and paused mid air. "But we never talked about each other to our friends. Not like other couples we listened to. They hammered away, beating the other down behind the back. We always talked to each other. Every dinner face to face. 'What did you encounter today? How's your mind doing right now?' But here I am talking about my wife. My wife. I'll never be able to call her that again."

"You learned an important lesson early on," said Travis. "Keeping each other's confidence."

Cord set down his glass and crossed his arms across his chest. "Yeah, Doc. And the good it did?"

"Funny how she came to dislike you," said Travis.

"Funny? Not the word she'd use," said Cord.

"But she trusted you," said Carly. "Do you think she misses the relationship as much as you?"

"No indication she does. Her sleaze lawyer is settling that."

"Bryan, I hope you won't be put off by what I'm about to say. For some reason, I feel I can be totally honest with you about ourselves."

"Thank you." Cord was moved. "I…appreciate that."

"Earlier you asked about good genes. Let me define that as a healthy family life. Trav lost his and I never had one. His father died when he was in high school. The man was everything to him. When he was gone, Trav's mom took a path no one would have guessed, married a dud who helped her waste the entire life insurance settlement and lose the house Trav knew as home. He wasn't invited to move with them to a single-wide, nor did he volunteer."

"I pretty much camped out in the home of my best friend," said Travis. "Bud's parents gave me refuge when I had no one. I've always been indebted to that family. Still am, because they became my family." He took his wife's hand and held it. "But Carly's story was worse."

"Yes, it was," she said. "My mother and father, church people by the way, divorced when I was thirteen. My dad had been my best friend. But he changed. They both took a few tumbles in the sack with others, most of them in the same church. They each eventually married—how can I say it kindly—also-rans. Neither wanted my brother or me, so he was packed off to somewhere I didn't know for years, and I lived with various relatives I came to despise and had to defend against. When Travis and I found each other, we couldn't come up with anything looking like a good foundation. We didn't want to just live together. We saw where that took our parents and a lot of our friends. We needed to be married."

"Needed?" said Travis, his eyes wide.

"Not that kind of need," she gave her husband a light kick under the table. "We wanted to give our relationship a chance for permanence. So we got married. But three years after the honeymoon…"

"And they were three gratifyingly active years at that." interjected Travis, feeling another kick under the table, her leg remaining next to his.

"…something went out of the marriage. So we talked with an older friend who'd been a mentor to Trav. At the time I didn't even know you could have friends who were over forty.

"Now here's where I hope you won't be put off, Bryan. To be blunt, we got to where we wanted Christ to be part of our marriage. I was resistant for a long time because of the false virtue I saw in the religious veneers of my mother and father. Over time we feel he's become more integral to our relationship. Are you okay with my telling you that?

"And just to be clear," she added, "Trav and I are not what you'd consider saintly. We've got unpleasant matters even in our recent past we're dealing with."

Travis tensely bit his upper lip. "How about that meatloaf while we carry on?"

Uncharted

Twenty-Two

HERE I AM ON THEIR BOAT, SITTING AT THEIR TABLE, sharing their food—the best meatloaf I've had. And she asks permission to tell me about their personal lives.

"I don't know much about Jesus or God," said Cord. "And from what I saw of church that one time, I didn't like it. If you're good with that, I'm good with what you've got."

"Those books on marriage that Travis mentioned," said Carly. "He's right. Like a lot of our friends, we grabbed onto the latest advice. We even listened to one radio expert. But we couldn't keep up with the demands. We were hurting ourselves trying to be better than we were. So one morning after a particularly wretched night—"

"I hated that couch," said Travis.

"We vowed we'd had enough," continued Carly. "There we were at the kitchen table, no breakfast, no coffee. I'm in my long flannel nightie and Trav's in his boxers, both of us staring at the table. We just asked, are we finished, or worth salvaging? We were through pretending."

Travis picked it up. "Crazy thing was, we decided not to see a marriage counselor. We didn't know of one who'd be a fit, and the guy we'd heard about, and steered clear of, was the top-down kind who had too many answers and not enough listening capacity. So we did something reckless."

"Yeah," smiled Carly.

"We figured what twenty counseling sessions would cost, because we knew we couldn't get by with just a few. Then we doubled that amount and spent it on a twenty-day round-trip cruise to Hawaii. A lot of days all we saw was the sea—its wideness, its calm, its power. Never chatted with anyone but the same two dinner waiters a little, spent the entire time only with each other. Talking, walking numerous laps around the promenade deck, resting, eating, talking, more talking. Interesting how after the first couple days of all that talking we started to get in some bed time."

"Yeah," repeated Carly. "Tossed the flannel nightie overboard."

Cord hadn't expected that. These people were recoloring his picture of an older couple.

"We discovered we wanted," said Travis, "to be together again. To hear each other, relearn each other's language, be honest about our pasts and our defects, apologize for some things. And we began to dream together. Our dreams turned to the water, and we knew we couldn't leave it. That cruise was like being on a saltwater IV for three weeks. That's also when I took up cigars. Carly puffed a couple too. In fact, I'm ready for one now. Like to join us? Let's step outside to cigar central."

Carly began to clear the table.

"Let's leave the dishes, hon," said Travis. "I'll clean up later."

He led the way to the enclosed cockpit and Carly grabbed a lap robe. He turned on a portable space heater to warm up the area and touched a match to a small oil lantern hanging from above.

"The smoking lamp is lit."

He opened a tabletop humidor with a selection of thirty cigars. Cord chose one with a large gold label.

"That'd be on the mild side," said Travis.

"Not being an experienced cigar guy, that's probably what I need," said Cord.

Travis also picked a mild for its hint of sweetness. After punching and lighting his he gave it to Carly for a few puffs.

"When we got home from our cruise," resumed Carly, handing back the cigar, "we started to hang out again with the older mentor of Trav's, and his wife became part of our picture too. They didn't teach us, but showed us by simply being themselves what a nurturing marriage looked like in everyday living. And it included a lot more laughter and ordinary fun than we had ever seen or read about."

"Give me an example," said Cord. "I can see where a marriage could show glimpses of enjoyment, but fun? I haven't seen that."

"Neither had we," said Carly. "Fact was, we couldn't for all the debris in front of us. Now, these days some of our friends still think we're eccentric, or in denial of reality—"

"Or both," added Travis. He took a pull on his Montecristo Classic and blew a satisfying smoke ring. Carly reached for the cigar and puffed a double ring.

"You're good, lady."

She handed it back with satisfaction. "Sometimes I love showing off."

Cord tried to form a ring, but only coughed. "Where'd you learn to do that?"

"A French-Canadian priest showed me when he and I were in our twenties," said Travis, nearly forming his own double ring. "Grew up to be an archbishop. The man will be pope yet."

"And Trav taught me on that cruise."

"A clear example of the student surpassing the tutor," he replied.

"Your relationship doesn't seem to take much effort," said Cord. "You both must be naturally easygoing, even with your childhood years being rough."

"In some ways, yes," said Travis. "In others, not at all. We've both had our intense moments—in marriage, and out in the field."

"In the field?" asked Cord.

"Call it a former life, another dimension. We did some traveling for a company."

Cord thought the answer intentionally vague, and he noticed a momentary hardness in Travis' expression.

Carly said, quickly, "Getting back to the present, we've come to recognize and accept our differences."

"Some days require concerted patience," said Travis.

Cord made no reply, smoked his cigar.

"Travis does make life an adventure," said Carly. "I'm still learning to track with his reasoning. Like for his fifty-fifth birthday."

"My double nickel."

"He walked through the brushless car wash on the hottest day of the summer. What was he thinking? Only Travis knew."

"I should have opted out of the spray wax. But the power drier was cool."

"You came out looking like a Smurf."

"I did it all for you."

Carly smiled and turned back to their guest. "Bryan, I mentioned how our faith walk changed our marriage, really our outlook. And by the way, thank you for letting us ramble on. I hope you don't feel you're being held hostage."

There it was again. She wasn't being apologetic. She was simply a gracious lady.

He showed his wrists. "I don't see any handcuffs or zip ties. What you're saying makes some sense, even to me."

"Well then, let's see if I'll chase you off with this," she said. "And I promise, no more preaching. Then how about some coffee?"

"Preaching? Is that what you've been doing? Pretty painless, especially with that awesome meatloaf and this cigar." Cord tried once more for a smoke ring. It came out a small cloud.

"Let me say it this way," said Carly. "If marriage is a treasured relationship, it takes attention and guarding and care. But that isn't such hard work, is it? Unless the individuals are too self-focused to cultivate relationship. Does that make sense?"

"Not to me, but if you say so."

"Those older friends of ours, Will and Ruth, asked why we kept struggling with unanswerable questions like, how can we be better people? Or, why aren't we getting it right? That night we stopped."

"So, what questions do you ask to keep things good? Any? Or are you beyond that?"

"As if we're over the hill, right?" said Travis, admiring his cigar's perfect inch-and-a-half ash.

"Can I ask how long you've been married?"

In unison they answered, "Almost thirty-six," and slipped each other a soft low five.

"Are we past all our questions?" said Travis, flicking the ash into the large ashtray on the table. "By that you mean, are we too grown up to have struggles? Like Carly said, we still have them. Hey, we live on a boat and someone's got to be captain." He casually saluted his wife.

Out of the corner of her eye Carly caught a glimpse of Brooke on the finger wharf under the marina's lights. She slowly turned her head and made brief eye contact. Carly started to smile, but Brooke backed into a shadow. The two men didn't notice.

"Tell me if I'm right," said Travis. "The budding love you had for each other was somehow sabotaged. An event or string of them set you on a different course and you both found yourselves edging away from each other. A mutual dismissal began creeping up. Fault was assigned, blame dispensed."

"Haven't said it in those words," said Cord. He chose not to tell them about Brooke's family reunion that seemed to be the pivot point when the marriage hit the rocks. He bit into a Moroccan olive from the bowl Travis kept on the table, and his mouth twisted at the salty bitterness. "But it fits."

"I knew you'd like the olives," said Travis, and took one himself. Setting the pit in the ashtray he said, "A number of years ago someone introduced a series on healthy leaders. I think his greatest contribution was rephrasing an old line, Catch your people doing something…right. Whether in the workforce or in the family, how do you make it a priority to observe the ones close to you doing well, and point it out to them? It's most difficult in the family, isn't it?"

"I'm pretty good at it in the office," said Cord. "But with Brooke I couldn't make that happen."

"Shouldn't be a surprise, really," said Travis. "Home is where we let down our defenses, where we're not at our best but our most natural. The one you love changes from confidant to combatant who knows your soft spots. Catching her doing right is the last approach you consider because you know she can turn an offering of peace into a weapon of war."

Unaware of Brooke's presence, Cord said, "I don't get it, Doc. She changed overnight."

"I've seen it happen. Not often, but I have." Travis lapsed into silence as if processing a matter concealed. Then, "A single event triggers an entire series of changes in outlook, even personality."

"She became a different person."

Travis seemed not to hear. "These minds of ours, so complex. What we suppress eventually boils to the surface. And we don't know what to do with it all." He grew more pensive. "Deep wounds don't heal quickly. Some never mend. So we cover them the best we can, for as long as we can. Until the dam bursts."

Travis went silent again and deeper into a private space. Carly touched her husband's arm.

"Trav, you still here?"

Catching himself, Travis made an attempt to reenter the conversation. "Sorry, I must have drifted off for a moment."

Brooke heard everything from her vantage on the wharf. Her rage welled up with each word that she translated as methodical dissection of her marriage and herself. Betrayal was expected in the abusive family she'd escaped. Now she felt deceived by Cord. I'll never lie to you, Brooke. Sides were being taken against her, as if she had single-handedly soured the marriage. Hearing enough, she turned, and with a heart weighted by grief, limped to let herself out of the marina and drive slowly home. In her car her abdominal pain struck like fire, and she dug her fingers into her stomach.

Cord asked, "You must have run into those times when everything unravels. Did one of you lay down the weapon and take the hit?"

Travis and Carly hesitated a long while. With tautness in his voice, Travis said, "We were trained not to take hits."

Cord detected a sudden tension in the couple. Travis and Carly looked at each other, neither showing signs of their earlier good humor.

"Tell him?" Carly asked.

Travis barely nodded.

Twenty-Three

TRAVIS AND CARLY EDGERTON'S EARLY WEDDED LIFE was marked by more delights than scars. The scars came later.

What began as a life of satisfying normalcy was relinquished for one of secrecy when they hired on to an unnamed federal enterprise for frequent unscheduled excursions. Employed under the heading consultants, they traveled to various parts of the country and more often across borders. Motivational training they put it, the extent of their work was purposely kept obscure. Bogus professional reviews, written in a back cubicle by a governmental someone who assumed many names and titles, were glowing enough to land them some legitimate corporate leadership development gigs. No one gave a thought to their jaunts to destinations unknown. For good reason the Edgertons concealed that span of their lives.

Their clandestine chapter in deniable operations was opened over a glass of wine on the deck of a neighbor's boat in their marina. The boat's owner was new to the area, not much known about him and little offered by him. He asked odd questions, why they had relocated out of the States and back—

Travis had completed a two-year visiting professorship at a private university in Victoria, British Columbia; if they were in good health—Travis' glaucoma was a non issue thanks to laser magic, and Carly remained disgustingly healthy; if they'd had any military experience—Travis had been in the US Marine Reserve; if they could keep a secret—Carly rolled her eyes; if they would be willing to meet someone. Carly thought she was listening to a new approach to Amway sales.

Three days later they were seated in a corner booth at Denny's tasting passable coffee, and introduced to a Ms Booth who was all business and no smiles. Ms Booth pressed the Edgertons with further questions ranging from their marital life to past regrets, personal biases, loyalties, friends and other associations. It didn't take but a couple minutes to realize they were being recruited, not to sell soaps and cereals, but to enter a world they'd only seen in the movies.

"Let me get this straight," Carly interrupted the questioning by the woman with a frown. "You want us to go take out bad guys, is that it?"

"Our cadre doesn't take people out, Mrs Edgerton," was the reply between thin lips. "Let's say you'd be a specialized first responder, looking over the scene, getting the lay of the land, as it were."

"For Jason Bourne to pop them later. As it were."

"Something like that. You'd not be placed in dangerous situations. Not at all."

Travis reminded Ms Personality she was talking to a couple married as long as the sum of her own years. Did she understand Carly was a homemaker, a former accountant, and her hobby was running short distance races, and his own Marine Corps assignment was limited to driving a troop truck on weekends defending the beaches of Southern California? "And that was many years ago, Ms Booth, or whatever your name is. Now I only teach college kids how to make it in the market-place, and we work out with them on the track." He added, "But you already knew all that, didn't you?"

He received a taciturn, "Yes."

"So," asked Carly, "why us?"

Without a reply, Ms Booth abruptly stood, thanked them for their time, set two fives on the table and walked out the door. Relieved they had failed the examination, Travis and Carly went about their business, with a cautious eye toward the boater who'd initiated the contact.

A month later Ms Booth showed up sporting a smile and warmth Travis thought might someday become genuine. Carly was convinced it had been rehearsed in the rearview mirror of the SUV in the parking lot. Like the black rental, her pleasant demeanor could be quickly surrendered for professional sour-ness.

Ms Booth, however, did have a first name, Parthena, and it really was hers. During that follow-up visit she described in detail the small cadre she was inviting them to join. Yes, they were assured, it was one of those almost black enforcement units—*closer to dark gray, Carly*—with three initials no one could decipher except readers of fiction. Yes, the Edgertons were chosen to work as a couple and they'd be trained well. No, they wouldn't drive a luxury sports car or need a double-O license, but they'd learn how to handle various weapons, just in case. Parthena Booth left that day saying, "You're the kind we're looking for. Take some time to talk it through. But with no one else! I'll be by this way in two weeks."

What followed was a chapter of life undreamed by two married people of middle age and medium stature and with uninspiring vitae of accomplishments. They attended several

two-week intensive training sessions—both liked wearing ca-
mo fatigues—at a facility in the forests somewhere east of
Donnelly, Idaho. *Only the big boys train on The Farm, Trav.* Nearly
six years of adventure consumed them as nondescript opera-
tives in drop-in secret junkets, filing secure sat phone reports,
engaging in and escaping a few close-call encounters.

They abruptly left the Cadre, as they too came to call it, after an incident forced them both into a program for post-
traumatic stress. Parthena Booth had promised they'd be kept
from violence, but when a curbside kidnap attempt in an un-
disclosed country was made on Carly, Travis instinctively
sprang into action. Disregarding the safety of anyone—himself,
bystanders, even his wife—he instantly threw himself at one of
the two attackers, adrenalin-wresting the gun out of his hand.
Carly, also quick to react, chose the oldest move in the books.
She lifted her feet off the ground becoming a heavy weight to
the other man who paid for loosening his grip on her with a
back head-butt to his nose. Travis later told the therapist it all
seemed so natural to turn the Vektor on both men and fire
point blank. One round each. Deliberate. Almost tranquil. The
hollow points fulfilled their mission, tearing apart everything in
their way until their drive was spent creating exits through cavities twelve times larger than their entries. Carly watched trans-
fixed. Travis grabbed her up and ran until he could run no
more. Agents at the safe house had to pry the gun out of his
hand.

The Edgertons told no one except the team of therapists.
Not even Parthena Booth, because they never saw their han-
dler again.

AT FIRST, CORD COULDN'T BELIEVE THEIR TALE of intrigue
and death and the Cadre trauma that nearly destroyed them.

But the more he listened, the more he understood their furtive glances at each other in silent communication, frequent searching gazes over their surroundings, occasional words interspersed in their dialogue sounding like code. He was beginning to see that this outwardly good-natured couple carried their own baggage.

"You were talking about God earlier," said Cord after listening to an abridged account of exploits he hadn't expected from the older couple. "I've never heard anyone talk about God as if they knew him. Can I ask, did God enter that brutal world with you? Was he there when you were attacked? Or do you just need a bigger reason to justify what you were forced to do?"

They were all silent. Travis still couldn't fathom his detached emotions when he ended two lives. Even in therapy he'd described the killings dispassionately.

"Was God there?" he echoed Cord. "I've got to believe he was. He's always everywhere, don't you know?"

"I wouldn't know." Cord stubbed his now-cold cigar. "He isn't on my friend list. I can't say that we've spoken. Probably never will."

"It doesn't need to be that way," said Travis.

Cord kept quiet.

Travis took Carly's hand, mostly for reassurance. He said, "We've got a long way to go in resolving our past, and understanding our current behaviors and lapses into anger, in light of…that event." Travis hated to admit to having killed, even in self-defense. "But did we then, do we now, count on God to justify our actions by sidestepping our responsibility for self-reliance? That's what you're asking."

Cord was slow to respond. "To be honest, I'm not sure what I'm asking. You've told quite a story. You don't look the part, you know, of a crime-fighting duo. Why are you telling me all this? Are you trying to aim me toward believing something about God more than I do?"

Twenty-Four

CONTENT AT HER DESK BEHIND the high counter, Brooke idly reclassified a stack of books she'd been putting off. She momentarily looked up and caught a glance of a familiar face. She'd seen the woman somewhere but couldn't quite place—

That woman in the marina!

Brooke took the first action that came to mind and ducked behind her desk. Trying to scrunch her five-eight figure under it, she smacked her knee against a desk leg, her curse well above a library whisper. A workmate hurried over and asked if Brooke had lost something she'd be glad to help. Brooke tried to shoo her away, but the affable assistant just waited there looking perplexed. Carly stood at the counter watching it all. No use, Brooke knew, and uttered a stronger oath seldom heard inside library walls. She crawled out from under the desk, stood, straightened her hair and covered in three long paces the distance to the older woman at the barricade between them.

"Yes." Brooke's voice was bereft of goodwill.

"Is there a time we can talk?" Carly's visit was intentional. She held Brooke's gaze. "I feel I should fill in some blanks of the conversation with Bryan on our boat." Her smile was genuine, but her manner determined. "I was thinking over tea."

"I haven't the time, nor the interest."

It had never been seen before in that room: two determined women staring the other down, speaking volumes in silent exchange in a space reserved for stillness.

Brooke was about to turn away, but Carly kept her focus locked on the taller woman. "Brooke, you need an apology from me, and an explanation."

Brooke's glower didn't soften. "If your explanation is an attempt at his justification, take it right outside those doors." Eyes not moving from Carly's, Brooke motioned her head toward the entrance.

"I understand you work out at the gym," said Carly. An unexpected turn.

"I kick-box. Care to join me?" Spoken with a humorless smile, Brooke's threat was barefaced.

"I'd love to." Carly's acceptance of the challenge was as clear as her recognition of the threat. "I'm a bit out of practice. I haven't gone serious rounds for a few months."

Few months. The woman was an artifact.

"I don't go easy on anyone, anytime," Brooke said, still the menacing smirk.

"I wasn't aware I made that request." Carly's retort came with a smile.

"I'm all yours."

"Or do you expect me to be all yours?"

The woman's reply surprised Brooke. But she was eager to spar.

"I'm off at four," she said, eyes steady.

"We'll make it five."

CARLY FOUND BROOKE at a balance bar. In the middle of a series of high kicks, the younger woman showed no recognition as Carly began her own stretching routine.

After ten minutes of stretches, quick muscle footwork and high kicks, Brooke said to Carly's reflection in the mirror, "I need to warn you I'm not a weekend kick boxer. When I throw the punch I expect to connect and cause pain."

"Sounds like our senseis learned from the same master." Carly threw a sidekick high above her head. "I like your choice of sweats, by the way. Unpretentious."

"Interesting comment considering your dotage. But let's see what you've got. Or would you rather Zumba with the millennial mommies over there?"

Carly turned to acknowledge three women who appeared most concerned not to perspire in their Spandex. LED blue was their predominant color. One of them, not smiling with her eyes, allowed a halfhearted *Hi there* in a whiney voice that Carly suspected had been surgically altered to bespeak the young woman's expectation of entitlement. Oddly, it fit her other enhancements.

Brooke impatiently assumed a set position on the large workout mat. No more talk. No after-you manners. Time to do what she knew best: deliver a cruel offense with little need for defense.

Carly was about to offer a bow of courtesy, but Brooke struck. Carly surprised her by easily blocking that first move, a frequently seen sweeping high kick. The older blonde didn't return a punch but began to study Brooke's moves. Twice she was thrown off balance when Brooke compensated for her shorter left leg that, like a change-up from the pitcher's mound, moved slower, forcing Carly to adjust.

For the next five minutes Carly kept to defense while she read Brooke's fight tells and vulnerabilities. Just one time her concentration drifted and she didn't see the jab coming to her midsection. With a grunt of irritation she pivoted to the side to create a smaller target for Brooke's follow-through.

Brooke drove in, showing no mercy. Carly, gasping for breath, dropped down and swept both legs, one high one low, against Brooke's planted leg. Brooke yelled her own surprise as she tumbled. The two women shot up, Brooke quicker to recover. Waiting only a second for Carly to stand, she screamed her loudest and thrust a stiff-knife right hand directly below Carly's face. A slim half-inch from the throat, Brooke pulled back, suddenly aware of her intent to mortally wound.

Carly said nothing, for now it was her turn to inflict pain. Seizing on Brooke's hesitation, she grabbed the girl's outstretched hand and turned her palm up and out. She stepped into the younger woman's stance forcing her backward and her hand higher until Brooke was kneeling with her arm raised high, her shoulder close to dislocating.

For the first time Carly heard a feminine whimper from her opponent. She immediately released the hold, took a pace backward and resumed her set stance. Brooke jumped to her feet and squared off. Now both women, adrenalin flowing, traded punches and chops to body and limbs. Their slaps audible, fists striking targets, feet skimming the mat, they hit fast and hard.

Their throaty shouts drew a sizable crowd. The locals hadn't seen two women attack so vehemently in the gym. The millennial moms, now double in number, kept safely distant, criticizing the rough display before them, whispering *absolutely* to anything they affirmed and to most of what they didn't understand but tried to fake.

Neither Brooke nor Carly granted solace on that mat, and after fifteen brutal minutes both reached their limit. Breathing hard, they ended the match as they'd begun, with no bow toward the other, but eyes locked and a slight nod of the head.

Carly wiped her face with the towel she was given when checking in. "Didn't see that early punch to the gut coming. Good follow up too," she said. "I could go for some tea. Wonderful place two blocks over. My treat."

"No."

Brooke made a grab for her own towel, missed, cursed, grabbed again.

Who was she fighting? This older woman who wouldn't back down? The torment of her past? Cord?

She headed to the showers, alone, angry. The spectators melted away.

Uncharted

Twenty-Five

A BIT INCONGRUOUS, CONSIDERING HIS GOOD looks and bearing, Cord was more reserved than assertive. Known by his friends and throughout the workplace for his sincerity, when he asked how you were, he actually listened to the answer. Cord was an anomaly in a culture of self-admiration.

It wasn't always that way. In his younger years he was severe, at times heartless. His world centered on himself and he grew accustomed to the fit. But two pivotal events changed his young adult life and prompted a different outlook to include his interest in more than just Bryan Cord.

MARVIN CORD, THE GRANDFATHER Bryan never knew, was drafted into the Marines in 1965 to serve his country in the jungles of Vietnam. The Marines drafted? And a young father at that? Must have been a mistake at the Selective Service board. Well, no, he wasn't married, not yet anyway, but he was no less a father of a one-year-old. With no one to run legal defense, Marvin could do nothing but accept an unjust classification.

In the recruiting building he was among two hundred young 1As herded into a hall and ordered to stand abreast, three files, no horseplay. Two uniformed men with stripes and campaign ribbons looked them over with noticeable keenness. One, from the light in his eyes, appeared to have at least a sense of personality. The other, with the strangest haircut, looked like he'd been nursed on bleach, couldn't have had more than a room-temp IQ, and yelled unintelligibly from deep in his throat. Marvin was glad the first uniform had more stripes on the sleeve and reckoned he could get along fairly well in that man's army. That is, until Sergeant 72-degreemental began choosing individuals from the files with a practiced disdain.

After an hour in line at the only phone booth for a short call to his betrothed, Marvin Cord was on a bus with a load of other dazed college dropouts headed for San Diego's Marine Corps Recruit Depot. Nine weeks later his company was trucked in cattle cars fifty miles north up Interstate Five to Camp Pendleton for four weeks of tortuous infantry training, followed by a two-week leave for Marvin to marry his wife and give his moppet son his name. Then back into green utilities for more training for war before getting his six delivered to Saigon and up to Da Nang to begin a thirteen-month tour of duty. Four months later and a world away he read his bride's handwriting, splotched with tear stains, that he'd be coming home to a larger family, and the one in the pot sure felt like another boy. That same day, his twentieth birthday, a war with an insatiable appetite gobbled the head of a young hometown household awaiting his return.

The nineteen-year-old widow watched from her window as the military green sedan pulled up to the curb and two Marines in dress blues slowly walked in step to her door. Never a nightmare so horrible could have been conjured. Two years later Marvin's platoon buddy, an arm lost from the shoulder his reluctant contribution to the war effort, went to visit the widow, fulfilling the strongest promise he'd ever made, ever. He handed her the last letter she'd written to him—the others were somehow lost. He hated reliving the battle scene, but at her insistence he told how her husband caught several VC rounds when scaling a minor hillock a few klicks from the compound that a backroom light colonel thought would be a nice spot for a family picnic someday. Both tried to hold back the flood of tears, each hoping the tap had finally been closed. They wept while her toddling sons quietly played with the box of Lincoln Logs the buddy had brought.

Marvin Cord's sons lived their adult lives with a longing for some sort of closure for their mother, and in a way for themselves. They knew the man they referred to as Pop only by a few faded photos and progressively fewer reminisces by the aging woman who guarded them deep in her spirit. Graced with the familiarity of many more years than their father's two-score, the brothers stood at the Vietnam War Memorial in DC trying to put to rights their loss. But finding Pop's name among nearly fifty-nine thousand others etched in black marble wasn't enough.

Bryan Cord, full of himself with a six-figure job, and having no idea the meaning behind the wild suggestion he was about to make, offered to take his dad and uncle to Vietnam. Never having visited a war zone except Chicago, he was looking for a little adventure. The overseas trip wasn't difficult to book; many hundreds made the pilgrimage. Procuring the help of an old guide who spoke passable English and knew his land and its story but remained silent about his part in his country's civil war, the three men located the rise of earth on which the senior Cord's young life ended. The local residents, not unmindful of supreme cost, had given the mound shrine status in memory of real men sacrificed in their homeland to war gods always active and never appeased. On a piece of dirt designated fifty-five years earlier only by a three-digit number, two middle-aged American sons knelt and openly wept while a grandson with a new heart stood watch.

THREE YEARS SHY OF HIS THIRTIES, another decisive event forever changed the life and mindset of Bryan Chandler Cord. The year after he took his dad and Uncle Steve to Vietnam, the stuffings—as his Aunt Meguiar called it—were yanked right out of him. His dad, Bryan's close-up real-life hero, died of massive heart failure. Present and vibrant one moment, lifeless the next.

Reaching his folks' house for their scheduled weekly dinner followed by the requisite card game with his dad, Bryan thought it odd the house was empty, door wide open, all the lights burning. Mrs Johnson next door rushed over from her porch and followed him into the house. The son of Francis Kenneth Cord stared down at the discarded wrappings from oxygen mask, IV start kits and EKG pads littering the living room floor. Kneeling and gently touching the medical debris, he vaguely heard the neighbor lady tripping over her words telling him his father suddenly collapsed and his mother called her to come over and no she didn't know how dear Mr Cord was doing but she believed in Jesus so things would be fine but he ought to get over to the hospital to be with his mother and not to worry she'd take care of the lights here and lock the door.

The last time Cord spoke to his dad was that morning on speakerphone over a bowl of Wheat Chex before leaving for the office.

"See you for our weekly game tonight, Bryan?"

"'Kay, Dad. Rummy or Stud?"

"Poker. I'm too far in debt to you to stop now. You mind if I cheat a little?"

"Long as I can."

"Love you, Son."

"I love you, Daddy. Dad." Strange he said that.

No final good-bye. No chance to whisper in his father's ear, "I need you, Dad. Please. Don't go." No pacing the hospital hallway waiting for the doctor's grim, we did all we could. His dad stopped being before he hit the floor.

The first few nights after the memorial service Cord slept in his old room. The TV stayed off and photo albums covered the coffee table. Each evening his mom spent a lifetime in pictures with him at her side. Most memories he shared with her, some she could only struggle through alone, because there is a depth of sorrow too great to be disclosed to another.

Back at his own place, he resumed his weekly Tuesday dinners at her house. A few weeks later sitting at his mom's kitchen table, shock turning to numbness, Cord revealed the inkling.

"Mom?"

"Yes, son."

"Before Dad died, did you have a clue, a premonition? Anything like that?"

"You did?"

"The last time I talked to him, I told him I loved him. But something in me knew I wouldn't say that to him again. I thought it was crazy at the time. I guess it wasn't after all. I miss him, Mom. Does this hole ever get filled again?"

"He was our life, dear. Sometimes he was bigger than life. There's a lot of young death in this family. First your grandpop in the war, now Dad. You're the man in the family now. I wish it weren't so. Not for a long time."

Eventually Bryan absorbed the ache of his soul, but there was always a part of him that wouldn't be raised back to life. He'd never claim another hero. His dad's presence was too large, his influence and inspiration lasting and good. A desire grew within Cord: he wanted to become more like his dad. A noticeable kindness began to flow inside the young man who used to think he was his world's axis.

People began to take on value.

Twenty-Six

Strange he'd heard no word from her lawyer.

Back at work a week now, Cord felt his head screwed on a little straighter. His boss, Marcus Elkin, in a spirit of empathy kept an eye on him just the same.

So did his neighbors at the marina. Frequent meals with the older couple were becoming part of an easy routine. This week they arranged for Saturday brunch. He was coming to value their bold honesty, and he had to admit the Doc's Moroccan olives were growing on him. The cigars too. Today he'd reciprocate with a box of real Cubans, easy to procure with the embargo briefly lifted. And for Carly, three pounds of French roast Ethiopian coffee he picked up in downtown Seattle.

"I was thinking, Bryan," said Carly after setting his steaming omelet and breakfast steak before him. "You asked us a while ago—oh, it's been a couple of weeks now—if we lay down our weapons and take the hit." She sat and sipped her orange juice. "I'm not sure we gave you a real answer."

"You told me a lot," said Cord. "You were trained in conflict tactics and forced to use them. The result was traumatic. I didn't need to read between the lines."

"It has taken effort to relearn not to strike back," she said. "We needed a different approach to living out life together."

"No other way to say it," said Travis. "We hit a wall."

"Did you both know it at the time?" asked Cord.

"Yes, we knew," answered Travis.

"You obviously made your way back."

"I believe we are." Carly said it quietly.

"Pardon me?"

She smiled kindly. "We're still in the process."

"Interesting how trauma can draw a couple closer," said Travis, "or send them to opposite corners. I'd pretty much left the room, deserting Carly to go it alone." He looked into her eyes. "I'm sorry to have done that to you, hon."

"Travis withdrew into a hole deeper than any man cave," said Carly, memories still recent. "And the further he escaped, the angrier I became."

"Her resentment was palpable," said Travis.

"I couldn't turn to him. He emotionally checked out. We became strangers, trapped under the same roof. We shared a bed, but the man I had known became someone I didn't like. And I hated making excuses for his remoteness."

"So, then what?" asked Cord.

"We didn't take another cruise, if that's what you're asking," she said. "And we'd already spent a few months with the crew of headshrinkers."

"We could agree on only one thing," said Travis. "We were lost at sea and needed rescue."

"We needed people in our lives," said Carly.

"You could actually admit that?" asked Cord. "And you knew enough to throw out a lifeline?"

"We had a few friends we could trust," she said, "and we began to let them back in. They didn't pry—some things we couldn't disclose. But they did listen to our hopelessness. In time we began to listen to them. They had real life stories too. All of them had encountered dark storms in their marriages. "Taking time to listen to them was our turning point."

"If we were pressed to give an answer," said Travis, "we knew we still did love each other, and we didn't want to stop."

"Then came the surprise," said Carly. "That one couple, Trav's mentor and his wife, Will and Ruth, introduced us to a marriage adhesive."

"A what?" Cord was confused.

"We call it laughter glue," said Travis. "Nurturing—reigniting—the marriage with more enjoyment than work. We had it as a young family, but managed to lose it."

Carly said, "We learned that laughing together reveals something good is going on between us."

Cord eyed them both. "Are you telling me you never get mad, I mean really mad, at each other?"

"Let me put it another way," said Travis. "Some couples struggle up so many high relational mountains they no longer have it in them to do much more than be cordial to one another. The best they can give is civility."

"We've been married almost thirty-six years," said Carly. "I think we told you that."

"Once or twice," said Cord, his grin off-center.

"That's plenty of time to prove that when two people live together, one of them will eventually become a huge pain in the spirit."

Cord laughed at the phrase. "I get that for sure. So…"

"Our new approach to life together included three basics. You can take notes if you'd like," said Professor Travis Edgerton. "One, we threw away the list of rules for a successful marriage. Two, we made it a point to respond more than react to each other's words. Still working on that."

"My toughest," said Carly.

"It is, at that," said Travis, raising his coffee mug to toast hers. "Third, listen to understand the meaning behind the words. You no doubt do this with your work team."

"Interesting you'd say that," said Cord. "My boss uses that one on me."

"The man I met on your boat?" asked Travis.

"That's the guy. He can be a chowderhead sometimes, but he's basically got good motives."

"Chowderhead," repeated Travis. "Haven't heard chowderhead in years.

"My dad would thump my head and call me that when I did something dopey, as he put it."

"'Dopey,'" Travis considered. "Another fine word from the past."

"You were saying about your boss." Carly brought them back.

"He told me to try listening closely to Brooke. Already happened. Struck out."

"Timing is everything," offered Travis.

"There's actually a fourth basic to our relationship," added Carly, "if you're still taking notes. Cultivating our friendship made us safe again. Safety was something we lost for awhile. A long while."

"Brooke and I began as best friends," said Cord, "but the friendship disappeared. So did safety. You got yours back. How?"

"We wanted to rediscover what we liked about being *us*," said Carly. "And that wasn't easy. At first we only went through the motions, trying to come up with positive words."

"But we were too stubborn to give up, and too scared to walk out," said Travis. "Eventually the activity of deliberately cheering for each other turned into a sport, if you will."

"And it grew on us," said Carly.

Cord shook his head. "How did you even know to do that? Did someone tell you to take five minutes a day to be nice?"

"Call it the power of observation," said Travis. "Our friends Will and Ruth didn't trade insults, but actually exchanged compliments. At times they went a little over the top to make the game obvious. We couldn't ignore it."

"So we gave it a try, on our own when no one was around. It didn't take long before the words we said took on meaning. I began to like my husband again."

"That's all? No magic touch? Just say pleasant things?" Cord refilled his coffee and gestured the pot to them.

"Of course not," countered Travis, accepting the offer for more of the rich darkness. "We've also had to stop some behaviors."

"And it's taking time," said Carly. "It hasn't been that long since we were in regular PTSD therapy." Her voice grew softer. "Memories float to the surface less often each year."

"And yes, we still argue, still get upset," said Travis, sticking with the topic. "But we've established new rules of engagement."

"And that means…" said Cord.

"We don't fly off and say things we'll later regret," said Carly. "That means we take a minute—"

"Could be longer," said Travis slowly. "It might require a stormy march alone to the all-night diner, a cup or three of bad coffee—quite unlike what you've brought today—and a slow walk back."

"To cool down," said Carly. "Plus, we don't use fighting words that blame and condemn. Avoiding the trigger words. Most of the time it works."

"Most," repeated Cord. "Not always."

"Right. When we're too angry to think straight. That's when we need to pause."

"We grew up in a church culture," said Travis.

"Trav, relax on church, okay?"

"No soapbox in the vicinity, Carly. I was about to say we were told never to let the sun go down on our anger. That's actually in the Bible. But it was rendered to mean we had to resolve every conflict before getting into bed. Well, for us that's premature. We tend to argue at the end of the day. Settle the problem before lights out? We're simply not finished being angry at each other. Sometimes we need to sleep on it to think clearly. Or we talk it through at two in the morning because neither of us can sleep.

"Here's our thing. We promise to see it through if it's important to our friendship, to being *us*. If it isn't, we chalk it up to yesterday's low point or bad chili and move on."

"And we began to ask," said Carly. "Why can't we simply be who we are, gradually accepting the flaws we both have?"

"We wanted to savor the journey of life together," said Travis.

Cord was silent for a moment, glad for the warm coffee mug in his hands, then asked, "What do you mean, savoring life together? Nice picture, but…"

Before either could answer, Cord changed course. "Got a different question. If you could do it all over again, what would you change?"

"Who are you asking?"

"I guess you, Doc."

"Killing those two men, watching them die, will always haunt me. However, that being unalterable, I wouldn't change much else. As if I could. The good times coupled with my mistakes, even my huge errors, have all contributed to who you see in front of you. Do I look in the mirror and ask how I could have done those things? Not so much now."

"Because you're older and wiser?"

"You underscoring wiser or older?"

"You got me there, Doc. I could use some help, Carly."

"Oh, I'm quite enjoying the moment." She nestled deeper into her chair.

Cord tried to smile. "It took both of you to want a better relationship. Not true for me. She just wants out."

"I like Brooke."

Travis turned toward Carly. Cord did a double take.

"I know," said Carly, "she covers her hurt with a harsh veneer, or so she thinks. She's a fighter. Something, or someone, forced her to defend herself. But I like that about her. I see a lot of myself in her."

Travis put his arm around his wife. "Do I hear a reclamation scheme forming?"

"You might at that. Isn't she worth the pursuit? Bryan, you still think so, don't you?"

Cord pressed his lips together, keeping to himself words he knew wouldn't help. Eventually he said, "So you've met her."

"A few times now."

"How did they go?"

"Awful. But there's someone inside her worth knowing. It's time I renew my membership at the gym. I could use a sparring equal."

Twenty-Seven

BROOKE AND CARLY FACED OFF ON THE MAT twice a week. Each time Carly suggested tea afterward and was declined without hesitation. But she was on a mission and changed her approach.

Before leaving the gym she said, "Would you mind a training partner more often? Say, three times a week. I've gotten a bit rusty on my moves."

Brooke stopped mid stretch, wary of the direction talking with this woman could take. "Up to you. I'm usually here every afternoon." She stopped short of adding, plan on someone sending you flowers.

CARLY FOUND HER GROOVE and Brooke learned to respect the woman as a legitimate challenge, open less often to surprise moves and offering a few of her own. Carly made one last offer for a chat over tea. If the girl shut her down this time she'd flatten her with a maneuver her trainer in the Cadre had taught her. *Your opponent won't see it coming, Carly,* the SEAL instructor promised. *Use it when you're sure there's no other way to end it. Then call the paramedics.*

Okay, Brooke didn't deserve anything that aggressive, but she did need a swift kick to wake her up.

Brooke for her part was less than eager to connect in conversation. She'd overheard Carly and her husband talking with Cord that one earlier evening on their boat when she'd gone to pick up a sweater on *Starstruck*. The advice she heard the husband spewing still grated on her. She knew she had made eye contact with Carly that night, who still seemed determined to make some sort of apology for her husband's loose tongue.

So, how else to be rid of the woman until she finally sat across the table and threw a few verbal punches of her own once and for all. Get it over with, sooner the better. And still enough time to get home and check what Vanna's wearing on TV. *Can't believe I said that!*

"I'll meet with you, Carly," said Brooke, saying the woman's name for the first time. "Get this straight. You're not bad on the mat. But I don't trust your motives."

Carly was pleased they'd finally meet over tea, and also a little disappointed she wouldn't see if the younger woman could block her covert move.

"Not bad? Who are you trying to fool? You've never had a good fight like I've given you. And you're thinking that's all I've got? As for motives, I won't hide a thing."

Brooke had to give the older woman credit. She still had the kicks, surprising her a few times with agility and an instinct to anticipate her next moves. *Where did she learn that?* And the lady was just as direct in her speech.

But Brooke was no less agile.

"Just know this for sure. My marriage isn't up for dissection. It failed. Let it. And you can keep your God in the box too."

Carly was never one to back down. Picking up her sport bag and making for the door, she said, "You like making the rules, don't you? See you in ten for tea."

INTO HER SECOND SET of fifteen high kicks to the bag, Brooke caught a glance of Carly signing in at the main desk. Not up for a sparring session on marriage, she was hesitant to say more than a brusque hello. Teatime had gone all right, but Brooke had no desire to make it a habit. Still, she was growing to respect the woman she found puzzling.

Carly settled in on a rowing machine. When Brooke finished her fourth set at the bag, Carly walked over to take a turn, duplicating Brooke's high kick and throaty shout, and adding a reverse kick to the bag's core.

She's still got the drive, thought Brooke, sure she also heard anger in the older woman's sharp kiai.

"Strong lady." Brooke tossed her a face towel after Carly did some quick toe work to limber up before starting her next workout routine. "Where'd you learn that last move?" she asked, curious.

"Some defense training a few years ago."

"Looked like you were on offense. You mind showing me what you did just then?"

After several weeks of sparring and liters of tea, the ice was showing signs of thawing. Carly agreed to demonstrate a tempered version of the sure-to-cripple tactical kick she was taught by her Cadre leader.

"Ready? Here it is in slowmo."

Brooke was on her back looking at the ceiling. She jumped up and would have delivered a fervid response, but Carly already had her back to her, walking to the opposite edge of the mat.

Carly turned to face her. "A little slower then?"

Brooke's hands said, *Bring it.*

She learned the move quickly, and caught on that Carly wasn't showing her all there was. *What is it with this woman? What else isn't she telling?*

They attracted a handful of spectators who watched awhile then went back to their own stations.

"Think you've got the hang of it?" asked Carly after a dozen repetitions.

Brooke nodded satisfaction. The two women sat on pads and leaned against the wall, oblivious to others in the room.

Unspoken matters have a way of demanding urgency. With legs straight out Brooke bent forward to hold her arches and stretch her hamstrings to release some of her inner tension. Opening the gate to let out the herd of elephants they both knew was waiting to be recognized, she said, "So, you've become familiar with my marriage—more than I want."

"Brooke, I want you to know I'm not trying to fix things for you. Can you accept that?"

"He doesn't understand. He doesn't care. The boat, that ridiculous car of his, his work. Those are his first loves, in that order."

Brooke stood and bent down to place her palms flat on the floor and hold them for a slow ten-count. "I tried to make it work," she said, straightening and going into back stretches. "I suppose we both did a little. But it's finished now. You can't build a marriage on selfish. Just give me my books, a heavy boxing bag and plenty of alone."

"I've forgotten what alone is like."

"And that means?"

"Trav and I have been married long enough that I no longer think of myself as a solo act."

"How many years?" Brooke's scowl was noticeable.

"Coming up on thirty-six."

Brooke didn't intend to communicate derision. She refrained from asking what her voice would have betrayed, *Why would a relic of a couple possibly want to remember any length of togetherness? And she counts down to an anniversary?*

Carly saw her displeasure. She smiled and stood.

"Why do you choose marriage," posed Brooke, steadying the bag for Carly and wondering why she'd just asked. "You don't seem to need the constancy of a mate."

"You're saying I'd do just fine on my own." A left kick to the bag.

"With all the rules to keep, learning each other's moves, opening yourself up to disappointment, why bother?"

"Valid question." Another left.

"I'm surprised you'd acknowledge that, being religious."

Carly threw two hard rights at the bag, forcing the younger woman to grab the bag tighter to keep her balance. "Not religious, Brooke. A follower of Christ. Or if you prefer, Jesus freak. That's what we called ourselves in the mid nineties."

"I was five."

An employee quietly went about cleaning and adjusting two elliptical trainers. Carly smiled her recognition at the young man. She picked up her towel and said to Brooke, "You asked, why bother with marriage. More couples would do well to honestly answer that for themselves."

"Refreshing idea."

"Marriage gurus told us to fix our problems so we'd be better people, live more happily with less stress. But the hoops they told us to jump through produced new tensions. One self-admiring authority maintained the exclusive reason people encounter difficulties was hidden sin. He didn't take into account that real people will always face real struggles. And sometimes our struggles are more than this life can handle.

"Trav and I flushed him down. All of them, without exception, promised a Neverland with sprinkles of pixie dust and no croc with a clock. And they guaranteed their sets of rules to work."

"But—"

"Yes. But. We'd had enough of them. We hid the books in a closet and set out to find healthy marriage reality without the pixie dust. First, we admitted we're just plain people and we'll always have problems. That was actually difficult, because we had to say right out loud, this is all we get. But we developed—still discovering, really—our own steps toward a marriage we can live with. You want to hear what guides us?"

"You're not offering a choice, so get on with it," Brooke said with not much resistance.

"We don't spend time looking for the end of the marriage rainbow. We decided to learn to enjoy the person we've chosen to share the toilet seat."

Brooke grimaced.

"Or if you'll allow the theological twist, we demonstrate our love because we believe God gave us to each other. As we are. What's so wrong with an ordinary relationship?"

"How many more guiding thoughts did you rehearse for this conversation?" Brooke showed her disdain.

Carly was okay with it.

"Only one more. We nurture the pleasure, and the entertainment these days, of being married, without trying to get it all worked out just right. Why look for perfection from people with limitations? We're taking a lifetime—"

"Close to it."

"—to explore the mystery of good marriage for the two of us, together."

"That's it? Pretty simplistic."

"Of course it isn't simplistic." Carly lazily snapped her towel in the younger woman's direction. "That kind of intentionality requires long-term tenacity, into countless unknowns. Is there anything more challenging, more risky? This is it. Don't you wonder why sweet and sour mix well?"

Uncharted

Twenty-Eight

CORD FINISHED HIS WINE AND POURED himself another. He topped his guests' before setting the Merlot on the table.

"Not bad for a sale item. Glad I bought a few bottles."

Carly tasted hers while Travis studied the striations forming on the inside of his glass.

"Nice legs," he said.

"Thank you," said she.

Cord merely smiled and shook his head, accustomed to the couple's repartee. Tonight he'd invited them aboard *Starstruck* for shrimp and beef ribs. A meal requiring a dozen napkins, informality was the rule.

"Mind if I ask you something?" he asked, reaching for his fourth meaty rib from the bowl in the center of the table.

"Anything you'd like," said Carly, another sip of her red.

"I remember you said you junked a plan for counseling and took a cruise."

"At first, yes. It gave us time to realize we had serious issues to deal with," said Carly.

"How long were you at sea, by the way?"

"The cruise lasted twenty sensational days," said Travis, reaching for a Moroccan olive from the batch he'd donated to the meal. "And you've phrased it correctly. More accurately, we returned home to find ourselves out to sea. After the terrific meals and time for each other, we still needed perspective from someone else who knew the signs of pain and could guide us through the mazes."

"So, then you did counseling."

"For the PTSD, and still do on occasion. But for the life of our marriage we began meeting with Will and Ruth, the couple who had something good in theirs. Learning from them saved our relationship. Saved our lives."

"And my sanity," emphasized Carly. "I never knew how far the bottom could reach…"

"You ever look into an endless pit?" interrupted Travis. "I remember working construction to get through grad school—"

"Wait, Trav, I wasn't finished with the thought, okay?"

"You have the helm, ma'am," said her husband.

"That cruise helped, no question about it. But later we desperately needed to rebuild underpinnings taken out by our Cadre episodes. That's when therapy began."

"It took awhile to get back the joy of being on the same page, together again, safe," added Travis.

"Does this make sense?" asked Carly.

Cord's gaze turned away toward the moored boats across the marina's fairway. Obviously these people hadn't entered their marriage *tabula rasa*, two souls unblemished from the wounds of raw life. Nor were they ignorant of the defects each brought into it. Thirty-five years of it. But something wasn't gelling. What was it about them? *Or is it me?*

They both sensed Cord's withdrawal. Rather than trying to fill the silence, Travis and Carly waited to see how this conversation might unfold.

Cord had encountered dead space before, in the workplace and in his attenuated marriage. He knew what was coming and how to handle it. Their next move would be their attempt to fit himself and Brooke into their picture of happiness. But would they permit the real question?

"I appreciate you telling me about your relationship." He turned in his chair to face them. "I'm going to be blunt."

"I think you know we're fine with that," said Carly.

"You're believable people, I admit. But I've been hearing cures from you."

"I'm sorry we're coming across that way." Again Carly.

"The problems in my marriage are different. No cruise will patch this."

Cord filled them in on Brooke's family secrets and the ridicule and resultant shame corporately heaped on her in her teens.

"You've described the erasure of her necessary innocence," said Travis.

"How do I get past the cruelty of her relatives? She's built a wall four feet thick. There's no chipping at it."

"Her past has impacted her future," said Carly. "And now yours. The two of you can adjust your course, but you alone can't do that for both."

"I thought I was willing to try, but she closed the door."

"I've been given that impression too," said Carly.

"You've seen her again?"

"Just last Tuesday."

"When is your wedding anniversary?" asked Travis.

"Not til September. It would have been our second. Yours?"

"Pretty soon. Thirty-sixth," said Travis.

"Yes, you've told me. Happy anniversary." Cord offered little enthusiasm.

"Try this on," said Travis. "Married life, like most of life, is messy."

"You've said that before. Why take a chance then?" Cord hoped he hadn't cleared the way for a tedious homily, but planned otherwise.

"Certainly a reasonable question. But tell me, where else can you experience all the emotions of relationship, where you have minimal control of the route ahead? You choose, both of you, to take countless gambles. And you navigate the complexities of togetherness. Not simple or orderly. Most of it topsy-turvy. What could be better?"

"You're saying you enjoy the constant unknown?"

Travis steepled his fingers. "Good clarification. You're right, endless mystery would be a mix of battleground and amusement park. Little chance of taking a breather, wouldn't you say?"

"Not mine to say, Doc. You're the one pushing for messy marriages."

"But not random or haphazard. Yes, you face uncharted waters, storms so fierce they just may capsize your marriage."

"It happened. Finished." Cord expected his last comment would pull the plug on Travis' oration. No go.

"But you can also set the anchor solid in safe harbors all along the way. You see, it's all unpredictable, but still intentional."

"Can't say you're much of a marriage advocate." Cord's patience was eroding.

"There's more to this extreme adventure," said Travis, lighting a Cuban Cohiba from the collection Cord had given him the previous weekend. "How about the doldrums, those seasons of aggravating boredom? With life, with each other. You think you'll never move out of being stuck with the person who used to be all you wanted. And those seasons last way too long for most couples."

"A real crusader, aren't you?"

"Hold on. Then something happens, and you don't know how or why, except that you just stuck it out and waited. On your own and together."

"You teach this, right?"

Travis puffed the cigar. "Carly and I, yes. Many times."

"And you haven't heard chairs scraping against the floor?"

"You're too kind."

"How do you give hopeless couples, the ones ready to capsize, a little optimism that there could be a future for them?"

"What do you think? We can only introduce them to the potential. They make their own discoveries. You see," Travis paused to savor the Cohiba, "it's like the faintest breeze. You begin to look at life and each other with a freshness you'd only heard about. And you begin to hope it could become real."

Cord slowly lit his cigar. "Isn't this straight out of the marriage books you threw away?"

"A little patience. I'm going somewhere with this. Each couple has the freedom to explore the satisfaction, and the pressures, of living out the two foundational mandates people have had from the beginning. To take a lifetime to work out what loving each other is like, and to know the pleasure of God himself because he's the third, and presiding, member of the marriage."

"Sorry, Doc, I have to be honest. I get the mariner symbolism, but you're trying to sell me snake oil."

"Too good to be real, right?" Travis passed his cigar to Carly. "Or too real to be good? Let me ask, what's the model on which you're trying to base your view of marriage?"

Cord took a few puffs and made an unsuccessful attempt at a smoke ring. "The only model I had was what I saw in my parents. But it was incomplete, cut short."

"We had no parental model either," said Carly, holding the cigar but not smoking. "But we did have the older friends who gave us close-ups of their marriage."

"And we were shown by those friends that there could be something good if we took the small steps," said Travis. "Not someone's prescribed stages to unity and happiness and contentment. While some of those ideas may work, the hot tips are unsubstantiated in the messiness of real life."

"Back up a minute to the part about God presiding over marriage. It still sounds like you're whipping up a magic potion. Tell me you're flimflamming me, Doc."

"Let me put it this way. Or have I lost your confidence?"

"Not yet." Another puff.

"But getting close? Well, this should ice it. If God were part of a marriage, it could look like a love triangle."

Carly took a couple of puffs. "Probably not the best word picture, Trav."

Travis deadpanned his wife and with a glint in his eye spoke in a voice he imagined was fairly professorial. "Given your approval, madam, I shall expand on my musings. However, and I say this with deepest respect, a significant lack of which I sense from your side of the table, I should ask if you would substitute another phrase for the one I have chosen."

Carly giggled. Cord had never associated an older woman with a giggle. He didn't know why. She giggled again, softly, and it sounded pleasant.

She slowly wafted her predictable double ring and handed back the cigar. "That's why I married you, Travis."

He grinned and continued. "The idea of God being in a marriage isn't mine, but comes from someone before our time. He said it something like this. A one-to-one relationship—marriage or friendship, whatever—is good to a point. The question arises soon enough, what happens when your reservoir drains of love or compassion? You've only got so much in the tank, and like it or not, most of that is reserved for sustaining yourself. That's just how folks are put together. Our capacity to love deeply is drawn from a shallow personal account. So isn't it fair to think that if God might be offering to enter into relationships, he might also focus on bulking up our love for each other out of his far greater capacity?"

"That wasn't bad, Travis," said his wife.

"Your servant, madam," he said, accepting her approval. "But, tell me," he asked Cord, "does this sound like another pitch for a questionable solution?"

Cord was about to reject the explanation, but the Doc's question stopped him. He was genuinely asking if Cord considered God entering into relationships was simply ludicrous, or possibly reasonable.

He ate a Moroccan olive, offsetting the taste of the cigar. He rubbed the bridge of his nose.

"I don't know."

Uncharted

Twenty-Nine

Y OU'RE MUCH TOO EAGER TO CREATE A FAIRYTALE where people play nice."

But Brooke did like the cozy tea nook, dubbed by locals, The Only Place In Town. Today the owner introduced her to a black Indian Nilgiri tea, unsweetened with only a suggestion of cream to allow its aromatic qualities to fill her senses. Whatever had she seen in characterless herbals?

Savoring her first sip, she set the flowered Colcough china teacup in its saucer.

"A patty cake marriage, that's what you want, isn't it?" Brooke didn't wait for an answer. "Why can't you bring yourself to recognize some couples will never have it easy? There's no potion, no amount of therapy, no savior, to make them change. If they stay married they'll be destined to live miserably alone under the same roof. Perhaps they don't divorce. For the kids? To sidestep financial ruin? Squirm out of their religion's disapproval? Your marriage works because you and your husband fit. Other marriages don't because the partners can't.

They bring or they build too many obstacles to allow a relationship. For them, and me, a lifetime of love and commitment is not viable."

"So what would you want for your marriage?" asked Carly, putting the peppermint blend to her lips, eyes warning, *I dare you to criticize my choice of tea.*

Brooke caught the silent threat, simply smiled and went on. "What was left of it?" Every reference she made to her former marriage she kept in the past tense.

"Fair question. But isn't mine too?"

"In short, I wanted simple, total, carefree enjoyment with someone I trusted."

"Enjoyment, trust. Two basic components of marriage. Travis and I want the same. So let me ask, does that happen because of a decent fit?"

"I don't expect you to accept this, but yes, I think fit is the main element. You and your husband…"

"Travis."

Brooke resumed as if she hadn't heard the name. "You're probably wired in similar ways. There's something to be said for being made for each other. I thought my ex and I were too. I was wrong."

"Isn't Bryan still your husband?"

Brooke's laugh was short and bitter. "Only on paper. And not for long. For once in my life I'm glad to know a lawyer."

"When does commitment in a marriage begin and how does it happen along the way."

"I wouldn't know." Brooke traced her index finger around her cup's gold-leaf rim. "My experience is limited to twelve months of sweet followed by eight of ugly."

Carly saw regret in the girl's face. "So you haven't had the opportunity to see what long-term can look like. Difficult to base your worldview of intimacy on a momentary marriage of love versus hate."

"Let me ask you, then, why you're so fervent to glue my marriage together, to package what you claim to have."

"As if I can?" said Carly. "I don't pretend to know what will work for you."

"Oh really? I think you do pretend to know. And you want me to join in your fantasy."

Carly accepted the censure, then pushed back.

"I see something in you that has the makings of a satisfied marriage partner. And I hear in you, though you camouflage it well, a longing to be loved as you are."

Brooke snickered and shook her head as if tolerating a child's reasoning, but she withheld her retort.

"I know," said Carly, "you see me as the adversary here."

"More like the tactless matchmaker."

"So let's stop that, shall we? I believe you're right about a couple fitting well. Some don't have good ingredients to create a relationship. Instead they do battle to have the final say, beating the other down. So they quit what was doomed from the outset, but which they told their friends they tried to salvage. But, Brooke, I don't see that in the two of you."

Brooke had enough. "Has anyone ever told you you're full of it?"

"Well, there was that man in New Orleans who's wearing two plastic kneecaps, and now there's you."

"Carly, you're a dreamer. You can throw a good kick in the gym, but across the table you're simply a deluded idealist."

"What attracted you to each other?" Carly hoped to throw a curveball.

Brooke smiled fiendishly.

"I'm sure it was more than sex," said Carly.

"Not much more, and it didn't matter."

"When did Bryan become unattractive?"

"Unattractive. That's a kind word. How about detestable?"

"Is it a question you're afraid to answer?"

"You don't give up, do you? No, your questions, as silly as they are, don't threaten me. Nor am I apologetic for the marital past, because there wasn't enough past with him to call substantive. The marriage was there for a moment, then evaporated. It didn't take."

"And now?"

"Now?" Brooke replied sourly. "Look, whatever picture you and your husband—Travis—are trying to paint, I'm off your canvas. There is no *now*. After seeing your moves on the mat I dared to think you'd be alert enough to recognize what's coming. Let me say this clearly. There is no Mr and Mrs. Not now. Not ever. Don't try to create what will not be."

They both reached for the last cucumber sandwich wedge on the flowered plate.

"You take it," offered Carly. "Your name's on it."

Brooke declined, but Carly eased the plate toward her. The gesture of simple kindness struck her. She looked down and studied the pattern on the tablecloth. Carly quietly sipped her tea.

With a bite of the sandwich, Brooke raised her eyes, a softer look. "You don't seem to drag an anchor around. Was your past better than mine?"

Carly told her about her troublesome teen years, then added, "I developed a thin coat of Teflon."

"And you're saying that helps your marriage."

"Truthfully—and we don't need to spar over this, but I will if you need to."

"Not at the moment. I'm trying to keep an open mind."

"You mean find an open mind, don't you?" Carly was a little surprised at her own audacity.

Brooke was about to challenge the rebuke. She narrowed her eyes. "Accepted."

"Relationships permeate every part of my life. With Trav. With you too. That means enhancing the friendship because there's something important in each one. I happen to be married. So Travis and I count it a privilege to have and to hold from that day a long time ago. Brooke, may I ask—"

"Carly, we both know better. Permission granted or not, you're going to say what you want, so get on with it."

"What are friends for?" said Carly, returning a smile. "What keeps you distant? When did you last allow someone past the moat surrounding you?"

"Did I mention I planted piranhas?"

"You didn't need to. Could you still be afraid of the tormentors from your past?"

"Not anymore. I've learned to protect myself."

"So, who are you protecting yourself from nowadays? People who don't know where to find you? Or from Bryan? Or is God your bully?"

Without a reply Brooke took her gym bag and left the table.

Carly picked up the tab.

Uncharted

Thirty

Y<small>OU LOOK LIKE YOU COULD USE A FRIEND, SAILOR.</small>"

Cord couldn't remember a worse come-on.

There he was, alone at a table in a pub that smelled more like a bar, slouched low in his chair as if he were creating an art form in slump, eyes fixed on a beer that hadn't made it past the first taste. He'd noticed her walk in and study the room, get her drink, sit with two friends at the next table, posing at a strategic angle to him. She looked his way, he looked hers; the second time their eyes met she stood. Not waiting for an invitation she pulled the empty chair up next to him. Strangely alluring, though her fragrance was a little much, her approach to make an impression would have been, at any other time, laughable. He thought of suggesting she find another victim, considered leaving her there to stare at fifteen and seven-eighths ounces of bad beer. He did neither.

He raised his eyes to hers. Very light brown. Decent. Lashes too thick, but not bad. Nose a little too pointed, but okay. Mouth fuller than what he'd expect to go with the face, but unique. She called it right; he wanted the company.

"What would you like to drink?" he asked.

"I'm good with what I've got."

"I'm sure you are."

He was drawn to her throaty laugh. She knew she controlled the table.

She reached around with only a hint of modesty for her half-full glass from the other table, repositioned herself closer to him, and he felt the hook set.

She took small sips of her soft drink; his beer sat untouched. She led the conversation, asking him questions he wanted to answer. So much like Brooke when they'd first met. But this girl was here, and his wife wasn't. He let it slip that he lived on a boat.

"Let me see it. Tonight." No subtlety there.

He walked her to his sports car, she taking long strides in very high heels. He opened her door, she got in with little delicacy. He forgot to ease the door shut.

TEN THIRTY-TWO. The Edgertons had turned out the lights. Carly was planning the next day's shopping with the granddaughter; Travis was asleep.

Not for long.

The girl's laugh came from the finger wharf separating their boat from Cord's. Loud. Coarse.

"Ooh," said the voice. "You really live on this? By yourself? Cool! Take me inside."

Carly whispered an oath and nudged her husband awake.

"What is it?" his voice already hoarse anticipating a full night's rest.

"Our friend brought a guest for breakfast."

They looked at each other, listened a moment. Travis muttered the same oath and kicked his feet over the edge of the bed. In running shorts and tee shirt he picked up his pace through the cabin and onto the deck with Carly following in her sleep pants and XL sweatshirt. She threw a pair of sweatpants to him.

"Put these on. It's chilly out."

They both slipped on flipflops at the door.

Just before jumping onto the wharf, he said, "He'll thank us for this later."

"Who are you kidding? Would you have at his age and single?"

"No."

CORD WAS MOVING much too slowly for her. He thought it appropriate to show her around the cabin, but she made for the vee berth like she knew the way.

"How much am I worth?" her back to him.

Cord actually wrestled with the question, taking a second to think it over. The girl, whom he'd never met, was offering a romp through the night, and he had the cash. He was about to toss out a generous figure to go with hers, when *Starstruck* suddenly shivered and he heard quick steps outside on deck.

Turning toward the footsteps coming down the ladder he was stunned to face the cold glares of the couple from next door. His only sound making it to open air was a stammer.

He moved toward the girl but Travis blocked his way while Carly strode past them, grabbed the girl's shoulder and spun her around.

"Curfew, sweetie. Time for your own bed and lights out."

The girl's spiked heel snagged on an area rug and she threw out an arm to regain her balance. Carly caught it and lifted it over the girl's head.

"Ow! Who are you? Chaperones?" The girl's words were interspersed with phrases uncommon to movies for families.

She tried to push back, but Carly held firm. With her free hand the girl took a swing. Carly easily blocked it and twisted her arm.

"You don't want this, honey." Carly was all business, back in the Cadre.

"That hurts!" The girl's face contorted in pain, seeming to justify more emphatic language.

"Protecting an investment," said Carly.

Cord stood speechless.

"I'll call a cab." Travis' wasn't an offer.

"I can take care of myself," said the girl trying to free her arm.

Carly released her grasp. "No doubt you can."

Cord found his voice and tried to recover his ownership of the space. "Don't talk to her that way."

Carly's glower burned a hole in him and he took a step backward.

The girl ran past, bounded up the steps, out of the cabin and off *Starstruck*. Her heels clicked in quick tempo between the two boats and faded away.

Cord, eyes bulging, stood astounded. "Get out! Both of you! No one asked you to be my guardian angels."

His neighbors didn't move.

Cord's voice became a forbidding whisper. "I said, get off my boat."

Travis scowled. "Sorry, pal. That isn't tonight's script." He motioned Cord toward the ladder. "Let's go."

Cord tried to wheel around Travis, but the older man nudged him on.

"What are you doing, Doc?!"

"We're going for a drive, you and I. Carly, you can lock up the boat, right?"

She stuck out her hand. "Keys, Bryan."

"I don't believe this," said Cord, the statement supplemented with an expletive quoted often by his erstwhile guest. But he reached into his pocket and gave her his keys.

"After you," said Travis and pointed him toward the steps.

Cord made an attempt to shake off Travis' grasp on his shoulder, but felt the grip tighten.

"Don't do it, Bryan. We're not here to play games."

It took some effort, but Travis conducted him off the boat and walked him to the Edgerton's Jeep.

"Get in."

"You're ordering me?"

"Yes."

"I could take you out with one punch."

"Don't give it a thought."

"You think I can't?"

"Just get in the car."

"If I don't?"

Travis sighed deeply. "You want Carly to come take over?"

Cord couldn't stop himself from snickering. But he got in. Seated, he made sure he slammed the door.

"Spare jacket in the back seat if you want it," Travis offered.

"Keep it," mumbled Cord. "I'm good on my own."

Travis glanced sideways at him, and refrained from a comeback. He started the Jeep and drove to the town's all-night diner. During the ride Cord asked himself why his neighbors would have the rudeness to interfere with his personal life.

The diner would have been empty but for a group of teens astonishing one another with limited views of life from their smartphones. Travis made for a far booth, and Cord didn't know why he followed.

"I'll get us some coffee," said Travis. He walked to the machine, beach sandals flapping to make the teens turn and stare. He took the black-rimmed carafe for the real stuff and nodded to the waitress on duty. "Sandi, how are things to-night?"

"Doin' okay, Doc. Boyfriend's bein' stupid. Thinkin' of dumping his clothes on the porch when I get home in the morning."

"Took off again, did he?"

"Across town to his ex."

"You deserve better."

"You need more than coffee?"

"This'll do. Thanks, kid."

"You always have a way with words, don't you, Doc?"

At the table Travis turned both coffee mugs right side up and poured. "You want creamer?"

Cord didn't answer and lifted his cup for a long swallow. Travis returned the pot and sat down opposite him.

"I won't mince words, Bryan. That could have been disastrous back there. You really wanted to tie up with that girl? She was poison. You could see that."

"Stop." Cord slammed the mug down, spilling hot coffee on the table. The teens looked over. "Let me clue you in. No one is asking you to step in with your morality to make my life or anyone else's better or any different."

"So you want to throw yours away."

"Who says I was throwing anything away? She wasn't poison. Just out for some fun. And sorry to spoil the image, but so was I."

"So you're saying the way you'll become fulfilled again is by looking for success in one night stands."

"You're the one talking about fulfillment, not me. You're not getting it, Doc. I'm not falling for your ideas of right and wrong or good and bad. Now, since I'm at your mercy for a ride home, can we just call this an unfortunate misunderstanding and get back? I'll forget this happened if you will. No harm done."

Travis pushed harder.

"I concede we're not tracking here. But there's something bigger going on than you finding a moment of gratification."

"Come on. Give it up and let's go home." Cord pushed his coffee away and stood.

Travis didn't budge and kept eye contact.

"Let's take a look into your future."

"No, Doc. Discussion over."

With Cord standing, Travis persisted. "There's no great story ahead."

"You don't stop. Let me say it again. Turn up your hearing aids this time." Cord began to tap his finger on the table for emphasis. The teens were staring again. He didn't care. "You've got nothing to say that I want, or need, to hear. Can I make it any clearer?"

Travis began to smile and it annoyed Cord.

"Okay, you've got a secret you're about to let me in on. Tell me then let's go." Cord almost liked this gutsy old man.

"Right, wrong, morality or dissipation aside, where are you hoping to find contentment in life?"

"As if it's attainable. You and Carly have something good. Bless you and all that. I'm happy for you. But your story isn't my story."

"Understand this, I'm not trying to convert you to a new belief system. I don't have much more to say, so would you like to return to your seat?"

Cord couldn't contain his own smile. "You sounded like my third grade teacher just then. Mr Briskin."

"Was he a good teacher?"

"One of my favorites. He looked the other way when I slugged Justin Thornton for making Darilyn Brookside cry in class. Dropped him to his butt."

Cord sat back down. The coffee, what was left in the mug, was still warm. "Now say what you need to and let's get out of here."

"My friend, and that's what you are, you won't look back with fond memories by settling for a corporate failure with Brooke—corporate meaning you've both had a part in it. Couple that with a feeble attempt at self-restoration in the company of the next person you'd hope to call your do-over. Dead end ahead."

"That girl was no do-over. Just playtime. That's all."

"We're looking into the future. Keep that in mind. You may have given up on this, but you and your wife—which Brooke still is by a thread—have something to grow from."

"You still don't get it, Doc. Stick to the present. The marriage is done. Hopeless. I'm moving on. Getting a new life."

Travis continued as if he hadn't been interrupted. "You don't know you're finished with your marriage."

"So, you know different."

"I know you're being a shmuck."

"Me? I didn't trespass onto your boat. I didn't throw your guest off. And, you know, I'm not the one who dug up the lawyer."

Travis looked into his cup and shook his head. "A real chowderhead."

"What?!"

"You don't know enough about anything to reason with an ounce of clarity."

"You listen to me. You're old, anyone can see that. You're somewhere in the 1980s and you want me to live next door."

"You do live next door."

"Cut it out, Doc! You've crossed the line." Cord stood again and pulled his cell from a pocket. Travis tried to stand but Cord put his hand on the older man's shoulder. "Know when to stop."

Travis froze. *Easy target. Right elbow to groin. He doubles over. Back hand to nose, hear the pop. Left fist to solar plexus. He's on floor. Game over.* He stared straight ahead, kept both hands flat before him and pressed hard to the table.

Oblivious to his potential danger, Cord punched a few numbers. "I'll get a ride. I'm finished here."

He took two steps and turned back. "My life is not up for public display. No one needs to take notes on how I make it turn out."

Cord walked away, past the teens with their phones, past the waitress on her way to the table where Travis remained seated, out into the cool night air. He felt blindsided by people he wanted to trust.

THANKS FOR THE REFILL, Sandi."

The waitress sat down where Cord had been. "Nice to take a load off for a sec." She slipped off her shoes and rested her feet on the cold floor. "Couldn't help but overhear the conversation. Didn't go so well, huh?"

"I think I may have pushed too far."

"You never know at first, you know. The walk home will do him good."

"Said he was getting a ride."

"Look out the window. That's him across the street, looks like. Someone told me awhile back that there are folks who can't learn from the mistakes others make, but have to make them all on their own. That someone sounded an awful lot like you, Prof."

"I guess I'm trying to prevent him from making the big ones."

"Like you've been trying with me?"

Travis kept silent.

"Like I said, Doc. You have a way with words. And I've been listening. Thanks." Sandi put on her shoes and went to clear off the table the teens had vacated. "I'll pour two take-outs. Tell your wife hi. No doubt you two will be up late tonight."

TRAVIS HANDED CARLY the cup of coffee. "From Sandi. Double cream, but it's real, not decaf."

"Nice of her. She doing all right?" She took a quick sip, then set the cup aside.

"Most of the signs point away from her finding a morsel of peace in the home. But she's got a new spirit. Not trying to win the happiness lottery all at once."

"How long ago was she your student?"

"Three years, wasn't it? Before her son started school. Took four courses from me as I recall."

"From your expression and the fact that he didn't come back with you, I take it things with Bryan didn't go well."

"Not well at all. He preferred walking home alone to my company."

"Quite an argument?"

"He left before it got bad. Grabbed my shoulder though."

"Uh oh. What did you do?"

"Sat very still."

"That took restraint."

"Did some deep breathing. Carly, what was that you said tonight about protecting an investment while we were making an assault on the friendly?"

"Oh, she was definitely friendly, the way she was dressed. Had every intention of being more."

"I meant Bryan. Did we step where we shouldn't have?"

"We may have gone too far, I don't know. We acted quickly, from the gut, thought we were right." She took a long sip of coffee. "It was too much like the Cadre."

"We may have lost a friend. Certainly lost his trust."

"We can't say that yet. It's only been—," she peered up at the chronometer, "two hours."

"I wanted to explain at the diner, reason with him, that he'd understand."

"Right, Trav. Like you at thirty."

"The man is headstrong."

"And you weren't?"

"I was different."

"You were worse. Talk about pigheaded."

"I wasn't that bad." He looked at her quizzically. "I wasn't, was I?"

She took one last swallow of her lukewarm coffee before dumping the rest in the sink. "I'll thank Sandi for the coffee when I see her. No, hon, you weren't beyond hope. Look at who you've become."

"Only took half a lifetime."

"So there's hope for Bryan."

"If we don't get in the way."

"I'll say it again, Travis. We're not privy to the outcome. This evening on his boat, and in the coffee shop, could be what helps him turn a corner."

"If not?"

"It's almost one o'clock. At this hour we can't search for answers to that kind of question. Let's go back to bed."

"You go. I need to stay up a bit longer."

"No, Trav. You need to turn off your mind, stop reviewing, stop second-guessing, get back to trusting your God to create good out of even the worst things. And he doesn't need the sleep. You do."

She sat in his lap and put her arms around him. "You can't save Bryan, Travis. Yes, you saved me that night on the street four years ago. But you've got to let him take his own path."

"I'm not trying to save him."

"I think you are."

"It's that obvious?"

"And I've been trying to rescue Brooke. We're concerned about them. That's fair, that's good. But we can't control their lives."

She stood. "Come to bed. You need a neck rub." She tugged his earlobe.

Travis stayed where he was.

"Maybe more, if you get off that couch."

"This late?"

"Could be."

He smiled and followed his wife.

Thirty-One

WE'LL HAVE THE HOUSE BLEND WITH YOUR afternoon tea-time selections." Carly thanked the hostess.

Moments later she and Brooke were treated to a teapot clothed in a knitted cozie, bone china cups and saucers, and a three-tiered assortment of finger sandwiches, hot buttered scones, and the darkest squares of chocolates.

Brooke took the smallest cream cheese and cucumber sandwich wedge for starters. Carly went for the nearest scone and smothered it with plum jam. "I've been waiting all day for this moment," she said with her first bite.

"Curious that you're not embarrassed to believe in your God," said Brooke without prelude.

"Oh, are we still in fight mode?" Carly partnered the taste of scone with a sip of tea. "No timeouts for you, are there? Okay, God is the topic. What else?"

"Your God. Big G, little g, have it your way. Nor, it appears, are you angry with him. I think about how much my life was trashed by the people who called themselves by his name."

She spat the words. "Then there's the guilt I carry, that I owe him something for not adoring those…people. As if I'm the one who should be punished for the pain they took pleasure inflicting. Your God can't be any different than those monsters I had to call my family. Have you ever stopped to think through your beliefs? God uses reprimand as incentive to stop your naughtiness."

Carly didn't need a roadmap. After patiently listening and making her way through half her scone, she asked, "What if God isn't who you've been told about? Is it possible he just might be different, and you might even like him for it?"

Brooke couldn't hide her revulsion. "You once asked what my attraction was to Bryan. Let me ask you, what do you find so attractive about your God? Distant—somewhere out there, not much more than a good luck piece for people dead set on summoning him to grant their whimsies. How could anyone with a sense of dignity be caught up in such rubbish? You and Travis seem to have more going for yourselves than the need for a celestial talisman. Why would you discuss God as if he's real? And if he were real, you're telling me he'd actually be likeable?"

"What if you discovered he loves you?" Even midway through the question Carly knew it was coming out trite.

"The love of God." Brooke shook her head in pity. "What has love ever produced but dependence and pain? Its payback is punishment. The founder of your religion brought that to light. You claim the purpose for his death was set up before the origin of time. And it was supposedly love that drove him to it. A useless gesture of unnecessary self-sacrifice. But that's love for you."

Carly simply nodded, which didn't calm Brooke at all.

"Open your eyes, Carly. Your God isn't what you've made him to be. But for the sake of argument let's say he might exist. And be loving too, if that's important to you."

"You're on a roll. Tell me more."

"It's good to have you back in the ring. Okay, I'm happy to throw the punch." Brooke ate a bit of scone and pressed her index finger to the plate for the crumbs.

"Here's my picture of the God you say is ultimately good. He's got a ledger. The big book in the sky. He's always got it open to each person's page, entering *You owe me* on one side, and on the other, *I might grant you but don't count on it*. Day after day, line after line. He'll let a few things slip by, not because he's neglectful. He doesn't overlook a thing. But once in a while he feels sorry for the likes of us. But never forget, he ultimately has it in for the ones 'made in his image'. And you talk as if he invented love."

Carly waited to reply. This wasn't the time for a quick comeback. What was it Travis taught his students when in conflict? Take the time and effort to understand the other person's position—to get it right. If Brooke would give her a chance.

She quietly said, "There's nothing we can do to reconcile the ledger. People try all their lives to amass points on the plus side. And I honestly don't know why."

Brooke was about to agree. Then, "You're trying to play me!"

"I'm not, Brooke, because here is where I do agree with you. The point system doesn't work. It never will. Why do we keep playing that tune?"

"All right, then, why not just come out and admit it? If there is a God, and I sincerely hope there isn't, he's simply biding his time to exact eventual eye-for-eye reprisal. Love? It isn't love, Carly. It's humankind's collective folktale about living forever. Talk about an opiate."

"Yours is an awfully bleak outlook, isn't it? But you're right on that one point—"

"I'm sorry to interrupt and have to tell you this. Just shove it, Carly. Your Jesus talk somehow gives you satisfaction. It isn't for me. Can we leave it at that?"

"We can. But don't expect me to clam up whenever you bring up the topic." Assuming the conversation was over, Carly took out a credit card from her sweatpants pocket. "So, do you have plans for the weekend?"

But it was Brooke who wouldn't be denied a few more jabs.

"I have a suspicion," she railed, "that the majority of people inside your churches have never experienced the intimacy with God as your preachers promise, nor do they know how. May I hazard the guess that most of them are lured to your organization because of a network of friends or a quest for kinship of political like-minds? And if they're younger, possibly a sense of mission. But if they were free to be honest, I doubt they would claim close familiarity with God. And there stands the open door your secularist enemy has been given to those who still declare commitment to your God but don't understand how to know him."

"Just a moment. How did an enemy enter this picture? You're building a case, I know. More than a little venting too. Care for more tea?"

"I'll admit you're the only person from the opposite side I've been able to talk with about religion without being given the ultimatum to accept Jesus or fry in hell."

Carly filled both cups and waited.

"For those of us who have dechurched ourselves, the secularist view offers a liberty from straining to reach the unattainable spiritual goal you people preach. Yes, I know, your answer that God sent his Christ to humankind to bridge the gap almost seems plausible. But life has too many question marks. Your claims overstep reality."

Carly didn't reply, wanting to hear more from the woman she was growing to like.

"And a personal relationship with Jesus?" Brooke wouldn't be interrupted anyway. "You say he offers it, but did he? Where is he? In your heart? Now there's unshakable evidence to take hold of."

"You try to come across as agnostic," said Carly after a sip. "My hunch is, you're not angry at God or his son, but at people who misrepresented him."

Brooke smiled benevolently, realizing she was rather enjoying the exchange with this woman. "Oh Carly, that wouldn't be entirely accurate. Anger stems from disappointment and fear. Tell me you don't know people who are afraid of God, and angry with him. I do agree, the ways his followers portray him makes him look like a Picasso. And if he is as they say, then frustration grows into disgust because the seeker confirms no acceptable evidence to support his compassion, or his availability. Your God hasn't met reasonable expectations."

"Where do you place yourself on a continuum of belief and unbelief?"

"You still don't understand, do you?"

"I do, Brooke. I'm just asking you to say it out loud."

Brooke's eyes held the other woman's. "I took myself out of the conversation when I was thirteen. I stopped hoping for an attentive God. Will I request dialogue with him again? Galloping horses couldn't get me back to the table."

"If you knew God were real, if you could sit across the table from him, what would you say?"

Brooke was about to role her eyes, but only closed them for a moment. She stared at Carly, her face taking on the look of a woman many times defeated.

"I'll treat this with honesty because I think you just might care to hear my answer."

Carly nodded as she reached for a dark chocolate wafer.

"I sincerely doubt," said Brooke, "that God could be real or that he would care to hear what I might say. But it matters little." Brooke lingered over her scone, pursing her lips to keep from saying what she'd been holding inside since she was a young teen. Then, "Were I to give God more consideration, I'd say one thing—and I'll tell you this only once. He or she or it would hear from me a simple demand, if you will. Don't hurt me anymore."

Carly was about to reply that similar cries for God's attention could be found numerous times in the Bible's Old Testament, notably in the Psalms. But she let it go.

"Thank you, Brooke."

"Thank you?" Brooke's eyes were unfriendly.

"For being honest with me."

"I am merely giving you a report. Do us both a favor, Carly. Don't look for something that isn't going to appear."

Dear Brooke, thought Carly, *so grown up, so unaware she's craving to trust the affection of another.*

Thirty-Two

I'M NOTHING TO HIM. CORD! I HATE THAT NAME. Just like my family. The only value they saw in me was what I achieved for them."

Sunday morning at six. Alone in the gym, Brooke attacked the boxing bag with a vengeance. With each hit she detailed the faults of her family and the man still her husband.

Her voice was strained, barely a whisper. "He doesn't care if I exist! Why should he? I can't think of one reason. Whether I live or die, who in this ugly world gives a —"

"Want a real workout?" the voice taunted.

No one else should have been there. Brooke needed solo time with the bag. She had a few tons of aggression to unload. So now this guy walks up, nobody around, and presents himself a willing target. Why did everyone view her as a challenge? She just wanted to work out in her way. She didn't need to display competence.

"No," she said. "Not interested."

"Sure you are. I promise to go easy on you." He had a boyish grin.

Brooke's eyes bored holes through him. A few years younger than her, about the same height, trim muscular, showing off a smirk she was dying to turn into fear.

"Easy? You won't find easy here." She clipped her retort before calling into question his character and lineage.

His eyes held hers. "I've been watching you. Brooke, isn't it? Not bad against the old lady a couple of days ago. Now how about someone with the moves?"

He had jet-black bunned hair, surprisingly smooth skin and perfect teeth.

"And that would be you," she said.

"Try me."

"Look. I'm just here for some aerobics, okay?"

"Not as I hear it. You've got something to prove. I'm here to help."

She rolled her eyes and, shaking her head, sighed loudly. Anger from deep inside immediately welled up and took over. She wanted to inflict pain, and if damage resulted, so be it.

She smiled sweetly at the stranger, "All right, dearie. Show me what you've got."

She didn't recall those being her last words. The lightning quickness of his right foot was all she remembered. Severe pinpointed pain in her abdomen, then cold throughout her core. A welcome darkness closed in while she stood. She never felt his left leg sweeping into both of hers, severely dislocating her right knee. She lay unconscious, blood trickling from her mouth and forming a small pool on the mat.

He looked down at her and smiled to himself. Not sure if

she might hear him, he said, "Sweet dreams." He added, grinning, "Dearie."

He vanished through a rear exit.

Uncharted

Thirty-Three

THE BOUQUET OF FLOWERS ROSA CORTEZ CARRIED could stand nearly as tall as herself. She spotted Cord hurrying to the same elevator and followed him in. He recognized the small woman, nodded briefly and touched the button for the third floor. She would have asked him to press Five for her friend's floor, but studying his face she amended her route.

Cord stuck to minimal politeness. He didn't know her all that well, and he had no interest in chitchat. When the door opened he bolted. And she followed.

Brooke lay in the far bed, alone in a semi private room. Hair snarled. Skin pale. Eyes half open and sunken. Leg braced and iced. Her chin not completely cleaned of the dried blood from the preexisting stomach ulcer ruptured by the kick to her torso.

Standing in the doorway, Rosa handed Cord her flowers and whispered, "The look about her, she opens her eyes, but where is life?"

Cord absently accepted the bouquet, not knowing why she had trailed him.

Brooke heard Rosa's words, though the source seemed to be coming from under her bed. Still, she answered the voice of foreign extract. "There's no life in me," she rasped. "I'm dead."

Rosa stepped around Cord and over to the side of the bed. "You have life within you."

In her anesthetized fog, Brooke imagined a tiny woman peering up at her from the edge of the bed. Such a little person. *Am I with Ewoks?*

"Life? What is life?" Brooke said in a stronger voice, not sure if she was hearing her own or another's expressing thoughts for her. "I'm lost. Too long. Why is it gone?"

"There is something missing?"

"No light. Where is it?"

"Living once, you will live again," declared her Ewok.

These little ones speak with conviction, dreamed Brooke. *Am I in a movie?*

Loopy on sedatives and stumbling over words, she readily spoke to Rosa. Cord listened from the door.

"I've never lived. I died when I was young, did you know that?"

Brooke snuggled in a warm confusion and didn't want it to fade. Feeling more coherent than she was, she glided in and out of clarity. *How nice of this little one to leave her tree village to visit.*

"You have been given a more sobered life than you want. But it can become a good life."

"Can you fly too, little person?" Brooke felt young and small herself. Defenses down, she said whatever came to mind. "Good life, huh? I don't know what that means. That's a word for other people. Not yours truly. No way, Ho-zay! The thing of it is, is," she giggled at her wording. "The memories. Bad memories." *Does she know Anakin Skywalker? My daddy's Bob.*

"Many memories, I am sure," said the Ewok. "They will not always be bad because you will give birth to new memories when you leave your tunnel."

"Ooh, are we in a tunnel? A birth canal? I'm not pregnant, am I? I don't feel pregnant. Cord! Cord must have done this." More giggling.

"I am sorry you stand in your darkness. Soon you will walk out."

"Walks are good too. If I can."

"If? There will be no if. One day you will, *chica*."

"I feel so alone." *I'm glad this little one is in my movie. How nice she speaks Spanish.*

"Only you can walk out of your tunnel," said Rosa. "But you have one waiting for you at the opening when you arrive."

"I do? Who-o?" She imagined she was clever imitating an owl.

"You do not know?"

"No-o-o. Not anymore. I didn't even know I was pregnant." Brooke grinned broadly. She waved her arms over her head then let them fall to her sides. "I don't know *anything* for sure *anymore*."

"Then let me know for you," said Cord, walking into the room and to the foot of her bed.

What's Cord doing in my movie?

"I wish I could have walked the darkest miles for you. I couldn't do that." He moved to her side. "But I have a new vocation, Brooke."

Is that my name in the movie too?

"I'm at the tunnel opening. Just keep listening for my voice. I'll never leave." He paused to think about his next words, then took a chance.

"Brooke, I'll never lie to you."

This is no movie.

Brooke felt a strange release washing over her. With the slightest smile she said, not above a whisper, "What color are my panties?"

Cord closed his eyes in relief.

Thirty-Four

A WEEK SINCE *STARSTRUCK'S* BEAM WAS BREACHED during the neighbors' nocturnal raid. Separated by only five feet of concrete wharf, the slipmates hadn't so much as said hello since. Just as well. Cord was glad for the break from them, and he had pressing matters on his mind.

I almost lost my wife. I'd like to find the guy who hurt her.

He wanted to protect Brooke. Funny how it was easier to think of her as his wife while seeing her vulnerable in the hospital. He didn't know what to do with that, but he did like caring about her again. She actually seemed to appreciate his after-work visits at her bedside.

But he had to admit his anger toward his neighbors wasn't ebbing. What had prompted the madness in those two? He had only been minding his own business, or trying to. They apparently felt justified in minding it for him.

For their part, Travis and Carly needed time to address the same question: why they'd done what they'd done, encroaching in ways they would have never allowed on *Soulmate*. They quietly questioned their motives, certain that a fine friendship was lost.

Were they genuinely sorry? Answering that would be a start. Could they reasonably defend their actions and still be repentant? That might justify motive, but question tactics. Bottom line, their conduct was inappropriate, intolerable.

They taught courses in how to conflict well, but trying to self-apply the tenets they passed along to students, they were drawing a blank. Classroom principles were coming off manufactured when taken off the page and dropped into real life.

Travis was standing between the two boats coiling spare dock lines when Cord turned onto the finger wharf to his boat. Discomfort filled the space.

"Bryan."

"Hello."

Silence. Travis deliberately broke eye contact. Cord was about to climb aboard *Starstruck* when Travis said, "I was wrong. Both of us were."

Before Travis could complete his apology, Cord, without a word, stepped onto his boat's swimstep and disappeared below.

Travis finished coiling his dock line and went into *Soulmate*'s cabin, pulling the sliding door shut.

"Did I hear you talking to Bryan?" asked his wife.

"Almost. Short conversation cut shorter by his dash to safety. I said nothing he wanted to hear."

"I saw him talking with the harbormaster yesterday. I hope he isn't moving his boat to another slip."

"I wish I'd said something more than telling him we were wrong." Travis shook his head. "Carly, why did we do it?"

"We made a snap decision. That's what we were trained to do. But we based it on a wrong premise, that we had more credibility with Bryan than we do."

"Went backwards a lot of steps in our relationship."

"Probably a few miles," she said. "But it isn't ours to say. Not yet. I've been asking myself why we want his friendship. Because we value him for who he is, or because we have plans for his better future? If it's the latter, how did we make ourselves his trainers? What we did was an insult to him."

Travis had to agree. "We weren't like this before the Cadre. We've become reactive, rushing headlong into the fracas."

"We're more combative."

"That we are," he said.

They sat on the sofa staring at a seascape on the wall. "Your sister is an incredible artist," said Carly, to fill the silence.

"I've got work to do," said Travis, standing to signal the close of the conversation. "Whether Cord appreciates what we did isn't our decision. Even if we were combative, as you call it, we saved his six from a lot of regret. And for that I won't apologize."

Carly flared. "That's rather arrogant."

Travis looked down at her. "Don't make this about us, Carly. I won't have it."

"So much for dialogue then."

"I'll be in the engine room."

"Appropriate hiding place."

Her glare told him her short fuse had been lit. He turned and walked away. She sat alone, smoldering.

THAT SLIP ON C DOCK is open, Mr Cord," said the marina's harbormaster. "Shorter by four feet than the one you're in now, so your stern will extend your maximum allowable into the fairway, which means you won't reduce your monthly bill in the trade. But it's yours if you want it."

"How about if I move now?"

"I should have said it'll be available in a couple of days. Didn't know you were in a hurry for it. But you can have the dock locker now. The outgoing tenant said he emptied it."

"Thanks. I'll take some things over."

Cord set down his cellphone and thought over the move. Why make a change when his was the ideal slip? Protected from winds, easy access to the entrance and the channel beyond, at home with other cruisers and blue-water sailboats larger than forty feet. A clientele of his choosing, mostly, whereas C Dock housed smaller runabouts and day-sailors, and seasonal commercial crabbers with their messiness, noises and smells.

CARLY WAS STARTLED out of her silent anger by the firm knock on the cabin wall. She looked out the window, surprised to see their neighbor. She quickly went to slide open the door and on the way called down to Travis.

"Please come in, Bryan."

The three of them stood uneasily in the salon.

"Have a seat?" offered Travis, wiping oil off his hands on a blue shop cloth.

"This won't take long," said Cord, standing where he was. He looked intensely at each of them, and spoke quietly but with an edge of hardness. "I'll just say this. You two were out of line, I hope you know that. But I've been thinking it over. In your thoughtless way you meant well. And for that I can thank you. But listen to me, both of you. Don't ever try something like that again. It would not be pretty."

The Edgertons avoided glancing at each other. They both knew either of them could take Cord to the floor in seconds. But this conversation was not about overpowering. It was all about reconciliation.

Travis spoke first. Thinking he was conveying sincerity, his words came out academic. "Bryan, you're showing me your proactivity by making this move." Then catching himself, he said, "I'm sorry. What I mean to say is, you didn't have to come over, but you did, and that means very much. I—"

Travis put his arm around his wife, a silent recognition of his own transgression moments earlier. She put her hand around his and not too gently squeezed, her signal they'd be talking later.

"We…," continued Travis. "We are, both of us, genuinely sorry for invading your privacy, taking liberties which were never given—nor should they be, for trying to manage your life."

"Thank you," said Cord. "You're sorry. I'm sorry. So we're good now, okay? Now we can move on."

Carly said, "It's kind of chilly for spring. I think some coffee would go good, don't you?"

"If you're offering, I'll take a beer," said Cord with a faintly uneven smile.

"I'll bring three," she said.

That night Cord left a message for the harbormaster, deciding to stay put.

Uncharted

Thirty-Five

RECOVERY, MY DEAR?"

It was the censure in the chief surgeon's voice that miffed Brooke. Authoritarian. Jerk.

"Young lady, you're lucky to be alive. Of course you'll limp. You'll have to learn to cope. But you've got two legs! And all your internals! Dr Paulford and I did exceptional work piecing you back together."

Well, two can play the attitude game.

"Doctor, your tutelage of the Almighty must leave him spellbound." Brooke spun her walker around and hobbled away from the white-haired medico in his dark blue three-piece ensemble. With the poise of old-school presumption, he squared his shoulders and turned on his wingtips.

In her room, Brooke retrieved her overnight bag from the closet shelf and threw it on her bed. She hastily packed her few items with one hand while holding onto the raised bed frame with the other for balance. Her back to the door and her mind rehearsing the rest of what she should have said to the physician, she didn't hear Cord's knock at the door.

"Brooke? You're walking?"

Her concentration still elsewhere, her reply was brusque. "Yes, I'm walking! Is that so unusual?"

"It's only been a week since the accident. Yesterday the doctor made it clear you'd be in a wheelchair for awhile."

"Right. I'm lucky you're not receiving sympathy cards for my untimely demise. And I should send the surgeon chocolates for his brilliance in the operating theater. The cretin."

Cord sat on the edge of the vacant bed next to hers. "What's happened? You were in good spirits yesterday."

She scratched her arm nervously. "Dr Deity outside. You see him?"

"I saw some old suit chewing out a nurse at her desk. You have a run-in with him?" He refrained from adding *too*.

"He tried his power play to churn up my guilt and gratitude. How's that for a prescription for healing? I told him to shove it."

"As only you can."

"Take me home, would you?"

"Serious? You've been discharged?"

"Just take me home," she snapped.

He didn't argue. She was mobile, and spirited—the right stuff to heal a body.

"On our way," he said approvingly.

"I can't squeeze into your car."

"I'll bring yours. Can you wait?"

"Not here."

"Let's go down to the cafeteria. You can chew on a coffee mug there."

It took effort, but Brooke pivoted on her good leg to face him, still holding onto the bed rail. "I don't want to be alone."

Cord held her gaze and nodded. "I won't leave you."

Cell in hand, he double-touched, swiped and tapped.

"Marcus, which car are you driving today? Good. We need your help. Could you get to the hospital for Brooke and me? Yeah, now. No, no one's permission but her own. Half hour? We'll be waiting."

He pocketed his cell. "He's got his old Navigator today."

Brooke was sitting on the bed, a wave of weariness coming on. "Thanks for not arguing."

"Not a hill to climb, or one you need to defend."

"Nor one," she corrected, ever the grammarian.

Cord took her overnight bag, wanted to retort, didn't.

Marcus Elkin pulled into the patient loading area. Cord effortlessly picked up Brooke, leaving the walker at the curb. She tentatively placed an arm around his shoulders and grimaced from the pain as he set her in the passenger seat. In the car she closed her eyes and kept them shut.

After a slow ride through the west side of town and into the driveway of the cottage, Cord got out of the back seat with crutches from the hospital.

"I don't want those. Not yet."

"Are you sure?" He saw determination in her face.

He helped her climb slowly out of the large SUV. Shakily she held onto the armrest then grabbed his shoulder. Already exhausted from the short drive, she didn't resist when he put his arm around her waist to steady her.

"Thanks, Marcus. Means a lot." Cord took her bag and side-kicked the door closed.

"You got it, my friend." The door sealed Elkin's voice in the car.

With fewer stairs to negotiate at the backdoor, Cord guided Brooke into the back porch, through the Pullman-style kitchen and into the cozy parlor. She stopped at the stuffed chair and collapsed into it.

"Not to the bed?" he asked.

She shook her head.

"I'll fix some tea," he said.

"No, stay."

Cord sat on the edge of the sofa across from her, hands folded between his knees.

After some minutes, Cord wondering if she might have fallen asleep, Brooke made an attempt at a smile.

"Thank you."

"Of course. You would have done the same for me."

"I don't think I would have. You don't think so either, do you?"

"I know you would. How about that tea?"

Brooke sighed deeply. "I need to say this."

Cord settled back uneasily. It seemed strange to be in the cottage. After a couple of months living on *Starstruck* this house wasn't his anymore. If he had to pick a word describing his feelings sitting here in what used to be a favorite room, it'd have to be…awkward. Not tense, not nervous. Awkward. Now she was going to tell him something. Okay, he'd hear her out then get to the boat. He'd have to call a cab back to the hospital for his car.

"You must hate me."

"I don't hate you," he said, not knowing where she was going. His own words tumbled out. "I never have. Angry, yes. Frustrated, discouraged, for sure. You want the truth? I didn't want to take this divorce path, but apparently there's no other option."

"You think there's still hope?"

"I'm not sure what you mean." He felt defensive, and didn't like it.

"What I mean is, if we didn't go through with the divorce."

Cord pursed his lips, never thinking he'd hear those words. "So, I've been talking with some friends the last few weeks. They seem to think we've got another chance worth taking."

"Is Carly one of them?"

"Yeah, her and Doc."

"She and Doc," Brooke rephrased.

"No, if you'll look this up, I believe you'll see it's her and Doc."

For the first time in months, they both managed a smile toward the other.

Cord couldn't hold back his concern. His voice catching, he said, "I almost lost you."

She was still for a moment, then, "I'm afraid."

Cord didn't expect that either.

"Of me?" he asked.

"No, you've never given me reason to fear you. I'm afraid of the future, of all we need to do to get good again."

What did he just hear? Now could be the right time to try out once more that line Marcus taught him. So Cord did.

"Help me understand, Brooke."

As if by magic, the words put them both at ease and led to nearly an hour of good conversation. Brooke, between yawns and trying her best to stay awake, did most of the talking. She described events Cord already knew about, and people he'd met at her family's reunion. More things revealing not only her fears, but how she'd collected them. During one pause Cord made that hot tea for them both.

"Herbal this time?" he asked.

"I'm preferring black these days."

Another faint smile shared between them. The last time he offered her tea she was ready to throw it at him.

Early evening crept in. Cord's car was still in the hospital's open lot. He never allowed his 1800ES to sit in a public lot.

Sliding forward again to the edge of the sofa, he said, "I ought to call a cab and pick up my car so I can get home."

"I," she said haltingly, "don't want you to leave."

He sat back with relief. "I don't want to either."

They didn't move from that room, fewer words and a relaxed silence filling their space. Their tea turned cold and both of them heard Cord's belly grumble. Their eye contact came more easily.

"Can you handle pizza," she asked. "I've been dying for pizza in the hospital."

"I'll order one."

"There's a large pepperoni and mushroom in the freezer. Under the TV dinners."

"Been eating well, I see. Same here. What's there to drink?"

"You left four stouts. They're still there and cold. I'll share one with you."

"One large pizza, one dark, two straws, coming up."

"I'll help," she said, trying to stand.

He waved her down. "I sort of remember my way around."

Setting the beer and hot pizza on the table, Cord was about to help her from the parlor, but she was ambling her way to the chair she always used. Their meal was quiet; they had covered much ground before dinner.

They sipped slowly from their glasses, wanting to prolong dinnertime, because both knew they had reached the moment of decision. Cord was the first to speak.

"I'll clear the dishes and call for that cab." He stood, this time making it to his feet, only to be surprised again.

"Spend the night."

Resting his hands on the table to steady himself, he puffed out his cheeks and slowly exhaled. "Is it a good idea?"

"I might need your help in the middle of the night."

"Oh, that. Of course, sure. I wasn't thinking."

"Yes, you were. About something else."

He caught that her remark was made without disapproval.

"I suppose I can sleep on the den couch," he suggested. "I'd just need a blanket, I guess."

"You might not hear me if I need you. The bed is big enough for the two of us. It used to be."

He was about to confront her about the mixed message when he heard, "You can be on your side, I'll be on mine."

Cord was feeling a new discomfort. He'd been living on his own the last two months, responsible to no one, unrestricted in moving about as he chose. He'd resolved to becoming single again. Now the woman he was estranged from was inviting him back into relationship. At least, that's what it sounded like. He started to back away.

"I think I should get back to the boat. No toothbrush here. I'll check on you in the morning. Wish there was someone who could come over at this last minute."

"There's a spare toothbrush in the lower drawer. You left it. That, and the beer. Would you like to share another?"

"I don't know what to say, Brooke. What's your intent in all this?"

"This is all new to me too. Can't we just take it one night at a time? I'm still scared. I don't know where it's going either. But in the hospital I had time alone. And time alone means I fill it with thinking and reflecting and pondering and, and… It was far too much time without distraction. And you wouldn't believe the dream I had after surgery. It must have been the anesthetic. I dreamed you came into the room and told me you wouldn't leave me. Well, that part's happening right now.

"And in the dream there was also this tiny Hispanic woman standing at the edge of the bed. I could barely see her face. And I thought she as an Ewok. She told me I was stuck in a tunnel, or some such. And then you were calling from outside the tunnel."

"That all happened, Brooke. Pretty much as you remember."

"It did, really?"

Cord nodded, amused, hopeful.

"So many blanks in that dream. Or conversation, if you say it wasn't a dream."

"Then I'll help you with the blanks. But not tonight. You must be exhausted."

"I am. And I'll sleep tonight if you're here. After that second stout."

"I'll open it."

She slept soundly after she downed most of the second bottle. Cord, however, was another story. Stretched at attention at his edge of the bed, he spent the night seesawing from worry to wonder. The first light of dawn crept through the window before he fell asleep. When he woke three hours later he saw a second blanket had been set over him.

And he smelled coffee.

Thirty-Six

STARSTRUCK RACED ACROSS THE WIDE PASSAGE toward the hidden bay. Travis held the wheel and his grin made Cord wish he could store smiles like that in a bottle to pour out on dreary days. This older man loved life.

"I've never skimmed across the water at forty-three miles an hour!" said Travis. He raised his voice only a little, more for the wind in his face than the humming twin marine engines.

"Give her a sharp turn and see how she responds," said Cord.

"Are you kidding? We'll both fly over the gunnels!"

"Go ahead. Hug the edge."

Travis was doubtful, but couldn't resist. "Okay. It's your boat."

"It's my boat." Cord sat in the mate's chair, his feet on the dash and arms loosely crossed, his own smile spreading.

Travis gripped the wheel tightly with both hands and swung hard to port, fully expecting Cord to be thrown in his lap. The props dug in and pushed the hull deeper into the water allowing for little side-slip, with a near-perfect compressed turn and a drop in speed of a mere fifteen miles per hour.

Travis was ecstatic. "We just pulled a ninety degree turn at almost thirty! Who designed this boat? Maserati? Can I do that again?"

After more spins and weaves testing *Starstruck's* agility, Travis reluctantly aimed for their destination. At the entrance to the small bay he relinquished the helm to Cord who brought her in and anchored in a cove of a seldom visited island some miles from home. Engines off, they sat quietly, captivated by the gentle rocking of the boat, the silence enveloping them.

The sun popped out of the scudding clouds. Travis took off his jacket while Cord went below for the lunches he'd picked up at Rosa's Mexican Restaurant. After handing the foil-wrapped plates up to Travis, he sliced a lime to go with the cokes. Seated around the cockpit table they dove into their huge burritos, washing them down with plenty of carbonation.

"Rosa calls these her garbage burritos 'cause she's loaded everything she could in them," burbled Cord with his mouth full. Travis ate and nodded.

Burritos finished and drinks refilled, Cord and his neighbor sat on opposite sides of the helm station quietly admiring the sandy beach only yards off their stern.

"Folks pay thousands of dollars to come out here for a few days to experience what we get to enjoy anytime at the turn of the boat's keys," said Travis. He patted the upholstery. "You've got a magnificent craft here."

Cord said nothing for a long moment. Travis sensed he was about to hear the reason for his being invited to lunch. He drank his coke, waiting.

"Doc, there's something I've never told anyone. Here's a letter explaining it all." Cord set an envelope on the table between them.

"Why should you be telling me?"

"Because you're someone gaining my trust. And if I'm going to re-enter a marriage with my wife, I need to go in with no secrets, no anchors holding me down."

Travis moved to refill Cord's glass, but Cord waved off as he began his story.

"It was a long time ago. I didn't like letting my insecurity show so I tried to make up for it by being mean, sometimes malicious. My dad warned me about it when I was in high school, which is when this all went down. I wrote everything out here." He gave the envelope containing three handwritten pages to Travis. "I asked you out here today because I also need to tell someone face to face."

"That's brave of you. Sure you want to?" Travis held the unopened envelope, then set it back down.

"Of course not, Doc." The retort was too quick. "But I need to confront this and get it settled, and I figure coming clean is a necessary surgery."

Cord's narrative was every bit as shocking as it was sad. He spoke with little emotion, but his eyes revealed a sorrow Travis had begun to recognize in the man since they'd first met. Cord held back nothing, but omitted most of the graphics. Travis interrupted a few times asking to clarify a point. Mostly he kept still, letting Cord dig deep to find his words. Cord held steady eye contact, though he occasionally looked out across the water at the shore, shaking his head often as he unpacked a part of his past rightly labeled heartless.

I GUESS THAT'S ABOUT THE WORST you could hear from a guy who's supposed to be an all-around nice person."

Travis began to run his finger around the rim of his glass, staring into it.

"Quite a story, Bryan. Quite a story." He kept his attention on the glass. Only a few years ago he'd opened a particular chapter of his own youth. He'd hoped at the time that when he finally confessed his wrong of earlier years to his lifelong friend he could close the book on it. Now it appeared he was to reopen that chapter.

"I would be disingenuous if I were to withhold from you a part of my past," he said. "I call it the worst wake-up I've ever had. No, it had nothing to do with the two kidnappers Carly and I told you about, the men I…killed. A couple therapists told us they deserved those bullets to the chest. They were out to do damage and they paid for it in a way nobody expects to pay. And no, you don't forget the look of a man's face almost dead. Surprise, remorse. And the light really does leave the eyes.

"What I'm about to tell you happened before Carly and I met. I did something very cruel to a girl. You said I was trustworthy. The girl told me the same thing. 'I trust you, Travis.' For that she paid dearly. I turned her life upside down, changed her into a completely different person. She turned cold and never believed anyone again. You see, Bryan, what you did was terrible behavior, no question about that. But, and I claimed to be a Christ-follower then, I treated her as if she was without value. A worthless piece of humanity to toss away."

"Did you ever address that?"

"Not with her, not ever. And with no one else for too many years. I privately held on to the guilt, longer than you've been holding on to yours, which makes me not nearly as sage as the nickname, Doc, implies. I finally confessed it to my oldest friend, Bud, a few years ago when he and I were on the water, like you and I are now. Telling him gave me the courage to unmask it and reveal more of myself to my wife. It's still the hardest thing I've ever done, telling the woman of my life that she'd married one abusive man."

"How did she take it? What I'm really asking is, what can I expect from Brooke?"

"Carly only knew me as her husband, not as the lout I had been. Yes, she was shocked, and it took a fair number of revisits with her to help me settle the past. They were more for my resolution, forgiving myself. She was actually quick to grant me mercy."

Travis screwed up his face. "And it meant telling her why this nose of mine leans to the left."

Cord tilted his head to the side to study Travis' face.

The older man explained. "I didn't break it playing college ball. Nothing so glamorous. No, the girl I hurt had the pluck to haul off and tag me hard so I'd never forget that this deformity is nothing compared to the lifelong emotional disfigurement I caused her."

"So maybe we're pretty much the same, aren't we, Doc? Each with a story. Both of us needing to get right with our past. I'm afraid Brooke won't be able to let this go, always wondering if I'll return to being the kind of monster I've been hiding from her."

"You two don't have the time and mileage that Carly and I do. So at this point there's no guarantee, is there? Let me ask, do you know if that couple you wounded, they're elderly by now, ever recovered from their loss?"

"They receive a yearly packet with ten new hundred-dollar bills sandwiched inside a few blank pages. A friend of mine who travels the country sends it—he doesn't know why. They see the postmark but they can't trace it closer than to whichever post office slot he slips it into. Always the same amount."

"To assuage your guilt, I take it."

"Hasn't worked yet. I've sent enough money to pay a few times over for what I did to them, but how do you recover from the loss of what you dearly treasure? I attacked them with a cruelty no one should endure. I'll never get over their horror. I don't think I deserve to."

Travis picked up the envelope Cord had given him. "What do you want to do with this letter?"

"Will you read it?"

"Do I need to? Is there more you've not mentioned?"

"It's in there, Doc. All of it."

Travis deliberated a few moments. As he did, Cord caught himself sighing deeply and yawning nervously.

In time Travis said, "This letter represents your wrongdoing. It was a serious offense, one you've kept deep down. Today you're taking a step. You've confessed it. So now we ought to demonstrate that it's being sufficiently dealt with. And I say we, because you've generously invited me to accompany you in your resolution."

"Generous isn't the word I'd use."

"Oh, but think about it. You've chosen not to go this alone anymore, and you've made a huge request to someone you said you trust. I count this an honor."

Cord almost replied, reconsidered, then waded in. "I don't have it in me to climb the mountain alone."

"Let me take a tack here you may not be ready for. Then again, you could be. You say you're not sure if you want to believe in God. Let's say you do. Do you think he might for-give you? I certainly do."

Cord's derisive laugh was reflexive. "Sure you do, Doc. Not nearly the same thing. You can forgive me, but it wasn't you who suffered, who had to watch me inflicting pain. As for God, since when is he the forgiving kind? That's why there's a Judgment Day, so he can finally settle the score, get even for the damage we do to other people and their possessions, our-selves, the environment. No offense, Doc, but why do you God-people think there's a loophole somewhere to escape the wrath to come?"

"Sounds like you've been to church."

"You know something I don't?"

"I think I might. Care to hear?"

"Can I be honest?"

"You always have been."

"At this point I'm not interested in hearing religion. There's no attraction in it. It's about your Jesus, right?"

"It is."

"You intend to get me converted?"

"I'm good with leaving that in your care, and…" Travis paused to lift his glass and smile, "and talking about my Jesus whenever you're up to it."

Cord was about to object, but Travis quickly shook his head to forestall him before taking a long swallow of his coke. Setting the empty glass firmly on the table he said, "But I do have a suggestion for this letter."

"That, I'd be open to."

Travis volunteered his idea. When Cord didn't immediately answer, he said, "Well then, why don't I hang on to your letter and you take some time to think about it? Give it a few days.

No hurry, is there?" He held it in his hand as if weighing the contents. "No one else will see this."

"Not Carly?"

"You're trusting me with an important part of who you are. This conversation goes no further."

"I appreciate that. And I won't divulge what you've told me."

"Only two others know about that strip club episode; Carly, and my friend Bud."

"And the girl."

"I wish it weren't so."

"Your wife ever meet her?"

Travis spoke softly. "She'd know if she had. Hatred doesn't remain unconcealed."

Cord emptied his glass and looked across the bay while chewing on the slice of lime, thinking. Convinced, he gave his head a resolute nod.

"I like your plan, Doc. Why wait? Where do you suggest we do this?"

"We're here. Nobody's near this island. Why not go ashore?"

Cord was up and to his inflatable dinghy to lower into the water. He rowed them the fifty yards to the beach. Travis jumped off the forward buoyancy tube onto the sand and pulled the dinghy ashore with the towline. He tied off around an end of a large beached log while Cord stepped out of the nine-foot boat.

"Pick your spot," said Travis, and immediately went in search of tiny driftwood pieces and kindling.

Cord uncovered a flat rock about a foot in diameter and set a circle of smaller stones around it to create a fire ring.

Travis came back with his supply of fuel and fashioned the dozen small dry twigs Boy Scout style. "I don't think anyone will mind our fire. No risk of burning down the island."

With the wood pieces arranged, Travis asked, "You have something to light this?"

Cord took a small box of wood matches from a pocket, struck three together and touched the flame to various points at the bottom of the kindling. He sat on the sand close to the little fire. Travis lay down on the opposite side to create a shield from the slight breeze. They both stared into the small blaze.

"It's a sacrifice of sorts, you know," said Travis, elbow in the sand and head resting on his hand, not taking his eyes off the fire. "You're releasing what you've been holding. Letting go."

One of the wood chips sputtered and crackled as its sap caught fire. They watched and listened. They were in no hurry, letting the fire burn down to red coals.

When it was time, Travis asked, "You ready for this?"

"I wasn't sure even fifteen minutes ago. When you were dragging the boat onto the beach I wanted to turn back. But watching the fire, hearing you talk about this being a sacrifice and letting go settles it. Yeah, I'm ready. May I have the envelope please."

"You sound like a game show host." Travis pulled it from his back pocket and handed it over.

"Now what?" asked Cord.

"Fire's ready, you're holding the letter. Seems obvious to me."

"Should I say something first?"

"No one here telling you not to."

"Don't laugh, but it seems like there should be a prayer or something."

"That might be good. Why don't you?"

"Me? What would I say? To whom?"

"How about talking to the God you say you're not sure about?"

"Right, Doc."

"Couldn't resist. Possibly something like, 'I'm giving this away; it isn't mine anymore.' I can help if you want."

"These need to be my words." Cord was silent for a moment, then began.

"So, I'm not sure who I'm talking to right now. Maybe myself, maybe God. Doesn't really matter, I suppose. Like the Doc said, I'm getting rid of this letter. All it represents, the guilt, the anguish. I'm sorry. Very, very sorry for what I did to those people. I'm sure I've got no do-over with them, but I hope someday I'll have the guts to ask them to forgive me. Right now though, I need to forgive myself. So here goes."

Cord slowly and purposefully placed the letter on top of the glowing coals. The envelope smoldered dark brown before a flame burst from its center. The two men watched as a tangible symbol of repentance burned, ashes floating on the rising heat.

Travis was about to sit up when Cord spoke again. "If there's a God watching this, he can hear too, right? So, um, Sir, thank you for people like the Doc here. Someone who knows what it's like to hurt other people and feel the pain himself. So, that's it. Amen. Yeah."

Looking at Travis through the smoke, he asked, "Was that okay?"

"You did just fine."

They both stood and looked down at the fire ring, the driftwood now mostly black from being spent.

"I guess we should smother the embers," said Cord. He scooped some handfuls of sand to spread over the stone altar. "That should do it."

They gave the rocks another once-over. A final wisp of smoke made its way through the sand.

"I know a young man who did what you've just done," said Travis. "In an empty parking lot, not an uninhabited island. After he extinguished his fire, he scraped away any evidence with his hands and feet to be sure he'd never find it again."

"Good idea," said Cord. And with that he jumped up and down on the remains, kicking away the rock circle, grinding sand into the flat slab. Then he began to laugh from the deepest part of his soul. A man had just discovered freedom.

Cord rowed them back to *Starstruck*. When they secured the dinghy on the swimstep by its davits he said, "I could go for a brew. Want a cold one before heading back?"

"You read my mind."

"Will a dark do? Closest I've got to a light is an amber." He checked the fridge. "Out of amber."

"As close to a stout as you've got. Seems a shame anything lite would be called beer."

Cord pulled two porters from the cockpit bar fridge. "My kind of guy, Doc. Never touch a beer you can count your fingers through. In a glass or out of the bottle?"

"It always tastes proper from a glass."

Cord opened the bottles and pulled two chilled glasses from the fridge. Handing Travis his bottle and frosted glass he said, "Since when do you religious people drink beer?"

Travis chuckled. "Some don't at that. Carly and I grew up in families avoiding it. But we both like the taste of a good beer."

"And cigars."

"Yeah. Don't tell my Aunt Sarah."

"And she is…"

"The family matriarch. Still loves telling me I'm naughty, but I've always reminded her of herself." Travis toasted his young friend.

After a few sips Cord said, "You mentioned you helped someone else find freedom. The little fire, burning the evidence."

"Once, some years ago now. A student of mine who couldn't get past his own obstacle. He's actually about your age now."

"What was his outcome?"

"Quite dramatic. I could see it in his face, like a load was removed, lifted right off his shoulders. I keep in touch with him, like I do a few others who want to update their old prof. He's a husband and daddy now, couple of kids as I recall."

"Do the memories ever come back to haunt him?"

"He texted last month. Interesting timing. Told me this: 'No plaguing memories, Doc. Not even the ashes.' I'd say that's a clear answer, wouldn't you?"

"Hope I'll be able to say that a few years from now."

Travis reached over to put a hand on his shoulder. "One thing, my friend. Don't give in to an overactive conscience."

Cord's eyes revealed confusion.

"By that I mean, don't rehash your past. The letter's burned. You put the match to it. You watched the smoke. You stomped the ashes. In time you'll internalize your freedom. Let yourself. I was there with you. Witnessed the whole thing. It's over. Done. We drank to it."

Uncharted

Thirty-Seven

CORD SPENT THE FIRST TWO NIGHTS at the cottage after Brooke's hospital stay. Thereafter he stopped over every evening for dinner, but left to sleep on *Starstruck* after cleaning up the kitchen. The arrangement, though clunky, was acceptable to both.

Her healing progressed well and her strength was returning. But she was bored. Alone in the house during the days while Cord was at work, monotony soon got the better of her. When he stopped to check on her at the end of his day, she astounded him with meals like they'd come right off the screen of Gourmet.com.

"I'm going back to the library tomorrow," she announced between bites of her fresh basil, kale, arugula and tomato salad topped with shaved Parmesan.

Cord looked up from his bright red Coho salmon slab with fresh dill, and baked young asparagus spears. "Timing seems right. You've been cooped up here for awhile."

"Twelve days to be exact."

"I'm surprised you've made it this long without going completely nuts. Are you sure you didn't go out and catch this salmon yourself?"

"Had it delivered. I've been going crazy all day. I can only watch so many reruns of NCIS."

"Did I ever tell you my mom went to school with the lead actor? The Jethro guy. I forget his real name."

"Mark Harmon."

"Yeah, that's the guy. She was in a class at UCLA with him. She and six hundred others. He was the team's QB."

"I'm serious. I need to get out of here. If I stay inside another day I swear I'll start watching the Hallmark Channel."

"You seem ambulatory enough. I'll come by to drive you to the library in the morning."

Dishes in the washer, kitchen sparkling, he slipped on a pullover windbreaker to leave, and a wild thought came to him. His head still inside the jacket, he figured the worst she'd do was to tell him to shove off.

"You want to spend a couple nights on the boat? Weather's supposed to be great this weekend. We could zip over to the island with the twin cedars." He popped his head out to see that she was looking at him.

She surprised him with her immediate, "I'd like that."

He almost replied, *Really?* But said, "Me too."

Then another surprise.

"Why wait for Friday? We can go tomorrow. I don't really need to be at the library so soon. "But are you sure you can take the extra day from your office?"

"No worries. That boss of mine has been exceptionally generous in giving me time away. I didn't tell you, but Marcus was pretty shaken seeing you when he drove us from the hospital."

"I was that bad?"

Cord said nothing for a long moment. Looking down and slowly nodding his head, he said softly, "I was scared, Brooke."

He lifted his head to meet her stare, and she saw his eyes tearing.

"I didn't know," she said.

THEY ARRIVED AT *Starstruck's* berth late the next afternoon. The tide was high, giving Brooke a nearly level walk on the gangplank to the boat slips. Still on the ramp she saw a small Mexican couple walking toward her. She tried to remember where she'd seen the tiny woman before, but couldn't place her.

"Ah, *Señorita*, you have quick improvement," enthused the woman. Brooke thought she recognized the voice, but from exactly where she couldn't recall. From somewhere in a fog.

There was little room on the walkway for all four people, and others needed to get by. So with only a short greeting, the couples moved on their way. But not before the woman grasped Brooke's hand in both of hers and exclaimed, *"¡La gracia de Dios!"*

Cord guided Brooke the rest of the way to *Starstruck*. She kept shaking her head.

"You're wondering where you've seen her, right?" asked Cord. "That was the little person who spoke to you in the hospital. You called her an Ewok." He chuckled.

She stopped where she was. "I called her a... Yes, I remember!" She turned around but the couple had disappeared among the cars in the parking lot.

"She was real then. She wasn't a dream."

"Far from it!" Cord was laughing. "If you're feeling up to it in a few days we can have dinner at their place."

"Right. Just invite ourselves over."

"Pretty much. They own a little restaurant near the docks. They'd love to meet you." To himself, he said, "I wonder if they were looking at boats."

Cord and Brooke decided to stay in the slip that night. After a simple dinner and an extra glass of wine, He offered to sleep on the salon's settee. She objected.

"The reason I wanted to be here wasn't just for a boat ride," she said, no subtlety intended.

Late the next morning, Brooke offered to hold the stern dock line as Cord released the others while the engines warmed.

"No need. I've got it," he said. "Just have a seat. I'll get us out."

She took the wheel while he untied the lines. "There's nothing wrong with my arms or depth perception."

Steering *Starstruck* past the marina's jetty, she pushed the throttles forward to cruise at a brisk thirty-five knots, and chose a roundabout route to their destination. Cord relaxed in the mate's chair, pleased with her steady improvement after surgery, and intrigued by the change in their rekindled relationship.

They stayed in the little cove for two nights. He was careful with how much on-board activity she could take. She thought him overly cautious, but appreciated his concern. When it was time to head for home she relinquished the wheel and sat close to him, their nearness feeling almost natural. Back in the slip she went below to pack her few items and he hastily washed the salt spray off *Starstruck's* hull.

"Nice to have you home. Good time out there? Perfect weather for a getaway."

The friendly voice cut into Cord's reverie. He turned to see Travis and Carly loaded down with bags of groceries.

"Couldn't have been better." Cord was all smiles, more than seemed warranted to his neighbors.

As Carly was noting his look of satisfaction, she saw Brooke appear from the cabin. She tilted her head toward Cord, gave him a knowing smile and left Travis' side to greet Brooke.

After commenting on her remarkable recovery, Carly asked if they'd stop by for evening dessert. She was fairly dazed to hear Brooke's quick and warm, "We'd love to."

"Wonderful," stammered Carly. "Seven, then?"

Small dishes of vanilla bean ice cream topped with blueberries drizzled with limoncello accompanied steaming mugs of decaf at *Soulmate's* salon table. Conversation was kept light, everyone guarding against leading questions or extraneous statements about marriage. An hour later Brooke's energy faded and Cord thanked his neighbors for an enjoyable evening. They agreed to a follow-up date to be arranged after the Edgerton's upcoming anniversary.

Brooke accepted Cord's help into the passenger seat of her car. When he got behind the wheel she said, "I think I could like those people."

"I know what you mean."

"But married thirty-six years. That's longer than we've been alive. It's beyond me."

Cord let the motor's hum fill the silence for a moment before saying, "I'd be okay with aiming toward our third year."

She didn't reply, but her body didn't stiffen in reaction, and he was good with that. They quietly drove the few blocks to the cottage. He walked her to the backdoor with his arm around her waist. He said goodnight but she held onto him.

"I'd like that," she said, her head relaxed on his shoulder.

"Did I miss something?" He held her a little closer.

"What you said, about our third year. I want that too."

Cord felt right being back in the California king.

Thirty-Eight

Oh, THAT WAS A DELIGHTFUL DINNER," said Carly, slipping her arm through her husband's.

"Happy anniversary, lady of mine."

Outside a favorite wharfside restaurant, the two strolled the parkway at the water's edge, taking the long way home. The evening had turned misty, but the temperature was pleasant for early spring.

"Shrimp and lobster," he said. "The perfect anniversary dinner."

"Good thing we only have it once a year. I'm waddling."

He patted her behind. "You'll never be a waddler." She pinched his.

They hadn't walked more than fifty yards when a man in his twenties came up from behind on Carly's side. Under a large overhanging tree, its branches budding, he made like he was about to pass when he slowed to their pace. The young tough gave Carly a head-to-toe appraisal and an unappreciated greeting, his words degrading. She rolled her eyes and moved closer to Travis. Travis put his arm around her. The man, on the greasy side and a couple inches taller, was eyeing what he assumed to be an easy target of two middle-aged people. He foolishly hid his hands in his jacket pockets.

Travis ignored the man's comment with a benign reply. "Nice evening, isn't it?" He knew the man anticipated no pushback or he wouldn't have kept his hands holstered.

The man eased behind them. "It is for some."

Travis did an abrupt about face with Carly mirroring his move.

The man hadn't expected the standoff but still supposed he had the advantage. He began to pull out his right hand.

Travis knew what was coming. He'd been here before.

He lunged forward with an uncharacteristic snarl. He grabbed the younger man by the throat with his right hand, and with his left slapped him repeatedly in the face while striding forward, holding him at arm's length. The man could do nothing but try to keep his balance while backpedaling. He lurched and began to fall backward, his hands darting out of his coat for balance. Travis felt the man involuntarily wrenching away, so he shoved him all the way down on his back and thrust his knee onto the man's right arm to restrain it. The man tried to tear away Travis' chokehold with his other arm.

Carly made the offhand suggestion that the lad may have had enough. "What do you think, sweetheart?" She added the endearment to emphasize that her proposal to let the man go deserved consideration.

They felt the darkness of their Cadre past enveloping them. Both later admitted to their therapist the thrill of the return of a forgotten adrenalin rush.

Travis loosened his grip a little and said, not too kindly, "Would you like us to call the police for you?"

The man fought all the more to get free, his legs flailing, a knee occasionally connecting with Travis' back.

"You ought to stop kicking, you know, or I simply won't quit," said Travis calmly. The thrill was indeed back.

The man emitted a gurgling sound. It was no death rattle for he still had combat on his mind.

"I sincerely wish you'd stop struggling," said Travis, a bit exasperated, "or I'll have to begin to hurt you."

Carly leaned close to the man and smelled cheap alcohol. With a look of sorrow she said, "You'd better do what he says. I saw him become angry like this once." She shuddered with exaggeration. "It wasn't pretty. Just humor us? Please?"

The would-be robber's eyes grew wild because he knew both of them were in it together, a tag-team. His fear was confirmed when he heard Travis say, "I'm getting a little winded, hon. You want a turn?"

The man tried to scream, and made the mistake of arching his back to squirm away.

Travis slapped the man once more but with less intensity. "Oh, do stop!"

He stopped.

"Are you sure we can't call the cops for you? Certainly the paramedics. How about it, sport?"

The man lay still for a moment, then nodded, and continued nodding, fear filling his face. Travis released the choke-hold, but kept him pinned down at the shoulders.

"Now, young man, before I help you up, let's see what you're carrying in your jacket. You think we should do that?"

The man gasped something unintelligible.

"I'll take that to mean a hearty yes. Wise choice."

The man attempted to move his free hand, but too quickly. Travis struck him in the left temple.

"Let's agree that I'll tell you when to move. You need only do what I say. Think you can go with that?"

The man closed his eyes and nodded again, his fight gone out. He knew he'd just been thrashed by an old guy he'd mistaken for an easy mark.

Travis reached into the right pocket and removed a small .32 handgun.

"Carly, you'd better take this."

He checked the other pocket and pulled out a wad of bills, mostly twenties, and handed the acquisitions to her.

She expertly turned the gun over in her palm. "Old S&W. Our unfortunate friend won't be needing this anymore. Let's keep it somewhere safe."

She emptied the cylinder and hurled revolver and bullets across the rocky shoreline and far into the salt chuck.

Hearing the distant splash the man groaned. "That's my brother's," he rasped.

"When you grow up, learn how to play nicely with big boy toys," she scolded in a motherly voice.

Travis helped him to his feet, and began to straighten the man's coat. But the erstwhile aggressor regained his vigor and his anger.

Carly knew he was about to charge, so without warning she threw a mean punch to the ill-fated man's left jaw. They all heard it crack. He screamed.

"Oh, sorry, hon," said Travis. "I thought you had opted out of a turn. He's all yours."

"Thank you, love."

And with that Carly tagged him a good one to his solar plexus to double him over. They watched the man crumple to the ground.

"Not bad, lady," said Travis. "Been working out, have you?"

"Not bad yourself," she said, brushing her hair from her face. "We're both a little slower, but it's kind of nice to be back in the mix. Even if the talent here is terribly disproportionate."

The man tried to kneel on all fours, but Travis pushed him to his stomach on the wet pavement. He pulled the man's wallet from a back pocket and removed a driver's license.

"Well, Mr Reynolds, now we know your name," said Travis. "This isn't turning out to be your best night. However, in a way it is. We're not going to prevent you from living through it. Time to stand now."

The man lay still.

"Ah, good of you to review the directive." Travis spoke as if admonishing an errant student. "Hasty moves wouldn't be in your best interest, now would they? You may stand."

The man slowly got to his feet, had a fleeting thought of a renewed attack, but when he saw Travis and Carly taking offensive positions in front and behind him, he knew he'd not make it another round.

He tried to speak, but the intense flash of pain in his jaw nearly sent him to his knees again.

Travis and Carly both helped him upright. "Poor dear," she soothed. "Have that looked at. Soon."

Travis hailed a cab driving through the adjacent parking lot. He assisted the hapless mugger into the back seat and flipped the wallet in his lap.

"Get him to Island Hospital." Travis' order was sharp. Before closing the door he handed four of the man's twenties to the driver. "That'll cover your care."

Travis tossed the rest of the cash to the moaning passenger. The cabby drove out of the parking lot and made a left toward the hospital.

"Looks like he knows the way," said Travis while absentmindedly turning over the driver's license.

"You didn't give it back?"

"I'll mail it in a week or so. Really shouldn't be driving in his condition."

"How will the hospital get his information?"

"I doubt…," he glanced at the card by the light of a street lamp, "Nolan is their first John Doe."

They both straightened their jackets and adjusted their caps, Travis pulling his lower on his head. He put his arm around her shoulders and she slipped her hand in his back pocket, a habit from their early years.

"Do you miss the action?" he asked.

"No, not really. Didn't it bother you hurting that boy?"

"Surprisingly not."

"It all came back too easily."

"We put him on a steep learning curve is what we did."

They approached a street lamp and watched the mist swirling in the faint breeze.

After a moment Carly said, "I'll call the therapist tomorrow."

"It's been awhile since we've seen her."

"More residuals from the Cadre coming to the surface."

Nearing *Soulmate* Travis said, "Watch a movie before bed? Without too much action."

Carly gave him a tight squeeze. "I'll make popcorn."

"Not our typical anniversary."

Thirty-Nine

SHE SIMPLY WANTED TO STAY HOME AND LOSE herself in a good book. Brooke admitted to a growing comfort with the Edgertons, but was reluctant to an evening over dinner with the older couple.

Requests for her immediate attention at the library had been unusually demanding today, and her workout in the gym tedious. She wanted nothing more than to skip dinner, climb into bed with a new novel, and fall asleep before finishing a chapter. She'd never heard of the authors, but they spun a decent yarn about slow cars and slower people. Perfect reading.

But here she was choosing a pullover top and a subtle shade of lipstick to go with it. She felt she was preparing for a last meal and execution by conversation.

Cord waited patiently in the parlor mechanically thumbing through pages of "The Journal of Academic Librarianship". Seeing no pictures, he placed the magazine back on the coffee table, and was about to open last month's "Northwest Yachting" when Brooke walked out of the bedroom.

"I'm ready, I suppose."

He stood and held a jacket for her to slip into. She marveled that he misplaced the memo on the demise of chivalry.

"We won't stay long," he said. "I just started a novel that's already got my attention."

Her eyes brightened. "Then let's call in sick. You read yours, I'll read mine. We can see Carly and Travis another time."

"We promised. They're good people, Brooke."

She nodded in resignation and trudged to the backdoor. "Dead girl walking," she mumbled.

WELL, THAT WAS INTERESTING." Brooke fastened her seat belt as Cord put her Honda in gear and drove out of the marina parking lot.

"Which part?" he asked. "When they told us about his walking through a car wash? I heard that one before. Or them hospitalizing the mugger? They're full of surprises."

"Not your typical senior citizens."

"Better not let them hear you calling them that."

Brooke laughed. "Oh, not a problem. I've learned Carly's kickboxing moves. She's become quite predictable in our sparring."

"I'm not so sure. They may have a few more they're not showing. What amazes me is how calculating they can both become."

"You mean when in action."

"That's exactly what I mean. I've never met anyone who has actually killed another person."

"Did you see her shiver when she described how she brought the assailant to his knees? Almost as if she were confessing a sin."

Cord agreed. "They know how to hide their pain, but those years moving under the radar must have changed them. They have a unique closeness."

"I'm content with our routine and the serenity of my library."

Inside their cottage Cord set two mugs on the kitchen counter for tomorrow's coffee.

"I'm exhausted," she said, after changing into a nightie that captured Cord's approval. She crawled into bed with her novel. "I'd just like to read a little. I don't think I'll be much company."

Cord shrugged, still amazed he'd be sharing their king bed, with no DMZ.

"Nice nightie," his overture not subtle, nor unnoticed.

"Thanks. You bought it for me," her reply kind but weak. She silently vowed to get rid of the ankle-length beige cotton nightgown he couldn't stand.

He found his book and opened it to where he thought he might have been reading.

True to her desire, Brooke fell asleep before she turned a page. Her book dropped out of her hands face-up onto her lap and she didn't awaken. Cord took the novel, reached over and kissed her forehead. Still asleep she sighed and slipped down under the duvet. He set his book aside and looked at the lump under the covers he was again calling his wife. He stared at her for a long time, her mussed hair and all.

How did it come about? Sharing not only the bed, but life again with the woman who just a few weeks ago hated him.

He doused the light and his head sank into the pillow. Eyes open, he didn't quickly drift off to sleep.

Uncharted

Forty

¡Norteamericanos!"

Ramon Cortez usually kept his opinions to himself. Not today.

"Bryan, *amigo,* I am seeing your people make the living of life most difficult. It is because they are bored with their days? Why do they add barriers to happiness? I would ask the purpose. Our ways are not your ways."

"But we too are *Norteamericanos,* Ramon," said his wife to soften the force of her husband's words. "Citizens of *Los Estados Unidos.*"

"Congratulations to you both," said Brooke, detached. She wasn't interested in conversation with the little Mexican couple around *Starstruck's* cockpit dinette. But there was no escape.

It was Cord's idea to invite them for the day on *Starstruck* as a gesture of thanks to Rosa for her part in the hospital room to begin Brooke's healing curve. And he wanted to hear about Ramon's dream of a return to the sea. Brooke had to admit the food they brought from their restaurant was delicious. So between small forkfuls of an oversized tostada, she struggled to find an occasional response to sound halfway attentive.

"*¡Muchas gracias!*" said Ramon warmly. "We were much happy to give back our green cards and to pledge our allegiance to the flag that has become our own Stars and Stripes."

"Tell me, what is it that's so different between us who have grown up in this country and you who have transplanted?" Cord found himself thoroughly engaged with this couple who observed wide-eyed their adopted culture, and who plumbed the depths of relationship.

"*Ah sí, ah sí.* Many things, I think. Luxury is one. Here there is so much. But people always are needing more. Life is never the good enough, no? Always you must improve."

"It's called getting ahead. Pursuing the dream. Pulling your weight and all that."

"I do not know about getting ahead, but I know dreams. And Rosa, she tell me we both pulling more weight these days. I think I enjoy our cooking too much." He patted his belly, which was not all that generous of proportion.

Rosa shifted closer to her husband. "Together we take care for the other," she said, smiling with a sparkle in her eye.

Brooke eyed Rosa's past-prime figure. Prone toward focusing on people's flaws, her own and others', she looked askance at overweight women who allowed gravity the last word. If they couldn't control their diet, Brooke suspected restraint in general took a short straw. But something about this little person in front of her proved oddly attractive. A liveliness, an acceptance of herself. No, more than acceptance. Happiness. In who she was. Ignoring the cultural call to perfection, the beauty of wholeness emanated from Rosa. The little lady valued people as if they deserved it, not for their potential for reciprocity. Brooke's respect for her notched up.

Ramon continued, "Now I must ask, Bryan, *mi hermano*. A matter I have noticed since our arrival from *México*. It is about the marriage."

Cord and Brooke glanced at each other, both feeling blindsided. He was slow to respond. "I'm…not sure either of us knows enough about that matter to give much of an answer."

"*Perdon, amigos.* I do not ask about you. It is more the observation of some of your people. Or no, better if I do not ask. I am sorry, my friends."

Brooke's interest was piqued. "I'd be interested in your observation, coming from another culture. Marriage is a dying value in ours."

"I do not know of the ones who would make it dead. I speak more of the people who are married and who do not like it much."

Brooke coughed; Cord chuckled. "I think you're speaking our language," he said, nodding.

"Then here is my question, *por favor*. Why do your people push the marriage up the steepest mountains and escape the quiet meadows?"

And why must he misuse the definite article? Brooke winced at Ramon's grammar. She forced herself to stay at the party.

"Is there nothing more to do than making the marriage your workplace?" Ramon was asking. "*Ay*, I make my speaking to you too direct. Again, I am sorry for that."

"We understand you're talking about the value of marriage in general," said Brooke. "No offense taken. Please continue."

"*Muchas gracias.* I was afraid I insult you. All right then. *Amigos*," he motioned from Cord with his left hand to Brooke with his right. "You are the husband, you are the wife, *sí*? You become one together by growing together. Can you, I mean your people, not let the river of the marriage run its natural course instead of building—*¿como te dices, Rosa, presas? Sí*, the dams to restrict its flow?"

"Fascinating picture," said Brooke, warming to the topic despite Ramon's syntactical liberties. "Go on. Please."

"Some people more educated than I say the husband must behave as king of his mountain, and the wife takes care of the mountain. I do not understand such thinking. Does that not separate the one from the other? *Rosa y yo*, Rosa and I, we know—how do you say—our shortcomings. We know when we overmuch our good traits so they become harmful, when we disturb the pathway of our love. But *señores*, we do not punish ourselves for being how we are made, or each other for how we are meant to be. We are accepting the painting of our marriage as artistry. You use the word *picture* just now. Well, the Painter has given us *mucho* canvas and many colors to work with."

"Marriage colors. Interesting idea. Which are yours?" asked Cord who noticed Brooke's interest at the comparison of a marriage to a work of art.

Rosa was about to answer, but Ramon's burst of laughter stopped her. She too began to laugh quietly.

"I think we're missing something," said Cord, unable to hide his own smile.

"*Amigos*, I am now embarrassed to tell you my colors. Rosa's, they are much more alive and wonderful than mine. Hers are with many shades of blue and green and orange, and sometimes bright red when she is not so happy with how often her husband paints outside the lines."

"And Ramon's, Rosa?" asked Brooke, playing along.

Without skipping a beat Rosa said, "Ramon. *Ra*-mon," placing emphasis on the first syllable and her hand on his knee. "Ramon's colors are bold, to be sure, and rich. Not a single

T&L Pampeyan

pastel would be at home on his palette. Instead he has exciting paints that jump off the canvas and mix together to make shades I do not think colors would create. It is only a man with many lively colors who can convince his wife to sail to America by saying only, 'I would like to go north.'"

Ramon suddenly wanted to take the conversation in a different direction, and later blamed his enthusiasm on the expensive dark stout he had accepted from Cord.

"*Amigos, El Serpiente,* the Snake of the ancient Garden, did the dear woman and *el hombre* no favor, is true? Ever since that beginning of marriage the man and the woman do much in effort to recover garden of happiness. Tell me, why do married ones try so hard to be at peace? Is it not under their noses?"

"Do you have answers for us, Ramon?" asked Cord, more to provoke a response than to show interest in a story he suspected had to do with the Bible.

"We do not write the books, Rosa and me. My English is never too good, so I read only a few books. Rosa is our reader, so she tells me what they say. Sometimes she gives the words her own meaning, but I trust her to say it right. And then, every anniversary of our wedding she reads to me a letter from *la madre superiora* at *La Catedral* in Oaxaca when we first become *los esposos,* husband and wife. She reads slowly, I listen carefully. *La madre* did not know the love of a husband, or his arguments, or the seasoning of his years. But how she loved *El Cristo,* as much as she loved anyone. She tell us good things, that everyone wanting *Cristo* would belong to him and he will take good care of his belongings. She say, he, above all others, always is the one we must trust to— ¿*Como te dices, Rosa, nutrir? Sí,* nurture our souls and our marriage. Many times we ask, how do we know he does this nurture in us? I look in the mirror and see difficult man to live with. Rosa look at me and see

281

same man, but she tell me she see someone more than me inside my eyes. Same thing for her. She is not the same woman I marry. *Sí,* she same Rosa, for sure. But she grows into more than my wife. She become part of me, and I part of her. Rosa not my sidekick, is that right word? She part of my lifeblood.

"English is not my favorite language, so I ask, my words are sensible to you? Or they sound *loco.*"

Brooke began to squirm on her side of the dinette. Cord knew she was uncomfortable moving into religious territory, and realized he was as well.

Rosa noticed their reactions and asked, more directly than even Ramon was used to, "The talk of *Cristo,* it makes you not relaxed, no?"

There was no immediate reply, so she let the question hang in the air. Now Ramon began to shift in his seat and run a hand through his salt and pepper hair. But, relying on his wife's intuition he kept silent.

Brooke surprised Cord by speaking first. "The town where I grew up had its share of regular churches and a few fringies."

"You say fringies? That is a new word to us," said Rosa.

"Another word for little pockets of people hanging around the borders of social life. Religionists whom people crossed the street to avoid. Most of them, it didn't matter what flavor they claimed, talked all the others down and tried to convince everyone, whether we listened or not, that they were the only ones who had the keys to heaven, or everlasting life, or God, or something no one could get without their advice—for a fee."

"Most of them, you say?" asked Rosa. "There were some different?"

Brooke hesitated a long moment before admitting there had been a few individuals who treated her well, not because of her privileged station as a member of the town's ruling family, but because they tended to be kinder.

"Some seemed…," she paused for the right word, "good. They didn't preach or wear Bible verse tee shirts. I don't even know if they went to church. They didn't keep to themselves like the nutbars."

"Another new word you give us," said Ramon. "What is nutbar?"

Brooke considered a moment. "That is an unusual word, isn't it? In this context it means the same religious obsessives. No one liked them. They didn't seem to like themselves either. Always frowning, irritated about something. And believing they were superior for it."

Brooke admitted the town folk weren't the ones who hurt her. She stored real blame deep down for her family who had no use for church membership except for political convenience. The ones she once called her people created their own social group and kept a closed roster.

"We are familiar with those people too. The ruling class," said Ramon. "In the south of *México* or in this North America, always there is the big fish who swims in all the water as if it owns the entire pool.

Cord said, "I noticed at your restaurant you don't treat your employees as if they're common hirelings."

"We work to make our business best we can. Without our people where are we? Without hard work, all of us, we could not prosper."

"And you are successful," said Cord.

"*Sí*, in restaurant business. But in marriage there is difference. We cannot work on marriage like that. Not same thing. More like we relax the tension, keep our lines slack."

"And you do that how?" Brooke asked, wondering.

"I think we look for how to help each other and enjoy the knowing more closely. Not work to make the other better. Or improve marriage to qualify for prize. By whose measure is it better, I ask? Who says they know more to make my Rosa feel valuable than I know? Somebody who live far away and make marriage study their business? They lump us into pile of facts and tell us what is best for us? *¡Ay que malo!*"

"You're not like most couples," said Brooke. "You evidently listen to each other and look out for each other's needs."

"So, that is *difícil*, difficult? I think only for selfish person. Or crazy person who isn't knowing treasure sitting across table and sleeping same bed. All is needed just keep eyes and ears open. Asking too. That help much. Only need to say, Rosa, what you need from me?"

Cord frowned. "That'll open a can of worms."

"Not worms, *amigo*. Not fishing trip we describe. It treasure hunt."

"Someone else called it that," said Cord.

"Smart person. Married long time, I bet."

"Thirty-six years, they told us."

"Often," added Brooke.

"Good number shooting for. We going on—Rosa, what our number this year? *¿Veinti-seis, sí? ¡Ay, siete!* Twenty-seven for us. One year that much closer to our goal."

"A marriage goal?" Brooke pondered. "How does that play into relaxing the tension of a relationship?"

Ramon squeezed his wife's hand. "You tell, Rosa."

"Our goal is platinum anniversary. Seventy years."

"And after that," asked Brooke, "you'll have no more goals?"

Rosa was quick to reply. "Then we aim for eighty. We both be ninety-five old then."

Brooke couldn't imagine the scene. "So, what will you do on your seventieth? Any idea?"

"Sure," said Ramon with a grin. "Big plans for us. What we do every anniversary. First, Rosa red special letter to us from *la madre superiora.* Then we make love, we get up, go early dinner—not *Mexicano* that day. Then we come back in bed, more love."

"And you'll be, uh, ready for that in your senior years?" Cord struggled to keep from shaking his head in wonder.

"Always keep practice," said Ramon. "That's what doctor customer tell us. He already in late seventies, he say."

Rosa patted her husband's knee again. "Ramon in the habit of filling that prescription."

Ramon's grin widened. "*¡Sí!* Rosa make sure."

Uncharted

Forty-One

This week's gotta-do list keeps growing. You don't have anything to add, do you, Carly? Say you don't. How did I ever fit in a full-time job?"

Teaching an occasional night course was more than enough during Travis' retirement taken early. Retirement? Just a different kind of busy. But a good busy, with deadlines only self- or Carly-imposed. This morning's short list would fill the entire day. Change out the starboard alternator; lunch; run over to Boater's Haven for six-hundred feet of floating five-eighths line for stern-tying to shore while at anchor; pick up a handheld VHF radio on sale; stop for coffee with a former faculty colleague on the way home.

Speaking of coffee, he'd better fill the mug with another round. Probably need more than half-caff to jumpstart the system. He dumped the remainder of the morning's coffee, reached for the real stuff in the cupboard camouflaged behind herbal teas, and brewed himself a new pot, adding, despite his physician's counsel, an extra helping for strength and pleasure. He might warn Carly of the switch.

Uncharted

While the coffee brewed he took a quick look at emails, something he tried to remember three or four times a week. These days he scanned his single account so infrequently that even Peruvian girls looking for friendship ignored him. Only four messages today, but one stood out.

"Hon, we need to make a quick trip to see the general."

"Something wrong?"

"Disturbing email."

Travis had met the general while on active duty. The gunnery sergeant in motor transport assigned Travis as the senior officer's driver during a weeklong base inspection of the expansive Marine Corps desert installation at Twentynine Palms, California. The four-star turned out to be a surprisingly good-natured man, to the point of accepting Travis' off-the-cuff invitation to forego the day's-end visit to the officer's club in favor of a favorite burger stand in town. Over Eugene's double-buffalo-patty-double-cheese-double-onion burgers, jumbo cokes and two mounds of fries, an unlikely friendship began to form between one of the Marines' five full generals and the young enlistee who had trouble controlling a quick wit. At the end of the week the man offered Travis the spot as his personal driver if he'd forget his preference for the Reserve and ship over for another four years, and he would see his way to approving the lad for officer candidate school.

Travis thanked the general, explaining he had a different star to follow.

"Suit yourself, lance corporal," adding, "Whatever I can do to help."

"PFC, sir."

"I'll see to your promotion."

"You can do that, sir?"

"Son, how many stars do I wear on my collar?"

288

"I'd say quite a cluster, sir."

"Now, which eatery tomorrow? Tonight's was a good choice."

The next night over pizza and cokes—*I do no alcohol on weeknights, son*—Travis asked, "General, did you mean it yesterday about helping out?"

"One reason I lay off the sauce until Saturday night. Yes, I do remember, and I did mean it. What have you got in mind?"

"Three years from now do the honor of awarding me my academic hood. Call it my knighthood."

"Happy to do it—doctor."

So it happened. The university was fine making the allowance, and the general, who was by then the Commandant of the Marine Corps, showed up in dress blues to slip the hood over Travis' shoulders. The standing ovation was thunderous, not for the commandant's guest appearance, but in recognition of Travis' fervent if not sometimes rowdy influence on the lives of students and faculty and the soul of the school. The following year Travis and Carly attended the general's retirement party in DC, the commandant telling Travis to wear his doctoral regalia to balance the military uniforms, medals and sabers. "And son, buy Carly a new dress; something short." Travis was delighted to follow orders.

The two men, separated by two-and-a-half decades and a few states, corresponded almost monthly. Today Travis opened the email to read his old friend's short note. Carly peered over his shoulder.

Dr T, just saw my internist. Not good news. Test came up bad for the pancreas. Imagine, at this age. Care to take another drive to that burger stand? Time to look after pressing situations with the One Upstairs. Thinking you can help, Travis.

Carly looked up from the laptop's screen. "When do you want to leave?"

Travis' eyes welled. "Quickly."

"I'll book the flight now. We can postpone going out with Cord and Brooke on *Starstruck* this Saturday."

"Yeah. Priorities. The commandant comes first." He wiped the tears with his palms.

Cord stopped by later that afternoon to check on his boat. Travis filled him in on the emergency flight to be with his friend and champion. Cord understood, told him he and Brooke would look forward to the rain check, even offer to toss up a prayer if he knew how.

"Thanks," said Travis. "Appreciate the thought."

"Do you and Carly need a ride to the airport?" asked Cord.

"Shuttle's picking us up. Don't know how long we'll be. Open-end tickets."

"I'll keep an eye on things here. No worries, okay?"

Travis nodded indicating he'd heard Cord, but his eyes couldn't conceal that his heart was at the side of his general.

Forty-Two

Pᴇᴏᴘʟᴇ ɢᴀᴠᴇ Bʀᴏᴏᴋᴇ'ꜱ ɢʀᴇᴀᴛ ᴜɴᴄʟᴇ, JT Shiller, a wide berth. Nobody stood up to him, but then nobody needed to. He was all-powerful in the community, and at the same time everyone's friend. It wasn't fear so much as respect tinged with awe. And that translated into devotion. Even the skateboarders thought him cool for an unrequested donation making possible their own park.

When he'd seen battle lines drawn between town folk and the skaters, it was JT—by then in his late eighties—who walked over to the youths' hangout at the 7-Eleven and asked why they stood around and smoked. He bummed a Camel to show he wasn't leaving soon. No place to go, they mumbled. Who says, he asked. Who cares, they accused. What do you need? A park. City park? No-o, skate park. What's different about it? All concrete, for one, and stairsets, coupla quarter pipes. Their language was strange, but JT read their young and ignored natures. That led him to introduce the skaters to the mayor, followed by weekly group meetings with a local developer where he and the kids drew up plans for the finest skate park within 200 miles of the sleepy river town of Shaw's Bow. Built according to the kids' exact specs, with a half pipe, seventy-foot stair rail, two bowls, an über smoking full pipe and one awesome snake run. JT made sure it happened for the skaters whom he named his Youngsters With Promise.

That was it. Everyone was in some way indebted to him. He didn't hold it over them, but they knew they owed JT—for dozens of low-interest loans he'd arranged, for advancing the money himself when the bank wouldn't swing it, for calming storms of dissension, for buying local no matter the extra cost.

Admiration. That's what they felt toward JT. Near reverence.

But no one could claim to love him. They didn't know how. He had all he needed. Self-made, self-sufficient. More than a touch of arrogance, but he wore it well.

So, admiration seemed enough.

JT had invested his fortune well. How much was he worth? Unsubstantiated rumors had him in the high nines—as in nine figures. But he never spoke of his wealth. Except once, when he identified Scrooge McDuck as one his more astute pupils.

These days he didn't leave his luxurious retirement suite overlooking the river and the town, his town. Nearing ninety-six, his legs were weakened by a mild stroke two years earlier. The mayor dropped by weekly out of duty—everyone knew JT bought the man's election. But his family, not participants in his fortune as planned, gradually forgot their favorite patriarch. They complained the two-mile drive to the care home and the elevator ride to his floor had become arduous, and the facility with its odor of elderly inmates depressing.

Most of his life JT had few lonely moments, thanks to attendant friends and followers consequent of his fortune and influence. These days he had too many hours of seclusion strung together, and caught himself contemplating the meaning of life. And he couldn't stand contemplating. In a weaker moment he understood: he was esteemed for his status, but couldn't claim to know what it was like to be loved.

Then it hit him. His life amounted to admirable accomplishments, all overshadowed by lifelong emptiness and a growing despair. Where the despair came from he had no clue. And he couldn't make his mind go deeper to root out the source.

He tried to cover his loneliness by repeating one-liners about the aged with others in the dining room. There were many, some even humorous, but all of them pierced what used to be his thick hide.

Despite the years, the family secret stayed intact. Younger brother Edwin never divulged a hint about the treasure he lifted from the former banker. He was given clemency and paroled at age eighty-four by a governor seeking to exhibit goodwill during an election year. Edwin lived out his days alone in his tiny cottage. Accustomed to small spaces, he kept to himself indoors with brief excursions to the back patio to feel the sun on his face. Edwin died content seven years later, bringing to a close visits from across the lawn by his older brother. Soon thereafter JT moved into his present lodging.

There had been concern that one of the in-laws, Sheena, the one JT's kin called the ditz, would slip up one day and disclose the affair of the strongbox's recovery. But in her early forties she developed a neurological malady no doctor was willing to classify, and she fulfilled everyone's expectation by becoming truly mindless. Once it became public that Sheena's endeavors were limited to drooling and soiling, her husband

Reeve, not one for protocol, saddled his favorite waitress. The family airbrain died, alone and ignored.

The other loose cannon in the family was Brooke's older cousin Barlow, who had filled her young life with constant distress after her discovery of the cache in the pond. One night—couldn't have been very long after Brooke disappeared, while loading up on weed and Schlitz he began telling his buddies too loudly a story about lost treasure. Another cousin with greater vigilance happened into the tavern and drifted over to Barlow's table, diverting the discourse by keeping two fingers of straight 180-proof coming all around until there wasn't one of them sober enough to identify himself in the mirror. The next day, all with outrageous hangovers, the little gang took a dare from someone whose voice sounded familiar but whose face remained out of focus to their bloodshot eyes. Clinging to each other for balance, they laughed and stumbled their way to the bridge over a shallow part of the river. There, Barlow, who always prided himself in his ingenuity, strung up his homemade bungee cord from an overhead girder. Attaching the other end—minimally frayed—securely to one ankle and with the applause of his three friends he scaled the railing, and before losing his balance executed a passable swan into the wide open. Near the end of his dive his friends heard fibers snapping. The coroner later said the elastic band would have been the right length had the bridge been built three feet higher from the rocks.

Yes, there were still a few echoes of the past that brought a chuckle to JT.

But he could never bring himself to dwell long on the treatment of his favorite niece, technically great niece. Brooke, her name was. Someone said she'd appeared for a moment at a recent family gathering, but he suspected that person had snuck a few too many from Gus Peters' moonshine.

What had become of that beauty? Gimpy gait notwithstanding, they called her the homecoming queen, and she was the smartest of the lot. JT judged she'd eventually become the brainpower of his monarchy. Upon reflection, some of her mistreatment had been overly harsh. And he was the one who oversaw her misery, some said. But he believed he'd judged her boot camp of training a good investment. JT had had high hopes for that girl. Till she left all that was good for her.

Now, alone with only a view of the river and his past, his eyes moistened at memories of his losses, two or three he considered significant. But loved ones? They were more like devotees. He couldn't describe what love might be like, and hadn't thought of the need for it.

Or that the maturity of a young girl now grown up might have been stunted by not receiving what he had no idea how to give.

Uncharted

Forty-Three

SHE SAVORED THE DAY SHE TURNED IN the borrowed crutches at the Red Cross. Brooke was standing solidly upright, her limp noticeably decreasing, even to her.

Her long-term recovery, however, required greater endurance than planned. Brooke's emotions began to sink into unshakable sadness. Childhood memories and doubts of being valued gripped her. Who was she to think she was worthy of love and acceptance?

Cord spent his nights at the cottage now, so he saw close-up her melancholy. This morning it was clear she needed to get out of the house. She'd said she would be fine and should probably get herself to the gym for some workout time.

But her listless response didn't convince him. He phoned her midmorning from work only to wake her. Unusual that she should be taking a nap. An hour later he called again.

The sun peeked in and out between high clouds, the temperature perfect for April.

"I've got the rest of the day free." He tried to sound cheery. "Let's go for a drive along the harbor road. Lunch at the Oyster Cooker."

"You just got to work. Marcus is putting you up to this."

"I'm not saying. Want to go?"

"He's a better person than I believed."

She just said something nice about Elkin.

He heard her stifle a yawn, then clear her throat. "Can we take your bike?"

That shocked him. The wind in her face might be just the thing.

HE TOOK THE CURVY ROAD through the forest to the seafood cafe on the far side of the broad waterfront, keeping a good ten under the speed limit. Leaning forward on the Triumph with Brooke snug against his back, Cord liked having his wife's arms around him—didn't want it to end. His wife. The idea was growing on him.

HEY CORD. BROOKE."

The proprietor wore a faded green produce market apron folded under at the waist. He splashed a combination of Olympia and Kumamoto oysters, sea scallops and Penn Cove mussels on the butcher-papered table.

"Sorry about your accident, sweets. Made some fresh focaccia bread. Still warm. Like some?"

"Thank you, Stuart. That would be wonderful," Brooke answered for them both.

Her first bite of the fresh bread dipped in a strong olive oil and balsamic vinegar blend brought a sigh of satisfaction. Cord opened the first oyster, gave it a single drop of Tabasco and handed it to her. Her sigh became a soft moan.

Looking across the shallow ocean flats from the bay window they ate to Celtic tunes on a hammered dulcimer. They kept their words brief, sharing a preoccupied absorption in the meal.

"How about a walk on the beach?" Cord suggested, setting the last mussel shell on the table. "Or would you like seconds?" he quipped.

"Can we?"

"The walk, or more oysters?"

"They were perfect. I want to overdo a good thing."

An hour and three more dozen shellfish later, the couple—and it appeared they had become just that again—left the diner to the owner's approving smile, with Cord's wallet lighter and the contentment of everyone greater.

Cord thought to himself, *This just may be what we need. Not Doc and Carly's cruise to Hawaii, nor the expense, but time together without demands or old arguments.*

Back on Cord's Triumph, it felt to him like she was holding on tighter. *This is very good.* He turned his head slightly toward her. "Nice beach up ahead. Want to go for that walk?" He didn't hear an answer, just her squeeze up against him.

At the beach Brooke slipped off her shoes and picked her way across the smooth rocks to the ocean's sandy edge and the tiny waves lapping at her bare feet.

"Chilly, but I like it," she said, the water above her ankles.

"It's been awhile since we stood here," he said, coming alongside to steady her, his shoes also off and pant legs rolled up.

"Another life, wasn't it?" She held onto his arm and dug her feet into the soft sand for sure footing. "I'm glad we're here. But you were urgent on the phone this morning."

"I thought we could both take in some salt air."

"And shellfish. Have we ever eaten so much? It was delicious."

We. She'd just included him again.

"Carly said something I considered interesting," she said. "About releasing the past." A sudden change in direction, something she was doing more lately.

"You get together with her often?"

"Quite regularly, actually. I don't know why I finally decided to have tea with her, months ago now, but I'm rather glad I took the chance."

"She's one feisty lady."

"She doesn't back down an inch. The story about their anniversary attacker. The way she told it, Travis was protecting her—old fashioned courage and gallantry, on their anniversary night. But when I pressed her, she was the one who broke the man's jaw."

"Glad we're on their friend list. So, tell me about releasing the past."

"She talked about forgiveness, but I'd heard it all before. She thought she was laying down religious principles until I told her it was nothing I hadn't read in monthly periodicals. Forgiveness is becoming the new cultural obsession. Like parsnip water. It's fashionable to show your Twitter world that you're a compassionate, attentive person and not an entitlement brat like the rest of your generation."

"What is forgiveness as you read it?" he prompted to keep her on track. Brooke was decidedly more talkative since her hospital stay.

"Do you want to know, or is this some sort of quiz?"

"I've been talking with Doc."

"I know. Carly tells me."

"That's good. Nothing held back anymore, right?"

300

"Time will tell."

Her reply startled him.

"I thought we were further along," he said quietly.

"We probably are. Trust comes slowly for me."

I've noticed, he was about to say when he surprised himself with, "Could be there's something in this matter of forgiving for both of us. Uncover the stuff you've got buried, I've got buried."

"I'll bet mine's buried deeper."

Another surprise: disclosure. Where did that one come from? Cord kept silent, hoping she'd expand on her statement. He kept his gaze on the wavelets drifting in on the breeze.

He felt her elbow dig into his side. "That was a joke. Get it?"

He tried his best at a polite laugh. It would take time to get used to the Brooke who wasn't always mad at him.

She read his mind. "You don't have to take everything I say to be out of anger. Not anymore."

"Tell me about forgiving people," he repeated.

"One phrase Carly taught me sums it up. Ya wanna hear it?" Now she was teasing, even letting her precise grammar slip. What did they give her in the hospital that hadn't worn off?

"I wanna hear it." He hoped she'd accept his mimic.

"You don't owe me."

"For what?"

"No. Forgiveness says, you don't owe me."

"Oh. That's it?"

"Pretty much."

"Can you unpack it a little? I'm not sure I'm following."

Brooke patiently explained, as to a third-grader.

"When I forgive, I let the wrong go, right?"

"Riiight ..."

"I don't hold onto a demand that you, or anyone else, surrender some kind of compensation for wrong done."

"Let bygones be bygones."

"That's a cowardly way of saying, don't bother me and I won't bother you and let's just forget it ever happened."

"So then, what?"

"You haven't been listening."

"I guess I'm distracted."

"By what?"

"You. You're different, Brooke. You've got a lightness I haven't heard before."

Her laugh was rich and deep.

He said, "I like your laugh. I mean, I like much more than your laugh. But I haven't heard it for so long. It's a warm laugh. Did you know that?"

"Want to give it a color too?" she teased, reminded of the conversation with the Cortez couple and their descriptions of each other's personalities of vivid hues.

"Never thought of laughter having a color. For yours I'd go with bright blue, like your eyes, and with silver sparkles, like those cake sprinkles—right out of the bottle."

"I'd forgotten how crazy you can be when you're relaxed," she said.

"Is that what this is? Crazy?"

"Um-hm. Pleasantly nuts. Makes me want to laugh."

"I like your laugh."

"You said that."

"Wanna hear it again?" He grinned.

She said nothing for a long moment. Then, "With sparkles?"

"Lots."

He put his arm across her shoulders and she drew close to him.

"Lately I've started to forgive people who have hurt me," she said. "Parents, relatives, people I wrongly assumed valued loyalty. Carly suggested I come to the beach and toss a few rocks."

Cord's face registered confusion.

"She explained, and I tend to agree, that it's important to see myself, feel myself, letting go."

Brooke pulled away and went to collect an assortment of stones, some large, and dumped them into Cord's hands. Picking out one at a time, she began naming them after individuals who had done damage during her teen years. She threw each rock as far as she could.

"I did something like this too," said Cord. "Travis was with me."

"We're both under their influence."

"For the better, don't you think?"

Brooke nodded and threw her last three rocks.

Out of stones and names to go with them, she went in search of a boulder she could barely lift and hoisted it to her shoulder.

"Awfully big rock," said Cord. "Does that represent a person, or a nation?"

"Just one person. The one I'm having the most difficulty forgiving."

"It isn't me, is it?"

Her attention absorbed in making it to the water, she said with labored breathing, "If it was you, do you think I'd have climbed on the bike with you?"

"Good point. Can you tell me who then?"

"This rock represents my mother."

He kept from remarking that he saw the resemblance. Instead he asked, "Can I help you with that?"

"Thanks, but you know I need to do this."

At the water's edge, she balanced the huge rock on her shoulder, both hands covered with sand.

"The last few weeks, while I was mostly lying around," she began, "were very revealing about what I've really thought of her, how much I've ached over the pain she inflicted and inspired others to cause. I never felt her love. But holding onto the hurt, and to the hope that she'd someday see the error of her ways has kept me in the past. I won't be living there anymore. Now if you'll excuse me…"

She waded out to her knees in the cold water to the edge of the only deep pool anywhere to be seen, as if it were created solely to gulp down the grief of her past. With a mighty shout and nearly losing her balance, she heaved the boulder as far as she could. It disappeared into the depths, and the huge splash doused her good.

It took a few moments for the ripples to calm. Cord came to her side and they both peered down for any sign of the boulder, but it was swallowed up in darkness. Invisible. Gone.

"I don't suppose we'll ever see that again," she said.

"I believe you, Brooke."

Her hand found his, and they walked out of the water. He held her close and kissed her fully on the mouth. They looked into each other's eyes, smiled, both thinking they could get used to happiness.

Approaching Cord's motorcycle Brooke admired a cluster of rhododendron bushes, some tall as trees. Deep blue blooms, variegated whites and yellows, purples, flaming reds. They matched the brightness of the day, a life brand new to her.

Forty-Four

THE SENIOR LIBRARIAN GENEROUSLY granted Brooke additional time away, reminding her she had amassed more than enough vacation days, and wishing her, as she termed it, splendid revitalization of spirit.

CALM WATERS AND A SWEET BREEZE. A few boats, most of them single-masted sloops under sail, passed by the hidden cove large enough for only one at anchor. *Starstruck* bobbed lazily on the small wake of a fishing trawler returning to port. Cord and Brooke lay on the jumbo stern cushions, staring up at the cloudless sky. Together again. Quiet perfection.

Why then, would he go and spoil it? But he knew it was time to bring up the topic.

"Brooke?"

No reply, so he lay still. He heard her slow even breathing, and turned his head toward her. The facial stress lines she'd developed during their yearlong struggle had, incredibly, disappeared.

As if she knew she were being watched, she opened one eye, turned toward Cord and smiled. "What are you looking at?"

"You," he smiled back. He couldn't take his gaze off her.

She looked deeply into his eyes. "Thank you."

She noticed the new worry wrinkle over his right eye. "What is it?" She traced a finger along his face.

He returned the favor and told her he liked her perfume.

"You must have something important to say if it requires a preamble," she said.

Taking a deep breath, he asked, "You think we might need to go back to your family farm to put a case-closed sticker on that file of your life?"

Brooke tensed, took a slow deep breath and squeezed her eyes shut. The only sound they heard was another passing motor-craft somewhere distant from their spot in paradise.

She murmured, "I don't know if I could ever go back. It was at JT's place. That's where it happened. Don't ask me to do that. I couldn't. I don't know. Perhaps. You really think so? I don't see how I could."

"You know I won't force the issue, babe. Brooke."

"Babe is good too. And you can call me B. I always liked it. Well, almost always."

THE JUMPER FLIGHTS TO LEXINGTON taxed them both. Cord considered scheduling a same-day in-and-out to give them only enough time to take care of business. They'd walk the grounds of JT Shiller's farm and drive past the home of her childhood, and possibly stop in to confront her mother face to face. But he decided to book a next-day return flight. Brooke was too nervous to help with the decision and left logistics to him.

DRIVING INTO HER HOMETOWN the Cords were met with questioning stares. It wasn't often folks thereabouts beheld a couple as striking as the two of them. The woman looked very much like the high school beauty queen whose disappearance propelled her to legendary status. It took only a fill-up at the full-serve pump to learn of JT's whereabouts. At the retirement home, the teenaged receptionist recognized Brooke from pictures. After an awkward silence for the young girl to sufficiently gawk, first at Brooke, then at Cord, she told them JT's room number and volunteered to call ahead. They thanked her and walked to the elevator for the sixth and top floor. Brooke's limp was noticeable.

Out of the lift the hallway arrows pointed left to rooms six-oh-one through six-oh-six. The right arrow directed them to a single number, seven-seventy-seven. JT Shiller chose not only where he lived, but unhindered by the actual floor of his suite, created his own number. Because he was old. Because he was rich. Because he wanted to.

At the carved myrtle-wood and koa door, the only one of its kind, Cord put his arm around his wife and knocked. They immediately heard from inside a strong, "Please come in," a good sign the old man was lucid.

"Here goes," said Cord, turning the heavy polished brass doorknob.

The opulently furnished suite with its four rooms and two baths took up half of the sixth floor. At the far end of the main room—the square-footage of a dance hall and covered with expensive imported rugs—they peered through a six-by-twelve-foot single-plate window overlooking the town of Shaw's Bow, the river beyond and the carpeted hills in the distance. Centered at the window was a plush revolving recliner and antique leather-topped side table.

The chair turned as they entered. Facing them was a shell of a man whom Brooke recognized as her family's chieftain. Gone were the strong shoulders, the stubborn chin, the pride of life.

Brooke and Cord stood just inside the door. As she described it later, her feet felt glued to the threshold, and at the same time she was drawn like iron to a magnet to the old man hunched in his rocker. Stepping away from Cord, she walked alone toward JT, her limp pronounced, and stopped five feet from him.

She began to assess him, calculating what he might do. But when she got to his eyes, she was stunned. Cord quietly came to her side to provide protection and support. But neither was needed. Tears had filled a broken man's stare. His chin began to quiver. No one spoke, and Brooke couldn't break eye contact with her great uncle. Cord looked at his wife. She was staring in confusion.

Glancing back at JT, Cord saw the old man's body begin to quake. What happened next no one had ever witnessed in JT Shiller's nearly ninety-six years. Weeping turned into deep mournful sobs. It seemed to Cord to last ten minutes. To Brooke it was more like three days.

She hesitantly drew closer. The muted fragrance of his cologne, *4711*, brought back memories, surprisingly pleasant.

It happened quickly, naturally. She extended her hand. He reached for it and she knelt by his chair. He raised her hand to his face and kissed its back. He held it tightly for a long while, then loosened his grip some. She reached for a tissue on the side table and handed it to him. He dabbed his eyes that never left hers.

He eventually released her hand and nodded as if to say, Things are good now.

Brooke then did something she never dreamed she'd have the fortitude to do. She held his hand again and softly kissed it. He pulled her hand to his cheek again, still looking into her eyes. She saw his face relax.

She couldn't be sure how long she knelt next to the old man. There seemed a peaceful endlessness to the moment.

When she stood, he raised his hand in a wave goodbye, and slowly swiveled his chair toward his bay window. Brooke and Cord quietly left the room. Pausing at the doorway, they turned toward the old man and saw his withered hand raised once more.

He never did acknowledge Cord's presence in the room. All his attention was fixed on the girl he had wounded and who demonstrated in no small way the power of mercy. Little did she know she was the only person to offer him grace. Nor did she know he congratulated himself on a final choice he would make.

Those few moments marked a reconciliation between two lost souls. Though unintended, they helped each other find a place of resolution. His pride, her rejection, had prevented rapport between the two. He had been the king and she a queen, but they had reigned separately. The meeting, if it could be described as such, lasted only minutes and not a word was exchanged. But those minutes were essential to both old man and young woman. She had been set free, and in a real way so had he. Weeks later Brooke learned that Jordan Trevaning Shiller, great-grandson of a teenaged Georgia cotton heir and his mammy's oldest daughter, had died of a massive stroke, leaving his world with a softened countenance.

After the emotional reunion with her great uncle, the Cords drove to the Shiller place, still immaculate because his estate provided for its maintenance. Turning into the long gravel drive Cord steered the rental beyond the old house toward the huge back lawn. The ancient willow guarded the pond as if its roots still protected treasure. Brooke was the first out of the car and, waiting for Cord to catch up, stepped with purpose, her limp gone, toward the mouth of the pond. Together they gazed into the water aware of something hidden, not in the pool but deep within Brooke that needed to be released.

She reached into a pocket for a wallet-sized photo and showed it to Cord. He nodded his recognition. She bent down, her knees nearly touching the grass, and gently set the picture face up on the water's surface. It stayed in place a few seconds before the soft current collected it toward the willow at the far end. The photo almost reached the outer overhanging branches when a small eddy caught it in its whirlpool and took her high school senior picture under.

They stood, her hand reaching for his and pulling it across her shoulders.

She was the first to speak.

"It's okay now. I think it's okay now."

"You did well, Brooke."

She turned toward him and he lightly kissed the top of her head. She tilted her face to him and he gently kissed her mouth then gave her a soft peck on the nose.

They slowly walked back to the car, she with an even gait. He opened her door and when seated together inside, he said, "It's a little way to the hotel and some dinner. You getting hungry?"

She leaned her head against the backrest. "I'm in no hurry. I feel like everything's in slow motion. It's nice."

"Sounds like you're putting the case-closed sticker on the file. You want to see your mother?"

"Not today, Cord. Another time. I'm not afraid to come back."

"Thank you."

She turned to him. "For what?"

"You called me Cord."

Uncharted

Forty-Five

THE 1940S BLACK AND WHITE ROMANCE movie put Brooke to sleep, her head deep in pillows. Cord felt for the single remote on the side table and clicked off their motel room's TV and lights, easing his head onto the one pillow he claimed for himself. The day had been exhausting but good. Tomorrow no doubt held more surprises, but those could wait.

Cord had just fallen asleep when his subconscious knew his full attention was being summoned.

"I wonder how my dad is." Brooke was facing Cord, her voice barely audible.

So much for sleep. He wasn't surprised. Her question didn't come out of nowhere. This was a business trip. And business was being done.

"Thinking about him?" He propped his head on his elbow and tried to cover a yawn.

"I don't know why. I keep wondering if he's okay. If I should call him."

She'd heard from her father, Robert Potter, a number of times over the years since she'd escaped the family. He'd left town too, moving to Maine where he vowed he'd never leave. The reign of JT's dynasty had become too great a burden to bear. Besides, being a Northerner he was never received into their inner workings or the community at large.

"That would be a monumental step," said Cord. "Why not sleep on it a little more? We can talk in the morning."

"But our plane tickets."

"Easily changed, Brooke." And with that Cord plopped his head into his pillow.

The king bed wasn't bad, but now fully awake Brooke couldn't relax. She tried to get comfortable, shifting to her left, then her right, on her back, and finally her stomach. From under one of her three pillows she took a peek at the digital clock on her side. It glowed blue, 12:23.

"Can't sleep."

Cord didn't comment on being wakened again by her restlessness. "Your dad?"

"Can't stop thinking about him. One minute I want to see him, the next I want to wound him, make him pay."

Cord swung his legs off the bed and ran his hands through his hair. "Like some tea? I saw a packet of chamomile. Peppermint too."

"Either's good."

He nuked mugs of both teas; she chose chamomile. Sitting up and leaning against the headboard, she took her time with the first sip.

"My dad deserted me when I was thirteen. Okay, he didn't leave home 'til after I did. But that night, there at the pond. The others ganged up on me like they'd burn me at a stake. He didn't say a word but just sat there in his old chair staring into space! He could have saved me. Why didn't he? I was thirteen. He was my rock, Cord!

"Oh, he tried to apologize, several times. But it was more groveling than owning up, standing up."

"You had no one by your side, Brooke. Sad place to be when you were so young."

"But I miss him. Is it wrong to want my daddy back?"

"Why should it be? He isn't dead, he just lives in Maine." Cord sipped his own tea. "Maybe for some that's like being dead, but he's probably only a day's drive from here."

"I'm afraid."

Cord took her free hand. "I'm here, Brooke. I'm never leaving you again, you understand that?"

"What if he says no? I can't take another rejection. It's easier speculating about what he'd say than actually hearing him tell me he doesn't want me."

"That he never loved you, is that it?"

Brooke couldn't hold back the sob. Cord tentatively put his arm around her, and she collapsed into him. Tears long stored deep inside gushed. He set their teas on his side table and held her. She clung to the man whom she now believed would keep his word, keep her safe. Cord held her tighter than he'd ever been allowed to hold this woman. Both arms around her, like shielding a little girl. His wife, all grown up on the outside, but young and vulnerable, and now fresh and exquisite inside. Their embrace, more intoxicating than romantic, flowed life into them both. They fell asleep clutching one another.

TOWELING OFF HIS HAIR, Cord looked out the window at a sliver of sun cresting the horizon. A soft knock at the door; it'd be room service. He tucked the towel around his waist and let the waiter in. The kid set a large tray of covered dishes and a carafe on the dinette table and was rewarded with two twenties and an apology for the early hour.

"No worries, dude," he said, then looked at the bills. "Dude! Like really, thanks!"

Brooke could smell the bacon and coffee from the bathroom. She threw on the hotel's white terrycloth robe and made for the bed. "I don't know why, but I'm starved. I'm glad you ordered extra of everything."

"You sound different. Like a load's been lifted."

"Maybe." She brought the covers over her legs.

Cord set the tray on his side of the bed. They sat leaning against the headboard and he parked a plate of fried eggs, bacon and grits on her lap.

Finishing half his buttermilk hotcakes, Cord slugged back one more jolt of coffee and tapped his iPhone. "Let's go look for your dad."

A quick Google brought up her father's name and town.

"He's in Casco, Maine," said Cord. "Ever hear of it?"

"Sounds right. We haven't spoken for awhile."

"Got his number. You ready to do this, Brooke?"

"No, and yes."

"I'll call.

"Isn't it too early?

"Six-fifteen? To hear from his daughter? I don't think so."

Cord tapped the numbers and waited. Four rings. Six. On the eighth ring he heard a groggy, "Yes?"

"Hello, my name is Bryan Cord. Am I speaking with Mr Potter?"

"Must be a personal matter," came a sullen reply. "No telemarketer would commence in this manner. Or this early. How may I help you—your name again?"

"Bryan Cord, sir. I don't know how else to begin except to tell you I'm your daughter's husband, and Brooke needs to talk with you."

A long silence.

"Hello, Mr Potter? Are you there?"

"I'm here. Where is she? Is she all right?"

"She's fine. I want to bring her to you. We're in Lexington and we can make the drive by tonight."

Another pause, shorter.

"Tell me your name again?"

He did.

"Is Brooke with you?"

"She is."

"I'd like to talk to her."

"That will happen. But in person. Will you allow that?"

"You said you'd drive? Don't. Get on the first flight to Portland. Here's my card."

"That isn't necessary."

"Take the number! It's been a very long time since I've done anything right by my daughter. This is one thing I can do."

Cord had to chew on that. Why give the man a foothold to self-adulation? But then, why prevent an expression of a father's concern, a first step toward reunion?

"If you'd like," said Cord. "But you don't need to."

"Oh yes I do."

Brooke's father gave Cord his credit card details.

"I'll text you our flight number," said Cord.

"This phone doesn't receive texts. Will you call me? And I'll be waiting at baggage." Brooke's father paused for a moment. "Bryan?"

"Sir."

"Tell her… No, I'll tell her myself when she's here. Thank you. I've waited so long for this call. Never had the guts to make it myself."

Cord let the man's admission hang in the air.

"No, I suppose you didn't. I'll ring back in a few minutes."

Forty-Six

A SIMPLE MILK RUN FLIGHT; SHORT, IF YOU BELIEVED the arrivals board. But tiring for the young woman in seat 2A. Brooke's father insisted she fly first class to avoid the deplaning tangle.

They immediately recognized each other. How he'd aged. She hadn't remembered his rounded shoulders, so weighed down, thin. But then, it had been more than a decade. She whispered to Cord, "He's in the green Mr Rogers sweater."

Cord stepped ahead of her. "Mr Potter, I'm Bryan Cord. Your daughter, Brooke."

"I'd know you anywhere, Broo...," was all that came out before his voice cracked. He stared deep into her eyes, his own filling.

Not again, she frowned. *How many times must I watch old men cry?*

Her father broke the stare and wiped his sweater sleeve across his face. "The truck's right outside. I asked the officer to give me a break and not tow it. We'll soon see." He extended his hand and tried to smile. "Bryan, Robert Potter. Bob."

The vehicle hadn't been moved from the tow-away zone. The policewoman pasted on a scowl that wouldn't stay put. Bob Potter thanked her for her lenience and was met with more civility than harshness. "But don't let it happen again, Bob." She sauntered off.

Potter opened the passenger door of his five-passenger Nissan pickup for his daughter while Cord stacked their two overnight bags on the backseat and slipped in with them.

"My house is a bit out of the way," said Potter, "so I rented a couple rooms nearby. You two have a suite on the fifth floor, my room's on the second. Hope that's acceptable. We can meet wherever you want, for as long as you want. Have you had anything to eat? There's a restaurant in the hotel. Coffee shop too, if that suits you. Is the temperature all right here inside? I can make it warmer."

For the first time Brooke spoke. "Dad, I know you're stressed. So am I. Don't worry. Let's just talk, okay?"

Cord sat astonished at the change in her; a quiet calm was replacing her fear of even a few hours earlier.

More to fill silent space on the short drive to the hotel, Bob Potter asked his daughter, "Well then, how did you two meet?"

"I doubt you'll believe it. We still don't either." She tried not to show emotion, but a short laugh escaped.

"We've got all the time you want," said her father, relaxing a little himself. "Lately I've found that I like good stories. The longer the better."

Those were not words he would have put together when she saw him last. Brooke took a chance and offered up an opener. "It was in a church."

"Is, that so?!" He stretched out the first word, just like she remembered. Something about hearing his unconscious declaration of genuine interest made her feel oddly pleasant toward her father. She gave a thumbnail of their marriage, not afraid to include the past months that almost finished them.

Her father surprised her with, "Do you two have a new foundation?"

"What do you mean?" she asked, again cautious.

"Your first one crumbled. How do you find rebuilding it?"

She wasn't sure the father who'd discarded her should be granted permission to step onto hallowed ground. Her reply was cautious.

"We're taking care of it."

Potter watched in the rearview mirror Cord nodding his approval.

Over a light dinner in the restaurant's back corner booth, Brooke and her father tested the waters of trust. Cord sat by alert, all of them knowing he was ready to jump in to defend his wife at the hint of her discomfort.

Bob Potter did not enjoy talking about himself, but the long separation from his daughter warranted some filled gaps.

The week after Brooke disappeared from home, it dawned on him that he had endured enough of a frog-in-the-kettle life he'd gradually grown to despise. Changing into one of his two suits he'd need for job interviews, he packed a weathered Navy sea bag with whatever clothing and anything else he might need for two weeks. He wasn't about to leave behind his most treasured possessions, so he stowed those few behind the seat in his ancient Chevy pickup: his favorite rod, reel and small tackle box, the Browning over-under—a sixteenth birthday gift from his father, a Bible still in the box—also from his father, a small photo album of supposedly happier days, his daughter's high school senior photo off the mantle, his harmonica. Before sunrise he set a note on the kitchen table, which Brooke had done six days earlier, and drove off the family plot never again to see it, or his wife, or anyone else in the wretched town of Shaw's Bow.

He remembered reading in his old Bible about somebody wiping the dust off their feet when exiting an inhospitable place. Pulling his truck to the side at the edge of town, he got out and, leaving the motor running and door open, proceeded to the house across the street—which happened to be owned by the current mayor, and took a full minute to wipe his shoes, treading across a good thirty feet of lawn before striding back to his truck and driving off in new-found deliverance.

"Those years married to your mother were the longest eighteen years anyone could string together. She was devoted to that family of hers. Kin—she called them—came first, husband second. She wouldn't dream of making room for me. Or for you. You and I, Brooke, we were regalia. I was the token Yankee from up yonder. Of course, anyone twenty miles north of Shaw's Bow was suspected of being laced with Northern blood. One time I wanted to buy a used Beemer. Old JT nearly shot me for being un-American.

"I got that impression too at their Fourth of July party," said Cord.

"You were waylaid into one of those, were you? I'm somewhat surprised you made it out unscathed."

"Brooke heard the warning bells long before I did. I was hypnotized by those pork ribs and collard greens."

Robert Potter grew somber. "I was weak, Brooke. I always let them have their way. Early on I tried to stand up to JT, and even your mother. You've got to believe that, honey."

Brooke flinched at the word but let him speak.

"They always overpowered me—by their arguments, their threats, JT's money, their high standing in that pitiless little town. I was chattel to them. That night at the pond, I should have walked into that circle of wolves, grabbed you away and kept you from their cruelty. But I couldn't. I let you down. I guess I didn't do you any favors when you were growing up."

"Mr Potter," interrupted Cord, "it wasn't so simple as not doing Brooke any favors. You abandoned your daughter. Dropped her into a pit of vipers. My wife has been dragging a sackful of anguish all her life. And she's been trying to make herself presentable to a world she's been convinced hates her."

Potter sat staring at the floor. When he looked up he saw his daughter's stare fixed on the same spot as if trying to imagine a design in the carpet's pile. His focus shifted across the table to Cord. Looking directly at him, Potter said, "You're right, I haven't been honest with myself. But, Bryan, let me ask this. Do you love my daughter?" It was the first sign of a father's care.

"I do indeed. And I won't have you minimizing your inexcusable behavior, no matter how long ago, as simple weakness. You were a coward, sir. Don't you think it's time you walked out of your room of fear and stepped into reality?"

Brooke's father kept silent through Cord's outburst. The man before him had determination, the same his daughter had to grow into while defending herself. *Now he's defending her. Rescuing his wife. My daughter.*

"He's right again, Brooke," her father finally said. "I've been denying it all along. I didn't just let you down. I sacrificed my daughter because I lacked the courage to protect you. I was afraid of them. You became the ransom to shield my coward-ice."

BY THE END OF THE DAY father and daughter had begun to rediscover one another. For the first time in as long as either could remember, they each slept soundly in their beds through the night. The guilt of one and blame of the other began to lift.

The next morning Brooke and Bryan Cord agreed to accompany Robert Potter to his lakefront home in the small town of Casco. Long days and late evenings of honest and painful dialogue, accompanied by forgotten stories of a parent-child past, began to stimulate a solidarity of father, daughter and son-in-law. In due course a modicum of trust became noticeable, and by mid-afternoon of their third day they found together a liberating laughter none had sought. The humor was unintentional, something her dad had said, she couldn't remember what it was. A slip of the tongue, not that funny, but appropriately timed, the evidence of the past losing control.

Evening meals on the deck overlooking the lake highlighted their stay. Their fourth night at the lakefront centered on three marinated inch-and-a-half steaks grilling to perfection by Bob Potter. Cord commented that they looked like New York cuts.

"We don't call them that here."

"What then?"

Potter poked the closest steak with a barbecue fork to turn it over. "Funny, I've never asked. I just go to the butcher and tell Lester I want his best steaks, and the thickest he's got. He wraps them in brown wax paper, charges me a wallet full of money and tells me to work on my accent."

Potter heaped the sizzling steaks on an enormous platter, rushed them over to the table and set them next to steaming garlic mashed potatoes, the two packets of which Brooke had deftly opened and dumped into a bowl to microwave. Cord completed the meal by digging out a bottle of wine from the pantry. The small family clustered on one side of the table to take in the lake view, the sun behind them casting its final glow on the forest across the water.

Over still-hot steaks and a respectable Shiraz, Cord asked, "How did you make your way to Maine. The butcher implied you're not originally from around here."

"Not at all," said Potter. "Short story, grew up in Detroit, escaped to Ann Arbor before the gang owning our turf could nab me, got into trouble anyway and barely graduated high school, left for the Navy the next month while the folks set off for Ohio. Met the missus—we're not officially divorced—through a buddy while on liberty. Had nowhere to call home after my stint so I settled in with her family. Big mistake."

"And why Maine, sir?" repeated Cord.

"Furthest north I could get away from those people and stay this side of Canada. Folks here all know I'm a transplant. I haven't lived here a hundred and fifty years, and I can't nail the pronunciation of *ah-yeh*."

Late that evening, their last together, Brooke and Cord chose their respective padded lounges on the deck. Potter served a light snack of assorted cheeses and clusters of grapes.

"Thank you, Daddy."

The words brought Brooke's father to a standstill. "I haven't heard that word since you were twelve."

"What word, Daddy?" She picked a small bunch and one each of the cheese wedges.

Cord glanced at his wife, seeing her profile by the porch light. She was content.

"That one, honey," said Potter. "Before that awful night at the pond. I can't tell you how I've missed hearing you call me Daddy."

"I've missed it too. I'm happy we're starting over."

"And Bryan, when I hear Sir, I think you're still upset with me. Make it Bob, please."

Cord's smile came out distinctively lopsided. "You okay with Dad?" He waited a moment before he finished with, "Mine died and I might need one again."

Potter was still for a long while. Brooke stole a glance at her father and saw tenderness in his face.

He replied softly and slowly, "I would be honored. Son."

Cord broke off a stem of grapes from a large red bunch. Popping a grape into his mouth, he took in the expanse of the lake. Out of the blue he asked his father-in-law, "You like the ocean?"

"I've grown to love the ocean. I had a boat for a few years, but needed to sell it."

"Oh? What was she?"

"She. You're familiar with boating then."

"A few years now. What did you own? Or what owned you?"

"Oh yes!" exclaimed Potter. "You and I, we speak the same language, we do." His laugh mimicked Popeye's in the old cartoons. It came out sounding like he was mispronouncing the Old Testament book of Habakkuk-kuk-kuk-kuk. "She was a converted fishing boat whose conversion experience was incomplete. As the former owner said, she needed a second act of grace, but more blessing than I could afford. Probably prayer too. I sold her back to the man I bought it from. He sent me a few photos of her resurrected state. Must have cost him a couple of children for it."

"What did you name her?" asked Cord.

"She was already named and I didn't change it. *Signs and Wonders*. Thought it was unique. The owner apparently still sees new life in her. More power to him."

"Do you miss the ocean, Daddy?"

"Sometimes I think I've got seawater in my veins. You know the saying about how once it gets flowing in you, there's no dialysis treatment to filter it out."

Brooke and Cord glanced at each other.

"What would you think of a personal tour of the San Juan Islands?" asked Cord. "Soon."

"Never been to West Coast waters. Do I hear them calling?"

"Clearly, we're thinking," said Cord.

"Knowing!" Brooke corrected.

The three of them moved closer to sit side-by-side, watching the stars shining high over the lake and the forest beyond. Bob Potter pulled his old harmonica from a shirt pocket.

Tapping it on his open palm he said, "The neighbors don't complain when I play. But it does belie my taste in music."

He put the instrument to his mouth and played the first measures of Mozart's Serenade Number Eleven. He stopped and held the harmonica out for Cord to see by the porch light in the gathering dusk.

"When I was a kid my parents tried to get me interested in an instrument. I tried piano, trumpet, even guitar, but it was only a few visits to the teachers before they each told my dad music might not be my forte. So, no more music until I found this harmonica in the alley behind the house. Didn't take much to clean it up. No one knew I played for a couple of years until my mother heard what she said was surprisingly sweet music coming from my bedroom. I kept at it, especially in the Navy. In every port the boys would go drinking and I'd make my way up to the bridge and serenade the officer on deck. This old thing has been my comfort all along."

"Play some more, " Brooke said.

"Sure thing, honey. But you know anything I try somehow comes out sounding like…"

Brooke jumped in, beating her father to the punch, "Oh Susanna," with Potter quickly adding, "Or Schubert's Unfinished."

"I suppose some things never change, do they?" he said with a chuckle.

She nudged her father's arm. "Some aren't meant to."

The moment of intimacy wasn't lost on Cord. His wife and father-in-law laughed softly, and they laughed in unison, revealing a strengthening connection beginning to repair the ache of lost years.

Forty-Seven

Got a minute?"

Marcus Elkin was standing at the entrance to Cord's cubicle.

"Just finishing this last sentence. There…we…go. Got it! You're going to be happy with this contract."

Cord pulled his jacket off the chair next to his desk. Elkin sat down and handed him a five-inch square envelope. Cord looked at his boss questioningly, then the envelope. Elkin offered no explanation, saying only, "You need to read it."

Cord hesitantly opened it and saw only a few words on the enclosed card. "You son of a…"

"Watch it, pal. I'm still your leader."

"You're really serious about this?"

Cord was reading a wedding invitation. The names embossed were Marcus Crenshaw Elkin and Michelle Kaye Elkin.

Cord set the folded card upright on his desk.

"Quite a surprise, Marcus."

"After all the talk about you and Brooke getting back together, I did some soul-searching myself. Michelle and I have been talking with each other, with her lawyer too. The guy floated a couple shots across my bow, you could say, telling us we'd be better off in a lot of ways if we'd stop arguing and getting even, and start loving each other the way we want to be loved."

"He said that?"

"That, and more. Bottom line, Cordo, I want you to be my best man. Michelle's sister will be the matron of honor. It's going to be a real wedding. Minister, flowers, full dinner, that almond champagne you talk about. I might even break a vow and take a sip, and chase it with plenty of water."

Elkin held out his hand. "Just want to thank you for helping me see the light."

Cord was pleased to take it. "Not my doing. I've been fumbling through my own marital maze."

"Just the same, I wouldn't have taken this step without talking your marriage through with you."

"Glad to help. If I have."

"You have indeed helped, you and Brooke. Call yourselves marriage counselors by coincidence.

"Accidental examples. Brooke will like that."

Elkin glanced at his watch and stood. "Time to think about work, buddy. Michelle wants to meet you and Brooke. How about Friday dinner at Rosa's? The place stays open for the cook's guitar concert."

"Or we could do a dinner cruise. The weather these days has been flawless."

"Still don't go for Rosa's coffee?"

Forty-Eight

PLEASURE BOATS, WORK BOATS, FISHING BOATS, ferries and tankers passed by not a quarter mile from his restaurant. And he remained sequestered on land, dreaming of life again on the water.

Decided. Ramon Cortez would tolerate it no longer, this idle watching. He launched a hunt for an open water sailing vessel. His wife, Rosa, not reluctant to tag along at the floating boat shows, did put her foot down when it came to listening to him scroll through and comment on scores of Web listings as he searched for just the right vessel.

The first sailboat they inspected in their quest was a thirty-six-foot Hans Christian. At first it seemed spacious, more than they'd ever need. Like most eager buyers, Ramon was ready to slap a deposit on that first one he stepped aboard. Like most wives of eager buyers, Rosa wasn't convinced. During ensuing days of deliberating, visiting and revisiting sailboats in a stimulated market, they agreed they'd need something bigger than thirty-six feet when sailing a huge ocean. Many sailors throughout history had circumnavigated the globe in far smaller craft. Ramon and Rosa made their own voyage along the Pacific Coast of Baja California to Newport Beach some nineteen years earlier was in a tiny sixteen-footer. But they were young then, and by all standards foolish. Now, despite their short height, they wanted a lot of boat around them. They'd need size and seaworthiness to match their dreams of a return to a world of water and water only.

Their broker had given them no listings for weeks, and with the restaurant business gearing up for a robust summer, they hadn't time to think much about their search. So, it was a magical day when their broker called. "Mr Cortez, I believe I found your yacht."

That afternoon, with necks tilted back they gazed up to the top of the main sail of the twin-masted fifty-two foot Irwin.

"Rosa, now there is a tall spire." Ramon's eyes were fixed on its peak.

"She is much more than the little one we stole to sail to America," said Rosa.

Inside the cabin they were both spellbound.

"*Ay*, Rosa, this is as big as our house."

"A king bed, Ramon. Look how it fills the stern cabin. Is such necessary? Promise me I will find you at night."

"I will call your name."

"Do not move from the middle. That is too much bed for the two of us."

"But just the right amount of boat for our adventure, *sí*? *Señor* Curtis, we will take this one."

After outfitting, day-sailing and trial weekends, they wondered if they shouldn't have opted for the smaller Hans Christian. That is, until their first shakedown beyond the islands at the edge of the endless Pacific.

"Rosa, you know, this ocean, it is much bigger than I remember."

ON A PERFECT JUNE AFTERNOON, Ramon Cortez locked their restaurant's door and handed the key ring to his chef.

"In four months' time, Paco, I will relieve you of these. Or six. *¿Quién sabe?* Until then, they are yours. Do well. You are the boss."

So many years ago Paco had driven their belongings up from California in his pickup. He became adroit as a chef, a virtuoso as a guitarist, and a man of integrity. Financial arrangements during his employers' leave of absence were simple. He would keep all profits, and the staff would receive liberal bonuses monthly. In dire emergency Paco could contact them via ship's radio. But he'd been a fixture of the restaurant for as long as the owners, so chances were a call short of the building collapsing would be needless.

"This is the call sign for our *Soledad* if you must hear my friendly voice." Ramon scratched out the letters and numbers on the back of a crumpled business card, his last one. He'd ordered two hundred when the restaurant first opened and used most for scratch paper. "You will limit your calling to once, *verdad?*"

Paco jammed the card in a side pant pocket already full with shopping lists and other notations, thought better of it and slipped it in his wallet. "For safekeeping. I shall hand this *artifacto* back at your arrival."

The men gave each other a quick hug, and Paco leaned down and kissed Rosa on the cheek. "*Navegan con Dios, queridos.* God grant you pleasant sailings to all your destinations."

Rosa was already in the car before Ramon opened the driver's door. He remembered a last item and said, "Ah, Paco, *y una cosa más.*" He couldn't see over the top of the SUV, so he stepped forward of the windshield.

Paco turned toward his boss, chuckling. "Is there no final one more thing, Ramon? *Sí,* what is it, *amigo?*"

"This one is the most important," insisted Ramon.

"Tell me, and then you will leave for your grand adventure, no?"

"*Rosa y yo,* we will order the Paco Special when we enter that door next."

"You give me great confidence, and as much responsibility. In all these years I have not yet come upon my *especiale.*"

"But now you will. It is time, *amigo,* to come to your father's house."

RAMON DROVE THROUGH the marina gate to his reserved parking space. Marcus Elkin, their most frequent customer, promised to pick up and store their car in his spare garage stall.

Ramon switched off the ignition and took his wife's hand. They sat tranquil, undisturbed, watching the sun set behind one of the distant San Juan Islands

"Can you believe it, Rosa?" he whispered. "This is the day we have longed for, you and I. Tonight we declare our sailing vessel our home. Tomorrow morning early, it will take us to places before we have only dreamed. Paco called it our home away from home. He has the good humor, that Paco."

She lightly squeezed his hand and said nothing for a few moments, looking out beyond.

"Ramon?"

"*Sí.*"

"Paco is a man trustworthy of the business, no?"

Ramon's smile was pensive yet broad. "I trust him without question. So do you, Rosa *chica*. Paco has become our family; he is a man of honor. *Sí*, I know others have warned us about giving away the business. But they do not know that man as we know him. The loyalty of a brother, that is what our Paco has. I trust him without fail."

"As do I, *querido*. Call my question a request for confirmation of my trust."

"Then it is confirmed. With our very lives we trust no one but *El Señor*, as we have always. All else passes quickly."

They didn't move from the privacy of their car, allowing its stillness to quiet their minds. Soon they would trade this tiny space for living quarters afloat, and a world of open ocean beyond their scope. Embarking on their great adventure gave cause for silent pondering.

"Rosa, is your mind at rest, or do you have doubts?"

"I am at rest. And I am excited, I am eager. And also some fearful. But doubts? I have none. No, Ramon. No doubts."

"I know what you mean. Inside I have both the courage of the eagle, and the fright of the canary. So now, let us go to see if our fears will be justified. We are risk takers, are we not?"

"Our biggest await us."

The next morning on an outgoing tide, the sailboat they had christened *Soledad*—solitude—motored out of its marina slip. Beyond the breakwater Ramon shut off the four-cylinder Diesel, and Rosa took first shift at the helm. Under two sails, main and jib, she pointed *Soledad's* bow into the westerly eight-knot breeze, then north to Alaska. Two restaurant owners, short in stature, Oaxacan by birth, seafaring by taste, would in due course set subsequent bearings toward the Hawaiian Islands and the South

Seas before thinking about a return voyage home. But only after satisfying themselves on the fragrance, the wideness, the calm and the passion of the great Pacific Ocean.

Forty-Nine

WALKING THROUGH THE DOORS OF THE GYM, Brooke was welcomed with applause by the entire staff.

"Long time no see," greeted the manager.

"Nice to be back. Almost three months," she said.

"Your workout room awaits. Seriously, Brooke, we're glad you're okay. You had us worried. Did they ever catch the guy who attacked you?"

"Not to my knowledge."

She thanked the manager, adding, "It's in the past now," her words hopeful.

She made it back to the workout area to observe a young woman, one of the millennial moms, attacking the bag.

The woman saw her and immediately relinquished it, saying shyly, "I was keeping it warm for you."

"Straighten your wrist and keep it firm when you jab or you'll break it." Brooke didn't know why she offered, but she heard herself saying, "Mind if I show you? Here, give me your hand."

The young woman did as she was told. Brooke gently shaped the forearm and fist and guided it against the bag. "See if that works," she said. "I'm Brooke."

"Thank you. Me too."

"You too? What, you too?"

"I'm Brooke too. It's my middle name. Betsy Brooke. My papa liked the sound of the two names together. Betsy Brooke. BettBrooke."

"Pretty," Brooke lied.

"You can call me Bett. Here's your bag back."

"The bag isn't mine. I'm just here to use it. When you're finished."

"But you haven't since your injury. Thank you for coming back."

"Thank you?"

"So I could watch what you do. You have something I need."

Brooke jabbed hard at the bag. "Like a body that doesn't work?"

The younger woman caught the bag and was nearly thrown off balance. "If that's what you call not working, I want it. You think you could show me?"

"Excuse me?"

"I want to know more."

"You're asking me to train you? I expected you were more concerned about keeping your hair and nails sculptured than exerting yourself."

"I was, I know. Your accident was my wake-up."

"My…accident?"

"Do you think me and my friends—"

"…friends and I."

"Sorry. Do you think we just happened to be here every day at the same time, to do nothing but talk about fashions and our kids' latest preschool advancements?"

"I can't say I gave it a thought, actually." Brooke poked the bag again, with less attack.

"We were all envious. You take pride in your skills. You're strong, confident."

"Was." Then to herself, *If ever.*

"While you were gone we tried to remember your moves. I guess we haven't learned so well. So would you teach me? I'll pay you."

Brooke tilted her head to one side and squinted her eyes, mystified by what she was hearing. The women she was convinced had not a full brain to share between them had been studying her. They admired her? Brooke was more embarrassed than flattered.

"I'll need to think about that. And your friends?"

"They're content to watch. I want to learn."

"Steady the bag for me, would you?"

Her aspiring pupil gripped the handles from behind, and Brooke tried a soft kick. Before connecting she lost her balance and fell to the mat with a grunt.

Bett offered a hand up. Brooke was about to brush it away but reconsidered. She needed the help.

"Not back to normal yet. Not even close." Brooke stood with effort and nodded. "Thanks."

"You'll say yes?"

"I said I'd think it over."

"Thanks—Brooke. See you tomorrow?"

"You probably will. Keep the wrist straight."

Uncharted

Fifty

A Sunday afternoon stroll in a country park. Two lovers together whose total agenda was to walk closely in the freshness of a mild summer day.

"Nice today," said Cord.

"It is," said Brooke.

"Are you glad your dad is coming out next month?"

"Very. Thanks."

"For?"

"Initiating the invitation."

Brooke's happiness grew in the last few weeks to a level she'd only read about in books she'd presumed were meant for others. Spontaneous laughter, from girlish giggles to loud bellows, was part of her new language. She had to admit, laughter was a fine relational adhesive.

She stooped to pick up a small fir cone to throw and one to give to Cord. She looked back and saw the stranger.

Straightening up, she drew close to Cord. At first she wasn't going to say anything. But this was no coincidence.

"Someone's following us. I recognize him."

He turned back to look, curious but unconcerned.

"Friend?"

"No. The one who put me in the hospital."

Cord wheeled around and looked hard at the man still approaching.

The man slowed his pace but didn't stop.

"I've seen him a couple of times before." Brooke's voice was quiet but showed no timidity.

"He's been stalking you? And you haven't said anything?"

The man stopped directly before them. He was younger than Cord, shorter, too buff. A boyish smile bordering on innocence, but the eyes revealed a malice touting he was used to having, if not forcing, his way.

The man disregarded Cord as a nonstarter and eyed Brooke. "Recovering nicely, are we?"

Brooke saw the same smirk on his face as in the gym that Sunday morning. She hated it. And she was concerned about her safety, but more for Cord's. He was no fighter.

Cord hadn't a clue what to do. Since the third grade he'd never raised a fist. Now he was confronted by physical opposition that would be no grade school pushover. He wrestled inside: before him stood a very real threat. He felt he should make an attempt to come to Brooke's aid, who admittedly could take care of herself far better than he could ever hope.

His anger welled, fists tightened. He wanted very much to send the guy into late next week.

Brooke read her husband's signs of aggression. To the intruder she said, "Please leave us alone." To Cord she asked, "Would you take me home?" and tried to put her arm through his.

Without thinking, Cord pushed the man away. Huge mistake. The man slowly turned away, his back deliberately to Cord, but within striking distance.

Cord didn't see it coming. The arm up, the back of the hand connecting with the front of his face.

Eyes watering, Cord involuntarily went to one knee and held his nose.

The man, his smirk larger, shook his head in ridicule and turned his attention fully on Brooke as the worthy opponent. Cord looked up helplessly, a bystander.

Brooke immediately dropped down to sit cross-legged on the bark trail, four feet away from Cord. Neither man had any idea what she was doing, especially the one standing whose attention was riveted on her.

Cord could only recall two times in his life he intentionally hurt another. Now, staring at the back of a formidable adversary, something in him snapped. He knew no retaliatory moves. Third grade was a long time ago. But he had to do something. Shaking his head to clear his eyes he stood unsteadily and took a risk. From behind with open palms he cuffed the man's ears hard.

The brain thunderclap threw the man off balance. Disoriented, his legs wobbled. He staggered, his back still to Cord.

Cord was stunned by the effect he'd just had, and his nervous laugh showed it. Adrenalin surging, he seized a handful of the back of the man's fitted workout shirt and what he could grab of the rear of his biking shorts. With one clean jerk he hauled him high overhead. Not the smartest move against lightning-fast arms and legs for weapons. But wriggle as he might, the attacker now facing the sky couldn't find Cord's arms below for a purchase.

Brooke jumped up to assist, only to stare open-mouthed as her husband lifted the man higher and began to spin. Cord, surprised with his ability to subdue, laughed, and his laugh grew. Brooke couldn't contain her own chuckle that also grew to full laughter. Two, three, four revolutions. The man on top flailed his limbs, but centrifugal force and seeing only spinning clouds kept him defenseless.

With a gratifying feeling of wooziness and his enemy still hoisted and helpless, Cord leaned against the path's guardrail. On the other side was a steep grassy slope. Looking down gave him, what he imagined in his giddiness, a splendid idea.

He hefted the man up and down as if pressing a barbell.

"In a way, one," he counted the repetitions, "I should, two, thank you for bringing the spark that, three, reignited our marriage. But on the other hand, four," and he tightened his grip as the man clawed and kicked, "you hurt my wife badly. Five! And I, *six*, really get offended when anyone, Seven! And I mean anyone, *Eight!* Does damage, *Nine!* To my *wife!*"

Cord whirled his captive around twice more, raised him very high and growled, "You should have stayed away."

He unceremoniously dumped him over the rail. "Ten."

The man landed on his face, rolled and slid down the wet grass of the forty-foot embankment and under low hanging branches of a large Douglas Fir, coming up against the base of its trunk. Semiconscious, he threw up on himself and lay hidden from passersby. He woke in a heap and flexed his limbs, pulled off his fouled tee shirt, discarding it. He made his way out of the protective canopy and shuffled to his car a mile away. Smiling to himself, he'd found his match. It had taken the two of them, one to distract, the other pretending weakness. But they had proven their mettle. Perhaps he'd meet them again. For now, he was happy to grant them their imagined supremacy.

Cord and Brooke resumed their walk. She tucked her arm through his. "Didn't know you had that in you."

"What in me?" he asked a little too modestly and still wonderfully lightheaded.

"That move. The pirouette."

"Oh, that." His pride knew no bounds. "Didn't I see my wife do that once upon a time?"

"Not unless you were married to a dancer once upon a time."

"Hmm. Thought it was you I saw. I could teach you if you want."

"I'm sure you could."

"Maybe later though," said Cord. "Whatever it is I strained just now could use a time-out."

"Then we'd better get you right home. I know just what you need."

Uncharted

Fifty-One

CARLY EDGERTON STOOD AT THE FLYBRIDGE helm toggling the transmission levers to maneuver *Soulmate* to a full stop in the hidden cove near Puget Sound's southernmost bay. Away from the congested waterways and shipping ports of Seattle and Tacoma, far from thousands of summer boaters making their lemming way north to overpopulated marinas.

She glanced at the small plaque Travis had set between the two tachometers. It read, *So they got in the boat and went off to a remote place by themselves*. The quote was from the Gospel of Mark. Fitting, she thought, and glad for seclusion and time alone.

Carly was happy to be back on *Soulmate* after bring away for the final weeks and memorial for the Marine general Travis called a mentor. A difficult few weeks, to be sure. But necessary, and ultimately fulfilling with that good man during his last moments.

Travis snoozed on the mate's lounge and woke when he heard the electric windlass lowering the anchor. He lifted his

cap and took a visual sweep of the cove, one they'd never visited.

"Final waypoint to destination, Captain," she announced.
"Enjoy your nap?"

"These little hideouts begin to look the same, don't they?"
he yawned. "All so idyllic, serene. I never want to lose this
awareness of tranquility. What's our depth?"

"We're at twenty-two six, ebbing to fourteen overnight,"
she said while the three-eighths-inch chain jangled its way
across the anchor roller into the water. She lightly reversed the
twin Cummins Diesels until the anchor grabbed the muddy
bottom with a slight tug. "I've trimmed out seventy feet for
now."

The sun warmed from straight up, and her stomach reminded her that last night's leftover steak might taste good
about now. She made a move to go below when Travis caught
her by the waist and brought her down next to him.

"Wanna play around? Nobody looking."

She gave him a peck on the cheek and gently pushed him
away. "Typical. You take a nap and you've got one thing on
your mind."

"Hope it doesn't change with age."

"I'm good with that too. But later."

"Later. How much?"

She leaned back into him. "Baby, tonight you can do anything you want," she whispered in his ear, stifling a yawn. "Just
don't wake me."

Travis' brief fantasy was interrupted by the deep rumble of
an inboard engine. The antique Chris-Craft runabout powered
into the inlet casting off a large wake and made straight for
Soulmate. At the last minute the man at the wheel cut the engine
and glided along their portside.

Travis mumbled, "Not the best timing."

A second man stood in the rear cockpit of the naturally varnished nineteen-forties barrelback classic.

"Good afternoon, Dr Edgerton. Mrs Edgerton."

Travis considered complimenting the man on his care of the gorgeous Chris. But his annoyance overruled.

"You know who we are, and you've had no trouble finding us. You are?"

"My name is Garey Jameson, Doctor. I'm an associate of Parthena Booth. I believe you know the redoubtable Parthena from your days in the Cadre."

Travis' irritation peaked, his acknowledgment was terse.

"Yes."

"She sends her regards."

Senses now alert, Travis quickly scrutinized Garey Jameson. Average size like himself, but trimmer and three decades younger. Dressed in wealthy casual, he sported shoulder-length dreadlocks. The standard issue shades didn't fit. Nor did his driver. Travis scoped the characterless but beefy man at the speedboat's helm. Blond hair too closely trimmed for anything but old Ivy League. Bodyguard from his composure. Same idiotic shades too.

Carly's eyes went immediately to the wheelman's slight shoulder bulge under an unnecessary windbreaker for the warm day.

"Igor, gun left," she whispered out of the side of her mouth. "Knife right wrist."

"Doctor and Mrs Edgerton—may I call you Travis and Carly?"

"Not at this time, Mr Jameson," replied Travis.

"Do excuse my informality. A few minutes from you?"

"A request, then, Mr Jameson?"

"No, Doctor. Not really."

Fifty-Two

THEY LAY SIDE BY SIDE ON *STARSTRUCK'S* double-wide settee, their eyes closed to the summer sun drying them after a quick dip in the tiny cove's cold water. The warmth of the day, a new tenderness radiating through fingers touching fingers. *This couldn't be more perfect,* thought Cord.

He rose on one elbow and watched his wife.

Gratitude.

That was the word. Gratitude. A new life, once a nightmare, now a wonder.

Together again.

Her eyes closed, Brooke could feel his attention. "You're staring again."

"I can, can't I?"

She turned her head toward him shielding the sun with her hand. He was like a schoolboy. She'd missed that gaze during their long season of discomfort, questioning, estrangement.

"Thank you," was all she said.

They were quiet again. The boat swayed gently on a small wake.

"Brooke?"

"Cord?"

Cord. She'd been calling him that again, after way too long. An indicator of her trust, she'd been saying his, and her, last name often.

Something else. He was hearing in her voice a lovely Southern inflection.

"Your accent, Brooke. It's soft."

"I always covered it because it associated me with my family. No more. It's time to be fully who I am."

"I love you just like you are."

The stillness of the air, fragrance of the firs, the mid afternoon sun still high overhead. If they'd wanted to listen, the only sounds to be heard were a pair of seagulls near shore calling *me, me.*

At length Cord said, "That monthly God and Gars thing Travis invited me to." He detected the faintest grimace from Brooke. "I'd like to pursue it. With you there. You can try one of my cigars."

She pursed her lips. "You're not serious."

"Just a couple of times. Wade into the God waters. Just the shallows. No higher than our ankles. Maybe after they get back from their trip."

"They didn't say where they were going. Carly was rather secretive."

"Doc too. After they got back from the South Sound, they left without much of a goodbye, except his imitating the Terminator, 'I'll be back.'"

"Carly gets a lot of practice rolling her eyes," said Brooke.

"So anyway, is God in a marriage so farfetched?"

"The idea works for the two of them. Isn't that enough?"

"I'm wondering if there might be something more than it working for them. That God might be real enough to be part of us. Look at where we were and look at us now. Different. A second chance. Could he be in this? Possibly?"

"God-talk really isn't for me. I don't want anything to spoil what we've gotten back."

"Don't be afraid, Brooke. Nothing, no one, will hurt you again."

"God is a pretty big concept. I can't compete."

"You're my first love, babe. He can deal with it."

Her laughter was explosive.

"Right, Cord! You don't know anything about God, and you're putting him on notice."

"Just giving you my word."

"Is it God you're interested in, or the cigars?"

"Both, I guess. Where we could observe and puff a few. Belong before believing, if we choose to."

"What will we give up?"

"That we didn't already lose last year? I don't see that Travis and Carly have given up anything. Their life is a journey, and they seem to have a goal in their sights. Loving each other tangibly." He touched her thigh. "Might even mean more sex. Ah, but at their age?"

"Don't kid yourself," she said. "I'll bet Carly's just as aggressive in bed as in the ring."

"Lucky Travis."

She kept his hand to her leg. "Lucky you. Just promise you won't turn monkish on me if you go for the God thing."

His eyes lingered long. "Not likely."

He leaned over and kissed her fully. "Let's find another cove to put in for the night."

She touched her hand to his face. "Promise me."

He looked at her questioningly. "Anything. You know that, don't you?"

"The phone call from JT's lawyer yesterday. If I'm part of his estate, promise me it won't change us."

"Of course not. We'll always be us."

"I mean it, Cord. Whether a lot or a little. You do promise."

"Yes, I do promise." He thought a moment. "But you could use a newer car."

"What's wrong with my Honda?"

"Maybe something a little nicer."

His grin gave him away.

"Like?" she said cautiously.

Before he could answer, she said, "You're not seriously thinking what I know you're thinking. Tell me you're not, because I can see it in your eyes."

"What am I thinking?" His grin grew broader.

"You want your uncle's Aston Martin, the one you said you took joyriding while he was on a business trip." Now she was grinning. "I'm right, aren't I? Please tell me I'm not."

"Don't worry. He wouldn't part with it."

"You haven't asked, have you?"

"No, I know my Uncle Steve. He loves that car. He doesn't drive it much anymore, just likes taking care of it. The paint job must have twenty layers of Mirror Glaze protecting it."

Brooke shook her head. "Runs in the family."

"Yeah, you've discovered. No really, babe, you'd look great in an Aston Martin. Not brand new, mind you. A few years old would be fine. DB7."

She laughed. "Sure, Cord. And every time I'd back it onto the street I'd say to myself, 'Cord. Brooke Cord.'"

"That has a nice ring to it." He pecked her nose. "But if you insist, we'll keep the Honda. I suppose."

He crawled off the settee and started the engines. While they warmed he threw on last year's triathlon shirt and sat at the helm. Brooke joined him, snuggling in the captain's chair against the man she was learning to love once more. She might even admit she had fallen in love with her husband all over again. And she liked the thought of it.

"Where to, Brooke?" he asked over the hum of the engines. "The ocean's yours. So is the skipper."

"I don't *even* care where we go."

"Even? You angry or something?" The word evoked the argument that opened the door to their separation, a long time ago now.

"No." Her sigh was just above a whisper. "Intensely content."

She stretched her tanned legs out on the dash and clasped her hands behind her head, closed her eyes and tilted her face toward the sun.

"Take me for a ride, Cord. A long ride."

Uncharted

God & Gars

THANK YOU FOR READING *UNCHARTED*!

In the final chapter, Cord mentioned Travis' God & Gars conversations. God & Gars: groups dedicated to fine cigars and great discussion about God, a question and chat lasting the length of a favorite cigar.

You might be interested in starting a God & Gars dialog group. Some sample questions to choose from as you light up…

‣ What do you think God thinks of when he thinks of you?

‣ What would it be like to have God's full attention for an hour? Just him alone, making no demands for your best behavior. Just the way you are.

‣ Carly asked Brooke in Chapter 31, "If you knew God were real, if you could sit across the table from him, what would you say?"

Uncharted

Enjoy the pathways the dialogues take you.

Other God & Gars-style discussion groups we've come across.

Clinton County Cigar Club

Rumsuckers

Sip & Serve

Women and Wine

Whatever name you land on, we'd like to know about how you talk about God with good friends.

Facebook@GodandGars

Thank you...

SO MANY PEOPLE HELPED make *Uncharted* a reality. How we thank you! For encouragement, affirmation and ideas. For the means. For believing the story was worth telling.

Mike Atkinson: God & Gars name and idea for healthy dialog about God over fine cigars.

Charlie and Annette Booth: purchasing the character name, Parthena Booth.

Les Campbell: the phrase, *Navega con Dios.*

Kathy Garey: purchasing the character name, Garey Jameson.

Matt Garman: the title *Uncharted,* and draft edits.

Nancy Gower: reading through an early draft.

Mike Guernsey: one-of-a-kind marriage proposal. Inspirational!

Jake Hatfield: sharing part of your story.

Don Jaques: editing the manuscript.

Doug Knighton: editing the manuscript and lots more help.

Gary Lucht: perfect description of Brooke's high-pepper-quotient personality.

Phil Moomjean: description of paramedic emergency debris left behind.

Carmen Pampeyan: *Uncharted's* trailer narration.

Matt Pampeyan: *Uncharted's* trailer vocal production.

Jon Skiffington: *Uncharted's* trailer conception and production.

Len Sunukjian: descriptive phrase, marathon of a marriage.

John & Jean Taylor: beach house and cottage to write, and John's favorite oysters.

Lyle Williams: God & Gars question, What do you think God thinks of when he thinks of you?

TO YOU WHO DONATED to publishing *Uncharted*. Thank You, Thank You for your generosity!

Gene and Jeannie Ashe, Mike and Stacy Atkinson, Albie and Annie Booth, Harry and Sandy Boucher, Steve Bowman, Phyllis Boyajian, Sharon Boyajian, Joey and Robyn Coffman, Kathy Garey, Melanie Hack, Keith and Sue Johnson, Tom and Pierrette Johnston, Doug and Maja Knighton, Roger and Lee Kolden, Rick and Margie Simpson, Len and Diana Sunukjian, Stephen Swift, John and Joan Young.

ADDITIONAL CREDITS

Dietrich Bonhoeffer, *The Cost of Discipleship*: the love triangle.
Nat King Cole, "Somewhere Along The Way", by Kurt Adams
& Sammy Gallop © Warner/Chappell Music, Inc., Music

Sales Corporation.

Vince Flynn, *Kill Shot*: the phrase, marital détente.

Spencer Johnson: wisdom in catching people doing something right.

Hugh Ross, article, "Integrating Argument and Virtue in Conflict"

Uncharted

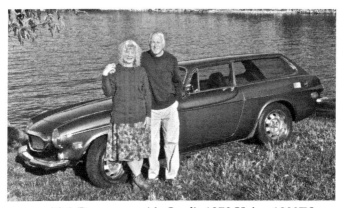

T&L Pampeyan with Cord's 1973 Volvo 1800ES

Ted and Linda Pampeyan live in the Pacific Northwest, away from the busyness of big city life, close to the water. Their motor vessel, *Renewal,* was their home for five magnificent years. They write, Linda teaches special needs kids and Ted is active in the men's retreats he began, Island Fathers.

The Pampeyans work with couples and organizations in crisis. They've been married 45 years, and take immoderate pride in their son, daughter-in-law and four grandchildren.

Information: navigating*renewal*.com
unchartednovel@gmail.com

Uncharted

Made in the USA
Columbia, SC
29 January 2019